# DOLLY AND THE
# NANNY BIRD

# Dorothy Dunnett

# DOLLY AND THE NANNY BIRD

Vintage Books
A Division of Random House
New York

First Vintage Books Edition, August 1983
Copyright © 1976 by Dorothy Dunnett
All rights reserved under International and Pan-American
Copyright Conventions. Published in the United States by
Random House, Inc., New York, and simultaneously in
Canada by Random House of Canada Limited, Toronto.
Originally published in Great Britain by Michael Joseph
Ltd., London, and in the United States of America by
Alfred A. Knopf, Inc., New York.

Library of Congress Cataloging in Publication Data
Dunnett, Dorothy.
Dolly and the nanny bird.
I. Title.
PR 6054.U56D6 1983   823'.914   83-5782
ISBN 0-394-71723-6 (pbk.)

Manufactured in the United States of America

*Dear Elizabeth, dear Edna, dear Sue:*

*This book is for you, and for all those other friends of the young who left, carrying with you the love of two generations. It is also, of course, for your children.*

# DOLLY AND THE NANNY BIRD

# Chapter 1

Everyone knows three boring facts about Eskimos. I'll tell you another. Whenever I think about Eskimos, I think about bifocal spectacles.

Ever since last winter, that is; when I was supposed to be between jobs and spent a week glacier-skiing in Canada. My college friend Charlotte Medleycott came along with me. Charlie had a job in New York and maintained boyfriends, like Barclaycards, in every country with a cheap postal system. When we set off to this party in Winnipeg, no fewer than six of them asked to fly with us.

One of them, I have cause to remember, was an ice hockey genius called Donovan, acquired from an organization entitled Data-Mate. He was large, long-haired and bracing, as if scoured and hosed-down with ice slush.

We borrowed a plane and Donovan flew it to Winnipeg. It turned out that he'd just passed the test for his pilot's license at the fifth time of asking. In my opinion, he should have asked a bit more before someone answered. We landed at the airport in tingling silence and he made straight for the loo bearing three brimming bags *pour la nausée*, and they weren't all his, I can tell you.

Winnipeg stands in the flat, frozen prairie bang in the centre of Canada, and even the city highways were deep in hard snow. The neon signs said Ten, which means degrees Fahrenheit, and the cab radio was also keen to spread the good news. "Bundle up, folks," it kept saying. "We've a low coming of fifteen to twenty below."

We suspected. I could see Charlotte's pinched face over her Fun Fur, and the escorts were all done up in Raccoon and Tibetan Yak and Scimmia and Alaskan Timberwolf and Natural Unplucked

Nutria. We arrived at Government House and the Aide simply stood there crying, "My God, the Wombles."

I could tell he was pleased. Once a year the State of Manitoba holds an art show of Canadian Primitives, and celebrates the opening with a bang at the Governor General's. Tonight was the bang, and Charlotte and I and the six Huskies were there to make sure it wasn't a whimper.

It worked, too. Charlotte, in lumps of Willie Woo and a dress slit to her armpits, brought joy to the Senior Citizens in between pointing me out all the richest, most unmarried Americans. The handsomest man in the room, it proved, wasn't American at all, but English like us. "Simon Booker-Readman," said Charlotte, consulted. "Simply gorgeous, I do agree with you. But Married to Money, name of Rosamund. She's currently in England, producing."

"Oh?" I said.

"But I guarantee, totally organized," Charlie said. "My dear, even the midwife will have a title. The Booker-Readman home is in New York. He runs an art gallery. Sultry Simon, they call him . . . You *are* a bitch, spending that kind of money on Italian knits. How do you do it?"

She didn't really expect to be answered. Which was just as well, under the circumstances.

After that, I worked quite hard for a bit among the City Council and the Legislature and then hunted out some of the exhibitors, who talked about quilting and Raku ceramics and splatter work. Ethnologists adore Winnipeg, which is a social porridge of Red Indians, Ukrainians, Eskimos, Japanese and what have you, which makes for a change at least in the chit-chat. I kept seeing the flaxen hair and godlike profile of Simon Booker-Readman, but I gave myself a full hour before making tracks for him. I fell hard once before for a married man, and I still remembered the pangs. I wasn't going overboard for Simon Booker-Readman, whose wife was in England, producing.

He was speaking to Charlotte, and since he was Married to Money I couldn't be accused of poaching. In fact, he turned his incredible jaw line and said, "You're Joanna Emerson, a sort of niece of the Governor. Charlotte tells me she's staying with you."

"Well, with my aunt in Toronto," I said. He was tall and slim, and his eyelashes were stupendous. "We missed the show, flying in late. Have you bought any Primitives?"

He opened his eyes. "Booker-Readman is better known than I bargained for. You know the gallery, do you? Actually, whisper it, I come mainly to chase up some ikons for a mad collector. But I did mark down one or two useful Primitives. And taped the opening speech. You made a mistake missing that."

Several people had told me I had made a mistake, missing that. It had apparently gone down as the most hilarious opening speech in the history of the Winnipeg Art Gallery, which would have thrilled me if I'd known whether or not Bob Hope opened it last time. I had opened my mouth to say something when a voice behind me said, "Having fun, Simon darling? He's sicked up his disgusting feed, so I've left him with Lady Carrington's girl. I want a very strong whisky, and some sympathy."

Rosamund Booker-Readman wasn't in England producing. She was here, having produced, and the product, no doubt, was upstairs in a basket. She was, moreover, a very upper-class lady, being at least five feet ten, and thin, and negligent, with brown Nefertiti hair tucked behind her ringed ears and beads falling in tiers to her kneecaps. She looked straight at Charlie and said, "I've seen you before, haven't I?"

"Charlotte Medleycott," said Charlie Medleycott, smiling sweetly.

If she thought that was going to get her off the hook, she was mistaken. "I have. At the Embassy. You're with the Mallards!" said Mrs. Booker-Readman, a little fretfully. "I don't suppose by any God-like chance you're free, are you?"

C. Medleycott is a nurse by profession, and is used to this. "I'm terribly sorry," she said. "I'm still with the Mallards: just on holiday. But congratulations anyway, What have you got?"

"A bastard," said Rosamund wearily. "Who won't take his bloody bottle, and won't sleep, and won't let anyone else either. He's upstairs. I don't suppose you'd like to look at him?"

We could hear him as it was, every time the talk died. He sounded like a piccolo with asthma.

Charlie, I must say, has her moments. She said, "Of course I should. What are you giving him?" and a few minutes later could be seen climbing the stairs, tracked by two bankers, I noticed.

Rosamund didn't go with her. The family nanny had died, the maternity nurse had departed and both the girls the agency sent her had left after the first week of four-hourly feeds, which are bad enough during the day, and ruin the night, of course, for all purposes including sleeping.

"I don't know how they do it," said Rosamund, referring to the absent Charlotte, as she fitted a menthol cigarette into a long silver holder. "It would drive me quite mad in a month. Poor Lady Carrington: someone's got her Eskimos pissed."

Everyone turned. From a corner solid with felt and cross stitching came at regular intervals arpeggios of Eskimo laughter, delivered from barrel chests whose lungs could scare an elephant seal into a stammer. Someone said, "They're not all that bombed, ma'am. I guess they're with that crazy dude who opened the exhibition."

Any man who can make an Eskimo laugh is a man worth saving up for a gloomy sales year. I said, "The Bureau of Ethnology must be rolling with the times at last. Let's go and meet him."

"Actually, it's not the Bureau of Ethnology," said Simon Booker-Readman. "They got someone better by accident. Would you like to meet him, Joanna? I may call you Joanna?" He took my arm.

It wasn't officially what I was there for. If there was any part of the bang which didn't need livening up, it was the segment in the far corner. But I was curious, and I walked over with Sultry Simon, and waited behind all the parkas while my escort cleared a path to the dude who opened the exhibition. And then I stood very still, no doubt changing color.

As a spectacle in itself, it would hardly have taken the drive-ins by storm. All I or anyone saw was a shortsighted man in a knitted tie and a nondescript sportsjacket and trousers. If you looked a little more closely, you saw he had a lot of black hair and odd cufflinks. His glasses, if you looked more closely still, were bifocals.

I didn't need to look closely. I didn't even listen as Sultry Simon confided: "Name of Johnson, Joanna. The portrait painter, *The* portrait painter, as a matter of fact. You've probably heard of him."

I'd not only heard of him, I'd met him. When I was seventeen. In my father's company.

He was a friend of my father. He might even know who my last employer was. He was going to wreck the whole flaming enterprise.

My father's friend Johnson set down his drink, glasses glinting, and addressed me plaintively. "I've been trying and trying to get my uncle in Brighton to knit me one of those, but the face never turns out quite right. You won't remember me. I was a friend of your father until he found out about your mother and me."

I remembered the sass, too; but this time I was old enough to answer back.

"I know," I said. "I've just checked the proofs of her memoirs. How are you?"

"Dazzled," he said amiably. His eyebrows, black as his hair, were the only guide to his expression, really, behind all the glass. He directed a flash of the bifocals at Simon. "We used to meet when she was a schoolgirl. I know her parents. Are you doing anything after?"

*Are you bringing Johnson?* my mother used to ask my father. *"Oh, good."* And even after I was at college she would write: *"Johnson came over yesterday. He's painting the duchess."*

"Doing anything after?" Booker-Readman was repeating, resignation in his voice. "Hardly, old boy. We've got this bloody brat with us. Rosamund is about to blow her mind."

"Bring it!" Johnson said largely. "It doesn't drink; it doesn't start fights, it doesn't run after crumpet. Most civilized gent in the province. Go and get Rosamund and the basket and make your farewells. Joanna is coming too."

I stopped myself on the verge of a "How can I?" bit. Something about the tilt of the glasses told me he knew all about Charlotte and the six Huskies and our invitation to stay at Government House till tomorrow. "You've arranged it," I said.

"I've got you leave of absence till midnight, sweetie," Johnson said: "The Eskimos are giving a party, and they won't let me come unless I bring the two prettiest blondes in the room. Truly. Charlie will be perfectly happy to stay in Government House, so long as you leave her all the Huskies."

I don't think Simon caught it, or would have resented it if he had. And it was true, of course, about Charlie. A wide gentleman with long black hair and a moustache pulled my wet-look silky Italian knit. "One for Sex," he said. "You come to my party?"

Another gentleman with flat cheeks, a round crop and a smile tugged the other sleeve. "Two for Sex. You are coming?" he said.

"Three for Sex?" I said. I had been set up by Johnson. I could feel it.

"No," said Johnson happily. "Three-Four Six is back home in Moose Jaw. But One-Two Seven and One-Four Eight are all waiting right here round the blow-hole."

There was a roar of unalloyed laughter. It was their standard leg-pull. Faced with five hundred folk-artists called Ahlooloo the only solution, I suppose, is to settle for painters by numbers.

They waited for me while I collected my skiing anorak and my boots, and made my excuses to my host and hostess and the others. Then I walked out of Government House with my four Eskimo hosts, two anthropologists, one Ukrainian, three Booker-Readmans (one of them in a basket) and Johnson.

Plus, he advised, a computer.


We drove straight to the railway station where we plugged the car engine heaters into a row of wall sockets, beside a policeman in pavement-length buffalo. Then we made our way through the station, out into the snow at the back, off the platform and down among the railway lines, which were also covered with snow. It was twenty-five degrees below zero Fahrenheit, and nine o'clock at night, and dark, and deserted. It was the kind of cold you feel first as a stiffening, crackling crust inside your nose, followed by a sparkling sensation all over your face, like stepping into a stiff gin and tonic.

The Eskimos were used to it. They walked along in single file cracking jokes about Indians which the Ukrainian also enjoyed: it was an undoubted tribute to something that in spite of all the well-intentioned hospitality they were all of them sober as housemothers. Johnson's state I was unable to assess, except that I knew he wanted me to ask where we were going and I wouldn't.

That is, with Johnson there, I knew I wasn't going to swell the white slave traffic and I am against pandering to rich portrait painters wearing old macs and tatty waistcoats knitted by their uncles in Brighton.

About the time I thought we were on our way by foot back to my aunt in Toronto there appeared a great deal of steam, and a long, dark shape sprouting cables and periodic bunches of icicles which looked uncommonly like an ordinary, empty, CNR railway carriage.

Ahead, Johnson abruptly rose dimly into the air; first, it became clear, with the aid of a foot stool and next up a pair of club steps to a doorway. There he turned and surveyed us. "And a great welcome, folks, on behalf of E2-46 and his friends to the Vice-Presidential Car of the Lazy Three. See you later."

It wasn't that he was going away: just that the heat inside the car steamed up his glasses like lavatory windows so that we had to undress him: a trace of a struggle with eleven folk and a basket all removing their slushmold galoshes and coats at one and the same time. Then Rosamund disappeared to park the basket in an adjacent bedroom conducted by E1-48, while Johnson sat us all down, and a whitejacketed steward came for the drink orders. In an isolated railway carriage in a railway siding on a winter's night in Winnipeg. With Eskimos. And Simon Booker-Readman. And, of course, Johnson.

One of the ethnology men, who were both professors, explained that the Eskimos were living on board for a day or two, before being hauled to the next station, so to speak, on the cultural circuit for short-changed minorities. They were all on great terms with the steward, who had their numbers off pat, and also their drink orders. Without their raccoon hoods and new cross-stitched parkas they were still twice as wide as anyone else. The Professors, who were thin and bearded, sat lodged between them like piano keys, but the Booker-Readmans chose the opposite sofa with Johnson.

I claimed the Ukrainian and he turned out to have lots of chat, which was a bonus. His name was Vladimir, and he painted ikons and ran a laundrette in Vancouver. We got deep into the laundrette, over which I could hear a learned discussion about Angmagssalik sculptures passing to and fro between Booker-Readman and the professors, interspersed with a six-sided ding-dong about the Hamilton Tiger-Cats' chance in the Grey Cup between Johnson, Rosamund and the Numerate Four who were drinking like pails, and showing a tendency to kick their feet into the air.

They had a tablelamp over twice before the steward came through to announce that dinner was served. Then E1-27, tripping up on the way to the dining room, hit the end of the buffet table with his chin and ran straight up the spare ribs and salmon in aspic, ending unabashed with his head in a flower bowl. E2-46, volunteering to wipe him off, discovered E1-27 was ticklish and they both descended sagging and chortling to the floor, where they rolled about for a bit. My Ukrainian, with his friendly smile, walked over and lay on them. They all three went to sleep, abruptly.

"Mr. Johnson?" ventured the steward.

Johnson, who had stepped back to survey the passage, re-entered the dining-room and addressed the affronted Booker-Readmans. "The other two Nanooks, I'm afraid, are out cold as well. Should we put them to bed?"

I could hear the cream of the Bureau of Canadian Ethnology putting the other two, puffing, to bed. I got down on my knees and took hold, with resignation, of Vladimir. By the time I got him into a bunk, Johnson and Booker-Readman had tidied the other two numbers away and the steward had redistributed the aspic. We all sat down to dinner, Simon, Johnson, Rosamund, the two professors and I. The candlelight pulsed on the stuffed peaches and cherries, on the dishes of roast beef and cob corn; on the fingermarks on Simon's mohair suiting and the lard-stiffened folds of my silky-knit, which felt like a fire curtain. One of the professors was going to have a black eye.

Not that the Eskimos had resisted. In fact, they had wanted to go to bed more than anybody, but not necessarily alone. For it is a well-known fact that very cold air will sober you, if you have been drinking heavily, whereas the first drink indoors afterwards will send you straight up and over the moon.

At least, Johnson said it was well known. He described his last client, who had been a Chinese dipsomaniac, and the one before that who had been a horse; and the one before that, who ought to have been a horse but in fact acted in koala westerns in Sydney.

It began to feel like a party.

At half past ten, over coffee, Rosamund Booker-Readman said, "Oh hell. What's the time, Simon?"

"Eleven," I said. It was none of my business, but I did go that far.

The Booker-Readmans looked at one another. He said, "Why disturb him? He's sleeping."

One of the Professors said, "They're all sleeping. You don't have to go, surely?" Rosamund, as I hope I have indicated, was, as well as select, quite excessively dishy.

Simon said, "We can stay for a bit. It feels like being let out of clink."

"That's *my* line," said his wife. " You haven't been stuck with him for four days. Have you a wife, Mr. Johnson?"

"No," Johnson said. "Although I rather like the sound of E4-257, who does twenty-foot stone-cuts of birdmen. We could set up a Druidic dovecote at Rankin with her models in twenty-foot pigeon holes."

The professors were unmarried also and had to spend their weekends with their mothers, fixing the plumbing and having their underwear mended. One of them asked, "How old is the offspring?"

Rosamund Booker-Readman was impatient. "Goodness knows, I've lost count. My mother's moron of a doctor got the date wrong and it turned up fifteen days ahead of schedule. I missed the Hartleymann wedding."

I remembered the Hartleymann wedding. There were twenty-two bridal attendants and no publishable group photograph. I said, "Then he's thirty days old at the most."

Nobody complimented me on my arithmetic. They all went on smoking and drinking. One of the professors was reminded of a funny story. I got up in the middle while they were beginning to laugh, and let myself out into the passage, and asked where the basket was. The steward took me into a single-bunk room reeking of baby. The light was off and the basket was dumped on the floor. I hooked a towel over the bulb, switched on and had a good look.

The Booker-Readman offspring was about twenty-five days old and a sturdy eight-pounder. His nightie was soaking and so were his smart cyclamen sheets. There was a patch of curdled milk under one ear.

He was asleep but hungry, his mouth making sucking movements and his face beginning to screw. He wouldn't be asleep for very much longer. A hunt round and under the mattress brought to a light a box of tissues and nothing else. I went back to the party and said, "Johnson, I'm awfully sorry to abandon the Numbers, but I've got to get back."

Simon Booker-Readman got up. "Oh, why? Are you feeling all

right?" he said. He had a boudoir voice too. His equipment was really unfairly prodigious. I smiled at him and said I was quite healthy, thank you. I was still smiling when I fell into his arms, and he fell into Johnson's and Johnson fell over both the professors, who struck Rosamund variously with their elbows and burst her beads.

Rumbling, grinding and squeaking, the wheels of the coach began trundling beneath us. The pullman trembled. The rumbling increased and quickened. A row of lights flashed by the windows.

We were moving.

That is, for an hour and a half, this had been a lone detached coach in a siding.

Now we were a part of a train leaving Winnipeg.

"Someone," said Johnson severely, "has stood on my glasses."

Rosamund Booker-Readman stopped screaming, picked herself up and began asking loud questions like everyone else. One of the professors fumbled with curtains. "No, no," Johnson said with mild irritation. "The telephone. If someone will guide me to the sitting room, I shall telephone the driver."

I thought it was a joke until we got back to the sitting room, but there it was on the wall. A barometer, a thermometer, a speed dial and a telephone. We were going at fifty miles an hour. Johnson lifted the receiver and said into it, "Driver?"

We all stood about.

"Driver?" said Johnson again. He joggled the rest, perhaps in order to alert the telephone exchange. Then he turned round, the classic expression on his unfocussed face. "The line's dead," he said.

My responding hoot clashed with another response we might have anticipated: an outburst of short-winded wailing. Rosamund Booker-Readman cursed and took a step, in a harassed way, towards the passage. The large figure of E1-46, appearing there, took her comfortably in its arms and said, "You are sleepy too? I am One for Sex." He had on a pair of Angora wool long johns.

Johnson, walking like Mister Magoo, said, "Oh, steward, you might take the bourbon before it rolls over," and handed the bottle to E1-46, who dropped Rosamund and retired with the booze to his bedroom. One of the professors, from the direction of the galley, said "The steward's knocked himself out. Help, someone."

My Italian knit was beyond hope anyhow; so I helped. The staff-rooms lay at the end of the carriage. We hoisted the stricken steward on to his bunk and I bathed and plastered the cut on his head and began to get him under the blankets. Through the door, I could hear the wailing going on, with certain vibrations to indicate that the wailer had been lifted and joggled.

Joggling a wet, hungry baby is a fat lot of use. I tucked up the steward and went back along the corridor. The Eskimo had not reappeared. The four Caucasian brains of the expedition were in the sitting room, pouring whisky and discussing the situation. Mother Booker-Readman was in the single-bunk room with the unshaded light blazing down on her son's rolling head. She was holding him like a rabbit under the arms, which were about the only dry places left, and he was bawling so hard his head was scarlet under the fuzz. She said, "He's dirty."

It didn't need mentioning. Also, everything he had was coming down, the longer she joggled him. It must have been a strain for her, too: she was gripping him as if about to hook him serially on to a curtain rail. I said, "According to Johnson, it may be several hours before we stop at a station. Or, if we're with an express train, the whole of the night." I followed her gaze to the pulsing fontanelle on top of her son and heir's head. "When did he have his last bottle?"

"Oh Christ," Rosamund said. She laid the baby back on its sopping sheet, whereupon it turned a darker red and set up a screech like a corn-crake. Green bubbles welled from its nostrils. Its mother said, "I'll sue them for this. We were to fly back to New York in the morning. And you're right. What about Benedict? He got his last feed at six."

Benedict. Oh, well. I said, "What's he on?" and wasn't surprised when she simply said, "Milk." The agency girl had left a formula and a bottle or two behind her, but these, of course, were back at the Fort Garry Hotel, together with the Harrington squares and the nappies. I said, "Well, there's milk and hot water. Why don't you clean him up while I heat something?"

She stared at me. There were bags under her handsome eyes where Benedict's demands had kept her up for a night or two. She said, "Are you joking? I'm going to bloody spew as it is. Get the steward or someone."

I treated it as a reasonable suggestion and said, "The steward's out cold. I'll do it, if you don't mind the legwork. We'll need a bowl of warm water and soap, and a bunch of clean towels, if you can find them. And a polythene bag, maybe the roasting size. Also a plastic sheet would be nice, or a tablecloth."

She found two, which saved the bed and what was left of my creative knitwear. Then while she was off boiling a kettle I picked up the poor bloody mite, stripped it, and ramming its nappies, its clothes and its sheets into the roasting bag, laid it on my knee and proceeded to soap and rinse it with a new dish cloth. After that, it got a folded table napkin between its raw legs and a towel rolled like a tube round its bottom.

By the time Rosamund came back, it was back in its cot with another towel and a plastic tablecloth under it, and a couple of blankets furled round its torso. It was still yelling blue murder and the smell hadn't dispersed so's you'd notice, so I suggested she went through to Simon and had a stiff drink while I got the milk going. I waited until she'd gone, and then took the carrycot through with me to the galley. I couldn't spare the poor sod a hand, but I could talk to it.

The galley had an enormous steel stove covered with gas jets. There were hot cupboards in steel up to the ceiling, and implements of every kind hanging all over the walls. There was also a refrigerator, with milk. I found a strainer, a cup, a spoon, a measuring jug and a couple of pans and scalded them all, prior to boiling up a pint of milk in one pan and a jugful of drinking water in the other. Then I added seven ounces of $H_2O$ to the milk, strained five ounces of the mix into a cup and sat it in cold water while I got some cottonwool from the bathroom cabinet and twirled it round Benedict's breathing apparatus, in recognition of the fact that he was shortly going to require his mouth for alternative purposes. Then I heaved him up, stuck a doubled table napkin under his negligible chin and dipped one finger into the milk.

It was all right. I changed the bowl of cold water for a bowl of hot, scooped up a spoonful of milk, and held it in front of him.

He stopped yelling. "Come on, Ben," I said. "You've got to start on spoons some time. This is your big moment, brother."

I tipped in the first one, to let him get the taste, but the next five or six he sucked off the spoon himself. It was the bluntest I could find, since I didn't want him to start life with a small, well-cut smile. After about three ounces he began to grizzle at the feel of the spoon and suck when it wasn't there. At four ounces he went on strike, and just cried.

He didn't cry very long, because his eyes were closing already with tiredness because of the crying he'd done already, plus the food and the warmth and the dryness. I didn't try any more, but stuck the cup back in its bowl and held an intelligent one-sided conversation with him, oscillating gently. He fell asleep, and I put him down in his carry-cot. Simon Booker-Readman burst in and said, "What's wrong?" sharply.

"I cut his throat," I said mildly. "I can't stand the smell." I said it mildly because he was the only one who had noticed the silence, even though he took the cause of it totally in his stride, being under the impression that the child had been induced to sit up and have a cheese hamburger. The carrycot back in the bedroom, I returned to where Johnson was playing cribbage, through fieldglasses, with one of the professors. Rosamund was lying back beside a neat bourbon, and the other professor was reading. "Meanwhile, back at the Orgy," Johnson said. "Have you done with the kettle? If I can find some sugar, I was going to make us all toddy."

"I couldn't find any sugar," I said. After viewing that nappy, I hadn't looked for it very hard. I added, "There's a pack of airport sugar somewhere in my anorak, if you can find it. The kettle is disengaged. Why is it so quiet?"

"Benedict has stopped bawling," Rosamund said. She didn't open her eyes. Johnson leaned over and switched off the cassette player.

Silence fell. "It *is* quiet," he said. The only real sound was that of Eskimos snoring. Rosamund's second bourbon, momentarily full, stood in well-behaved immobility, which was more than the rest of us did. We swung, as one man, to the speed dial.

It registered nil.

Our cries as we ripped back the curtains wakened the Ethnics. Our further cries, as we flung open the Vice-Presidential door, would have untangled a Kajuraho carving.

We had stopped. We had stopped on a plain, with no buildings in sight, in total darkness in the midst of a snowstorm.

And the rest of the train, and the engine, had vanished.

# Chapter 2

Of Johnson, eyeless in Manitoba, I had no great expectations. You couldn't say of the anthropologists that they were stoned out of their skulls; but neither were they in the way of dealing with what you might call emergencies. The steward was still out cold. The Booker-Readmans had, at public or finishing school, never even met a Boy Scout. But you would expect, alone in the howling wastelands of Canada, in a deserted railway carriage with the temperature at twenty-five at least under, that the men for the job would be Eskimos.

Not so. Even after we got them outside, they merely stamped about in the snow on the railway track. Tracking them from the light of the windows, the professors reported that, far from hunting, fishing, or erecting an igloo, the quartet were snowballing each other.

About that time, I got into my boots and my anorak and, prising out my private Ukrainian, set off to see what observation could do.

I had a torch, because I always have a torch in my anorak pocket. We walked along the snow on the track, with the car's row of brilliant lit windows above us. Then the coach came to an end, and we were in the dark, looking down at the trampled snow where some person or persons had unhitched us.

Some person or persons, it was apparent, who could only have come from the train that was pulling us. The footprints, half obscured already by snow, led along the track and ended in nowhere, where the bastard or bastards had got themselves back on the train. Vladimir, in whom the running of a laundrette had induced a suspicious nature, said, "But why did the train stop in the first place? There is no station."

There was no station. There wasn't even a tepee. We walked by mutual consent along the rails to where the head of the train must have been, and saw nothing. There hadn't been a Red Indian ambush, a trappers' demonstration, a moose asleep on the line. "He stopped," my Ukrainian said, "because he was before time? No. He did not stop long enough."

"He stopped," I said, "by my guess, because someone pulled the communication cord, and then made up some story while someone else broke the connection. Let's get back."

"Christ my Saviour," said Vladimir in a very reverent manner. "The Vice-Presidential car has now gone."

It hadn't, but the lights had gone out and it smelt, as we climbed in, of wet Eskimo and panic and whisky. There seemed to be a great many more than twelve of us, or eleven not counting the steward. Rosamund's voice said, "Heavens, you're cold," while she fended herself off my anorak. She had her own fur coat on. In the light of the torch, I saw they all had. Of course, with the connection gone, we had no heating.

Or lighting, it appeared. Or . . . ?

I said, "Can we get heat on the stove?"

"The toddy!" said Johnson's voice. He sounded aggrieved.

"Never mind the toddy," said Simon Booker-Readman. "When is the next bloody train due?"

"Not, I hope," said Johnson, "until daylight."

There was a short, heavy-breathing silence, interrupted by a familiar caterwauling. It was forty minutes since Benedict Booker-Readman had had an irregular and less than satisfactory feed and he was intent on lodging a complaint. He also appeared to have either colic or wind. Recalled to his existence, his mother said, "My God, the baby!"

Now was not the moment to question the intelligence of bringing a three-week-old baby out into sub-zero conditions in the first place. I said, "There's hot water still in the taps, and hot water bottles. Why not pack them round him, with a few extra blankets, and put the rest in a thermos to heat his feed with? There's enough in the pan to keep him quite happy all tomorrow."

"Joanna is right," said the calmer of the professors. "The coach, after all, can sleep seven. There are blankets. There is food. There is water. We are on a main railway line. Life is not threatened so long as there is no collision through the night. One of us must keep watch, with the torch."

"And through the day," Johnson said. "The snow will cover the carriage. Especially if there isn't much heat on the inside."

There was a gloomy European silence, underlined by the jabbering of the ethnic element, who were holding a meeting with the German professor on the opposite benches. You could only track them by the sound, since Rosamund, in even deeper gloom, had gone off with my torch to round up hot water bottles. I said, "Can't we work out where we are from the time we travelled? There must be a timetable somewhere."

There wasn't a timetable anywhere, and no one had looked at the clock when we started. Or when we stopped, for that matter. No one, either, remembered the stations. "It goes through Moosejaw," said the Canadian professor tentatively.

"Eventually," said Johnson. "On the other hand, the northern line goes to Prince Rupert on the Pacific, also eventually. I don't suppose there's a quick shuttle on either."

"What I can't understand," said Booker-Readman, "is how it happened. All right, they made an error at Winnipeg and hitched us up to a through train. But how did we get unhitched here? That was deliberate."

"Someone," said Johnson, "wants a corner on Eskimos. What are you worth, professor, in ransom money?"

The professors weren't worth a button, and neither was Vladimir or the Eskimos or, he swore, Johnson. But Grandmother, we all knew, would come up with the odd million if need be for Rosamund Booker-Readman's life. The discussion petered away at this point, especially as Johnson had cleared the windows and we all sat looking at one another in the eerie blue light from the snow. It stretched unbroken for miles and miles and miles.

Rosamund Booker-Readman's voice called, "I can't find the bottles, but I've filled a thermos flask. Simon? The battery's nearly done."

She must have kept the torch on all the time. I said, "I'll come," and felt my way into the passage just as the German professor was saying, "It may, of course, be the work of a band of deviationists. Or nationalists. Or those who do not approve of mixed races . . ."

"Or quilting," said Johnson seriously. He had got out and lit an old pipe, which illuminated the underside of his unremarkable nose, and his hair and his eyebrows, and nothing else whatever of his physique or his intentions. His Christian name, I forgot to say, is also Johnson, which results in a certain formality, even if you were as friendly with him as my father was.

I struggled through to where Rosamund had indeed parked the flickering torch on a bed, shut it off and pulled back all the curtains. She had found some blankets already. Working partly by touch I managed to locate the hot water bottles while she picked up and joggled the unfortunate Benedict. I used the torch a moment while I filled them and wrapped them in towels, then packed them with blankets into the carrycot. I retrieved the pan of feed from the fridge where I'd jammed it, filled the bowl of hot water and used it to warm up a cup of the mixture. The cup wasn't scalded, but that couldn't be helped.

Mother Booker-Readman was sitting down in the bedroom with her offspring, largely unfurled, yelling into her bosom. I draped them both with a fresh towel, shoved Benedict back into the crook of her arm and handed her the cup of feed with the spoon in it. She tilted the edge of the cup against the baby's pursed mouth, and half the feed ran down his face, while the spoon missed his eye by a fraction. They both opened their mouths and screamed with frustration.

I took Benedict from her while she went to get the milk off her skirt. There were only two ounces left in the cup, and he was as full of air as a bubble bath, but we managed. I had him hitched on my shoulder and was massaging his round shoulders absently, when I had happened to gaze at the window.

It was still dark, and snowfilled, but the plain was no longer empty.

Instead, like the teeth on a snowman, a line of minute black dots had appeared in the distance, enlarging second by second. Dots which, in the dimness, might have represented very large men very far off on skis, or very small men rather close to on skis but which, since the ground appeared flat, were probably travelling much too rapidly to be man-powered at all. I yelled "Johnson!" and Johnson's voice said peaceably from the sitting-room, "I see them."

I could hear everyone saying "What?" and the coach trembled as the complement lunged for the windows. It was not the moment to go into the matter of whether or not Benedict should have a dry nappy. I planted him down, to his annoyance, among the blankets and bottles and joined everyone else in the sitting room, which was reeking of alcohol. One of the professors was saying, "snowmobiles! Thank God they've found us!" As he was saying it, one of the snowmobiles, which are sort of powered toboggans, gave off a burst of red sparks followed by a succession of reports.

The Eskimos all lay on the floor. The professors and the Booker-Readmans stayed upright, thinking perhaps that the toboggans were merely pinking. I got hold of Rosamund round the knees and felled her. Johnson also lay down, on one elbow, while his pipe gently pulsed in the darkness. "The point is," he said thoughtfully, "who has found us? And which of us have they found?"

We were all prostrate by then, mostly on top of the Eskimos. The Ukrainian said, "It is a kidnapping then?" He sounded hopeful. No one bothers to kidnap a laundrette owner. On the other hand, Challenger power toboggans cost about eight hundred dollars apiece, and it might have been an anti-Soviet capitalist plot financed by Big Business. The Canadian professor, his nose rammed into sealskin, had gone into paroxysms of nervous sneezing, while the other, I noticed with surprise, had got out a revolver.

I said, "I suppose we'd all fetch a few pence, but they'd be better to try and kidnap one man than twelve. They can always relieve the rest of us of our cash and our watches."

Simon Booker-Readman got up and crouched at the window. "Why do we need to let them take anyone? A train is going to come sometime. Meanwhile they're out there in the cold."

"With guns," said Johnson.

"I have a gun," said the professor, waving it. "Living in New York, you understand, I am never without it." I got on my knees too.

There were six rushing black shapes on the snow, with possibly two men on each. I said, "If they come through the doors and windows at the same time, there's not much one revolver can do. But the galley's steel-lined and ventilated."

Rosamund was already halfway there. I just had time to pick up her son's carrycot and shove it through the door before it shut behind her. I hammered on it, and when she opened, dived for the drawer with the knives in it. Emerging, I prodded people and handed out knives.

The two professors and Vladimir had pulled the curtains across and were manning an eyehole apiece: the flower arrangements were in ruins. I said to Johnson, "Why don't you get into the galley? You're worth a mint and you know it." Five thousand smackers a portrait, so my father used to claim. More, for royalty. I discovered I was offering him the point of the knife, and reversed it. There was another volley of shots.

"You're right," said Johnson suddenly. He turned his back on the knife and fumbling out of the room, made his way into the passage.

The next moment there was a bang, and a blast of cold of freeze-shrinking intensity. Through the window, England's best-known portrait painter could be seen hurtling feet first from the coach doorway into the snow, there myopically to begin an advance, waving his knitted waistcoat and calling.

The snowmobiles which had fanned out in a halfcircle, came to a halt, with Johnson in the eye of the daisy.

One of the professors said hoarsely, "There is Hope for Mankind, while one man can do that." Slowly dismounting, the snowmobile riders were stalking forward. One of the Eskimos burst into tears. The intruders closed around Johnson.

There was an exchange of sentences.

Then the intruders, grasping Johnson, resumed their purposeful march to the railway carriage. It was the sequel the Boys' Own Paper always avoided: where the Hero Who Gives Himself Up becomes the Schmuck Who Ends Up a Hostage. Booker-Readman got the gun off the professor and I hung the tablecloth out of the window. Then we all stood about with our hands up.

Which made us look pretty funny when Johnson climbed back into the carriage followed by a line of hefty young men clad in Timberwolf, Raccoon, Scimmia, Tibetan Yak and Natural Unplucked Nutria.

We stood still in the glare of their torches. "Hi, chick!" said the Bank of Canada, and leaning forward, planted an enthusiastic kiss on my face. "Jeeze, you've sure had a party. O.K. Lights on, folks. The new talent's arrived!"

The lights came on, followed by a clicking sound. Heat flowed into the room. Those who were standing on Eskimos got off Eskimos. I said, *"Johnson"*.

Johnson blinked. "I told you," he said, "that I'd got you a free pass till midnight. Naturally, when your Huskies all went to meet you and found the coach gone, they did the right things. There'll be an engine along in a minute."

"The lights?" I said. "The heat?"

"Joanna," said Johnson sadly. "My glasses were cracked. If there was a switch, I must have missed it."

"You saw the snowmobiles," I said. It had become a private, and embittered dialogue. Behind us, hysterical laughter was breaking out. I said, "You scaremongered all the way through. You created panic. You flunked out of everything. You risked that bloody brat's life. Why?"

"I didn't," he said. "Honestly. In fact, I'll tell you a secret. I'm the guy who got the train stopped. The telephone wasn't out of order at all. I knew all the time we'd be rescued."

"It wasn't," I repeated. After a bit, I got my teeth apart. "And who coupled the carriage on to the train in the first place? The Huskies again?"

"No," said Johnson. "No. In fact that is a mystery. A railway mistake, one might venture. An act of the Lazy Three Fairies. Does it matter? It threw us together. Have a whisky."

He put one in my hand, topped it smoothly with water, and passed on his hospitable way. It was Natural Unplucked Nutria, I believe, who laid down his sporting rifle and gave the first howl. "What the hell are you drinking?"

"Whisky," said Johnson, surprised. "We've been drinking all night."

"Well," said Natural Unplucked Nutria, "have you *seen* what you're drinking?"

We hadn't. Held in the hand, our glasses contained what appeared to be an attractive straw-colored whisky.

Held up to the light, it still looked like whisky. Except that, coursing briskly around it was a large pack of frilly grey foreign bodies filled with intent, and for all I know, winking. I said, "Sea Monkeys."

I was the centre of attention. Everyone said "What?"

I said, "They're Sea Monkeys." I was furious.

One of the professors left the room quickly.

I said to Johnson, "That sugar."

"In your anorak pocket," he said. "I got it. I tipped it into the water. You remember. Then we couldn't make the toddy because we'd no boiling water."

I dipped my hand into my anorak pocket and came up, in silence, with an untouched pack of airline sugar. Johnson dipped his hand into his mac and came up with a torn pack of something else that he laid on the table between us.

*Instant life* it said, in yellow and red. *Ready-to-hatch Sea Monkeys, with a Supply of Special Growth Food. See them HATCH ALIVE. When fully-grown, they can be bred for even MORE adorable pets.*

"Murderer," I said to Johnson coldly.

The other professor left the room. Vladimir said, "What is this? Monkeys?"

"Brine shrimps," I said. "There's no need to fuss. Fish eat them with no ill effects whatever."

Until you put them in water, brine shrimp eggs look like dust. It would be perfectly possible, if your glasses were broken, to mistake them for sugar. Unless you were Johnson.

Simon Booker-Readman said, "What in God's name were you carrying these about for?" He looked, blessedly, more entertained than revolted.

Johnson picked up my anorak. "You'd be surprised. You don't mind, do you, Joanna? And without waiting, he turfed out my things on to the table. The sugar, which I'd saved from the airport. A picture postcard of a plane and two cocktail stirrers. A miniature pepper and salt. A pack of fruit gums, a box with a Mexican bean in it, a Matchbox tractor and three very poor cracker mottoes.

"I've got nephews," I said. Simon Booker-Readman was looking at me in a very odd way.

"You have no nephews," said Johnson precisely. "I, personally, am going to blow your cover."

"Shut up," I said. I knew, from the amused looks on their faces, that I had turned tie-dyed magenta with annoyance.

"Don't tease her," said Simon, but his voice had a questioning ring.

"I wouldn't dare," said Johnson mildly. "I only thought you would like to know that our gorgeous Joanna is a fully-qualified gold-medalled graduate of the world's finest college of nursery nurses. How do you imagine Benedict got the perfect handling he did, despite everything? The girl is a Margaret Beaseford trained nanny."

I scarcely felt Raccoon and Scimmia settle one on each side of me. Nurses of any kind only mean one thing to Huskies. Simon Booker-Readman said, *"You're a Nanny?"*

I've heard that tone of disbelief before as well. I had hardly finished nodding before he had streaked out of the room and was unfastening the galley door. Rosamund's questions and Benedict's screams died before the sheer violence of Benedict's father's voice, explaining.

Silence fell. Then the Booker-Readmans came back, all three, and gazed down upon me and my furry companions. Rosamund said, "We will pay you any fee you care to name, to come back and look after Benedict."

I agreed, after persuasion. It was, after all, why I had been sent to Canada. To pay for my original Italian knits I am not only a Maggie Bee nurse. I have another profession.

I thought no one knew about that. I was wrong.

We got back to Government House at five in the morning and were met by the Governor and his wife, who hauled me off for hot coffee and a family post mortem in their private sitting room. I was sitting in the aide's camelhair dressing gown inhaling steam with both eyes semi-closed when the door opened and Johnson came in, wearing striped winceyette pyjamas and a kimono.

His hair was on end, and if he had bags under his eyes, the glasses hid them. He said, "I've been a hell of a nuisance: I'm sorry, beautiful," and kissed his hostess, who got up and left, followed smartly by her husband, the rat. Johnson said "Two minutes" to me and, pouring himself a mug of coffee, sat down.

"I'll time you," I said. My eyelashes had been filed off with emery board and my nose in the steam was expanding like a Japanese paper flower in warm water. Even for a family friend, I wasn't going to volunteer anything more.

"All right. Listen," said Johnson. "I helped arrange that because I know a bit about you. Your father is one of my friends. So was Mike Widdess, your last employer, whose kid's toys you have in your pocket. I know that Mike lost his life in a car crash and that's why you're out of a job now. I know how he really died. And I know what you and he were doing together."

With some of his friends, my father is too friendly.

I said "Prove it."

The glasses flashed; perhaps with approval, perhaps with irritation. "All right," said Johnson mildly. "Mike Widdess was a lawyer who did some confidential work on the side for the government. He found you had some spare time and were bright, so he got you from time to time to help him. Then came the car crash."

The car crash which ended it all. I was coping with his kid to let Mrs. Widdess sort things out after the funeral when I got the news that the crash had not been accidental, but connected with Mike Widdess's job. And further that the people who had rigged the accident, whoever they were, had also been discreetly through all Mike's classified papers.

They had known what he did. And now they knew what I did also.

That much, Johnson had found out. He also knew about the alternatives which Mike's Department had offered me. To hide, or to help them by carrying on as if nothing untoward had been noticed, either about Mike's accident or his papers.

It had been tempting to hide. But I wanted to help flush out Michael's murderers; and perhaps I had. For, one week after his death, a Mrs. Warr Beckenstaff had applied to the Margaret Beaseford Nursery Nurses' Training College for a nanny with my qualifications. My qualifications down to the smallest detail. And at a time when no one outside my own friends and the Department knew that I was out of a job.

I turned down the offer when it reached me. I carried out orders and turned down every offer the first time. This one wasn't renewed.

But at the same time, Mrs. Warr Beckenstaff refused every other nanny they sent her. Refused even after the grandchild was born for whom the nanny was wanted. The grandchild being Benedict, the son of her only child Rosamund Booker-Readman.

"Then," said Johnson, "Rosamund and the baby went back to New York. The Department thought they were on to something, but didn't want to appear too keen. They knew Simon comes to Winnipeg every year for the Gallery. So they sent you to cruise all over Canada. If Simon came north, it was half of a coincidence. If he came north with the baby, it was more than half a coincidence. If he went all out to engage you for the baby, it was too much of a coincidence to ignore. Which brings the story to date. My bloody coffee's cold."

He drank some, and his peculiar glasses turned white. "And now you're wondering how I come into it."

"I know. You're my protection," I said sarcastically. "Does my father always blab this much?"

"Always," said Johnson blandly. "No. As a matter of fact, no one asked me to come. I'm just interfering. I had a bone, rather, to pick with Mike's murderers."

I supposed I should have to report it to somebody. I said, "So you agree with the Department? You think the Booker-Readmans have some ulterior motive in booking me? But you know, I could have sworn that neither of them knew I was a nanny beforehand. The mother especially."

"You were acting: why shouldn't she be?" Johnson said. "Or perhaps Simon was the prime mover. He was pretty keen to show you in action with Benedict. I don't blame him. I thought that sexy knit was going to do in your chances."

"I'm glad you noticed. I thought your glasses were broken," I said.

"Sight," said Johnson, "was the least of it. No one, at any rate, can suspect you of a burning wish to attach yourself to the Booker-Readmans. The Department has organized that. You've turned down Grandmother Warr Beckenstaff. Far from advertising your occupation, you've gone to some pains to conceal it. Whoever hooked the coach to that train achieved two things. They exposed you as a nanny, and threw Benedict into your arms so that when the job was offered, you took it. And that is something you hadn't promised the Department you'd do. Am I right?"

He was right. I had thought my mind was made up. If Simon Booker-Readman had engineered that car crash, I didn't want to look after his baby. If I was offered the job, it would be significant enough for the Department. They could take it from there.

So I had told the Department. But that, as Johnson said, was before Benedict had been thrown into my arms. Thrown into my arms and firmly kept there, it came to me, by the subsequent actions of Johnson himself, thus aiding and abetting whoever had hooked up the coach in the first place. I said, "You wanted me in this job? Why?"

His voice didn't change. He didn't put down his coffee. Damn him he didn't even blink. He said, "Mike's murderers want you in the job. And I want Mike's murderers even more than the Department does."

"So?"

"So you have a new job in New York. So have I."

"Doing what?" I said suspiciously.

"Painting Benedict and his mother. I forgot to tell you. Grandma Warr Beckenstaff asked me in England. That is, we bumped into each other and she—"

"—Made you an offer you couldn't refuse? The way," I said cautiously, "you and I are going to bump into one another?"

This time he did put down his coffee-cup, shaken, "Good lord, no," Johnson said. "You play your game. I play mine. Different boards. I shall be surprised, really, if we meet again."

*Johnson came,* my mother once wrote. *I thought for once we were becoming quite close, and then he sort of melted away in my hands.*

Like Sea Monkeys.

# Chapter 3

The status symbol supreme in New York is a Silver Cross pram with a Beaseford nanny in uniform pushing it. Beside that, a Rolls Royce is rubbish.

Manhattan is full of Maggie Bee nurses. You can tell us by our pudding-basin green hats and green coats and brown leather gloves over our varnishless, closely pared fingernails. By our lavender dresses with their bows and belts in uniquely dyed ribbon; by our stiff collars with studs and our crackling, box-pleated aprons. By our handbags filled with clean tissues and crayons and monogrammed spoons wrapped in handkerchiefs. By the indefinable odor of disinfectant from finger to elbow, and of sour milk about our left shoulderblades. By the fact, if you care to investigate, that under every stout skirt is a matching set of close-fitting knickers. You can't make a lap with your knees together which has, as Charlie Medleycott says, been the downfall of many a nanny.

Charlie's green coat and hat were the first thing I saw, flying in from Toronto. The next thing was the relieved face of Rosamund Booker-Readman, my new employer, as she hoisted a basket towards me.

She said, "I thought I would know you again. Listen, I'm going to lose my flight unless I go now. That's our address in Bermuda. There's Benedict. Charlotte will show you where the house is, and your room and everything. The freezer's full. Ask the help if you want to know anything. Have you money?"

"No," I said. I took the basket. Charlotte's face was bright red.

"Oh." Rosamund took out her purse and slid out three five-dollar bills, which was modest enough considering that she was paying me two hundred dollars a week. Or Grandmother was. I said, taking it, "And when will you be back?"

She turned back, looking impatient. She had a cloche hat over her large handsome eyes, and a 'thirties beaver collar which suited her. "Oh, in about a week, I should think. Simon'll wire you."

"Have a good trip," I said, but she was off already. From red, Charlotte had gone pale with fellow-feeling under the pudding-basin. I said, "Scrub it. I'd rather have that than be fussed over. Look, is this your time off?" to Charlie.

"No. The Mallards," said Charlotte, "have lent me for the morning. What a rotten—"

I let her talk herself out on the cab ride. I hadn't enjoyed my reception, but I recognized it. Not all mothers grasp the idea that babies are people. Or even that people are people, come to that.

My future home was a brownstone house in three storeys, plus a basement in which Sultry Simon stored the surplus objects from his Madison Avenue gallery. Every window was barred; there were three locks on the front door, and you had to walk round a mat in the hall, or it let off an alarm system. The house itself had had no attention in recent years from anyone except woodworm larvae but that was all right. For the first time for quite a while I began to feel safe.

Because Benedict, removed from his basket, proved to have a temperature of 104, I was safe for three weeks, in as much as I never stepped over the threshold. One Dr. Joshua Gibbings, at unthinkable cost, arrived daily and the Brazilian help went back and forth to the drug store with Portuguese notes stored in her bosom. Rosamund phoned from Bermuda three times but didn't come home for ten days.

Other people telephoned, such as Charlotte and her Data-Mate boyfriend Denny Donovan. I had a single innocuous conversation over the phone with Johnson. Johnson, installed at the Waldorf, was painting tycoons, tycoons' daughters and occasionally, he said, tycoons' mistresses whose tycoons didn't understand them. He wanted to know when he could paint Rosamund and Benedict, and when my first outing would be. "Go with someone else till you get used to the traffic," he said. "You know. They drive on the right."

"Separate boards," he had said. I didn't know what to do about

Johnson, so I'd done nothing. The Department had told me I'd be protected, but not by whom. I believed Johnson when he said he had nothing officially to do with it. He was a public figure. He had engineered that commission because he was Mike Widdess's good friend, not mine. Rosamund came home, and I gave her his message.

I took my weekly telephone call, also innocuous, from my mother, and had Donovan in for a chaste cup of tea in the kitchen, without Charlie's knowledge and with Rosamund's affronted agreement. Then she decided to produce *coq au vin* instead of cold beef for supper and Donovan was turned off the breakfast bar by the spice wheel. I was sorry, since he was the only guest I could have who could infect nothing more than a hockey team.

Then Benedict recovered, and the decadent stuff really started. That is, I could have a private life three evenings a week, and during the day could join the pram-bashing league with the rest of the nannies.

I met Charlotte Medleycott in the Carl Schurz Park just two days later.

The British Embassy being prolific, Charlie had three Mallard kids on the hoof and one bawling its head off in a push chair. Despite that, she looked the same straight-nosed, leisure-class athlete who had cut a swathe through the boys in Toronto and Winnipeg, or at hunt balls, or at the Maggie Bee back in England, for that matter. She had her hair waved to her ears, and then tonged out sideways under her hatbrim. I thought about growing my hair again. "Well?" she was repeating.

I knew what she was asking. I'd just had my first evening off between the six and ten o'clock feeds, and had spent it with a boy of Charlie's providing.

There have been more successful evenings. I must have been the only female in New York to fall asleep three times into the Breast of Peach Blossom Duck when out on a first date at Trader Vic's. I said, "He was sweet, Charlie; and I'm meeting him again, when I'm down to four feeds a day and only half dead."

Charlie peered into the expensive piece of coachwork rolling in front of me, with the hood up and Benedict slumbering neatly inside it. "How is he?"

He was well over seven weeks, and eleven pounds five ounces in weight, and was taking an average seven ounces per bottle of newly thickened feed containing two drops of Adexolin, five grains of sodium citrate, and lactose. I said nothing and Charlotte said, "He's filling out. Thank God you got rid of the petunia blankets."

Some mothers spend the pre-natal months buying midnight-blue buster suits, chocolate nighties and trendy black pillowslips. I'm all for contrast, but most kids are less often peach-colored than a blotched shade between green and yellow. I said, "The girl with the pink pram is calling you."

We went over and Charlotte did her standard, and slanderous introduction. The girl with the pink pram was called Bunty Cole and I'd heard of her. Among other interesting things, she and her employers lived in the luxury flats next to my brownstone. I remember quite clearly paying attention to her face and her clothes so that if we crossed paths again, I should know her.

As Charlotte and I stood together, Bunty Cole came to our shoulders. She had a tip-tilted nose, brown spaghetti-hoop hair, and lashes glued on her eyelids like draught-excluders. Someone had kitted her out in striped coffee nylon with a smart buff gaberdine trenchcoat. With it, she wore twenty-guinea zipped platform fashion boots to match the high fashion pram that sat perched on its wheels like a penny-farthing. A good-going breeze would have blown any child out of its socket, if not overturned it: the Maggie Bee would have nothing to do with them.

The world is full, however, of nursery nurses with full-scale N.N.E.B. qualifications and Health Diplomas who have not been trained at the Maggie Bee. Bunty Cole, introduced, offered a small, taloned hand. "Just a peasant from Liverpool, love. I keep telling Charlie. You either love kids or you hate 'em, but it's a great way to flush out the fellas." She turned to Charlotte. "You know yet what Donovan does?"

"Plays ice hockey," Charlotte said.

"In his spare time. Sure," Bunty said. "That's on his Data-Mate card. You want to know what he really does? He's a plant doctor."

Charlotte sat down. "A what?"

"A plant doctor. He spends his time paying health calls on pot plants."

I didn't really believe it and neither did Charlotte, but it was worth discussing. We sat there under the bare wintry trees on primrose benches and went on to other items of gossip from nurseries on both sides of the Atlantic while Benedict slept and Charlie's four pottered about between the swings and the chute and the climbing frame.

There were two other Maggie Bee's, and about two dozen mixed au pairs and helps and mums in jeans and headscarves and jackets, and the odd dad on his hunkers. And there were at least fifty kids, with pails and bikes and balls and bats and an epidemic of low pedal bikes with "Tristan," "Claudia," "Grover," "Melissa" and "Sanchez" painted groggily all down the axle-shafts.

There were, as I have said, a lot of English nannies in New York, and English nannies go to English families if they can manage it. I watched, idly, the pedal bike labelled "Sanchez" until it was appropriated by a three-year-old lumberjack in earflaps, a dummy and Wellingtons. Bunty said, "I got all the dirt on the Booker-Readmans when I was over in England at Christmas. The County said they'd either get a Maggie Bee nanny or smother it. You'd better watch the Warr Beckenstaff shares. I bet Grandmother is paying your salary. What's Sultry Simon like when Rosamund isn't there?"

"Rosamund's always there," I said.

"I bet," said Bunty again. "But he'd make a lovely rich widower. And what about the portrait man, Johnson? He looks a mess in his pictures, but you don't run a yacht and a Porsche on peanuts. When's he coming to paint her?"

Nannies know everything. "She's had a sitting already," I said. "At the Waldorf." The lumberjack was maintaining possession of the pedal bike in the face of bodily assault by a black-eyed child in a fur coat and a crash helmet. The baby in the penny-farthing started to grizzle and Bunty rocked the contraption with one booted foot. I added, to get it clear, "He's rich, single, thirty-eight and a friend of my father's."

"They're the worst," Bunty said cheerfully. "Some of them start early and never leave off. Even Grover got down to undoing my buttons on Saturday. Just like your father, I told him."

"Talking of Grover," Charlotte said. "You've forgotten to take out his dummy again. If Pa Eisenkopp sees you, he'll flip his lid, dearie."

Bunty leaped to her feet, swearing mildly, and tripped off, teetering, among the pedal bikes, where she pounced on the lumberjack and evacuated its plug with a plop. Grover let out a wail which sharpened audibly as he was lifted from the pedal bike labelled "Sanchez" and replaced on that marked "Grover." "The Eisenkopps," Charlotte said, "are hell on hygiene. Fortunately, Bunty couldn't care less."

A park attendant with a leaf badge on his left shoulder went by, wheeling a large oil can with brooms on it and a small boy riding outside talking, his fists on the rim. Someone fell out of a swing and was taken, yelling, to the Mister Softee van. A girl in pigtails went through on roller skates, narrowly missing Grover and Bunty.

In the pram, Grover's sister had begun a further series of more insistent complaints, ending in a short squeal of the kind that means "nappie pin." I was nearest, so I turned back the fur coverlet, the merino blankets and the Viyella sheet, revealing Sukey Eisenkopp, who had all her fingers stuck through different holes in her fine fancy shawl, and scratch marks all over her face from her fingernails. She also had both the terry and Harrington squares between her bare, mottled limbs, and looked like a two-legged terrapin.

I said, fixing her, "Do the Eisenkopps know they're going to have a hen-toed daughter and a son with bent teeth from dummy-sucking?"

Charlotte put down the child whose nose she was wiping and came over to help. "I did tell Bunty to alter the nappies," she said. "The shawl's a new disaster, and so are the scratches: she'll have to get gloves. Will you tell her? Or shall I?"

With good reason, non-Maggie Bee nurses do not appreciate Maggie Bee nurses telling them their business. I was therefore surprised, and Charlotte saw it, and grinned. "Bunty doesn't mind. Bunty's trouble is that she has three serious boyfriends and can't make up her mind which one to bypass her pills for, or whether to save it all up for her trips back to England. I tell you, she gets more Friendship Club letters than I do. But she's all right. She likes kids, when she remembers."

There was nothing reassuring about that statement. Charlotte's address book is maintained with the help of roughly five hundred male correspondents in both hemispheres.

"Even when she remembers," I said cautiously, "isn't it rough on the kids?"

"It won't be, now she's got you next door," said Charlotte with, as it turned out, push-button accuracy.

Then she said, "Joanna?"

The last time I heard her whisper like that, the incubator lights had cut out in a premie ward. This time, she was staring at Benedict's baby carriage.

It was still there, braked at the end of the wooden bench, shining. But the hood was eased back and the cover half off, instead of mitred and tucked as I'd left it. Nor, like a wren's egg in its nest, was Ben's bullet head bedded under it.

I got to the pram before Charlotte's next breath and tore up the merinos. The pram was empty but for one knitted bootee. Benedict Booker-Readman had vanished.

Two of the Mallard children, frightened by the look on Charlotte's face, started to cry. Charlotte said, "I didn't see *anyone*."

I was looking round. "There's a pram over there. Run. If he's not in it, try East End Avenue. I'll go out by the river." The Carl Schurz has a very small tots' lot. Unless he'd been chucked in the loo, or another pram, he was out in the streets in a basket, a bag or a car, in which case the Booker-Readmans had lost him. There was also the network of paths between the rest of the park and East River.

He wasn't in the lavatories. I affronted a number of kids of both genders and then hared for the riverside exit, shouting to Bunty, who had stopped there with Grover. She said, her hand over Grover's mouth, "No one came out this way. Wait. Someone did. The attendant." She turned suddenly and made a grab at one of the kids staring at us. "You had a ride on the oil can. Where did he go? The man with the brushes?"

Fast questions don't work with children. The kid's mouth remained open but silent. Bunty didn't wait. She was quicker than I was. Abandoning a thunderstruck Grover she took to her heels through the gate and past the play-courts and down the paths where old men in overcoats were sitting playing chess on stone benches.

The attendant was no more than a flying shadow among the bare trees: he must have seen us coming. But in his wake were two irate cardplayers sounding off in a mess of broken cigars and bent court cards while beyond, an oil drum lay on its side, screaming hollowly.

Inside among the cigarette packs and toffee papers and popcorn lay Benedict, still padded like a hand grenade in his matinée jacket, hat, coat and two shawls and tearlessly emoting throughout three square inches of naked face. I pulled him out, cheek to cheek, and held him until he began rabbiting away at my ear, while Bunty, platform soles chugging, made across the park after the attendant.

After five minutes she came back red-faced with a stitch and a crumpled park jacket, found on the grass, The man had disappeared. "Isn't that something else?" said the older of the two card players, standing with his tablecloth clasped to his waistcoat. "The judge give you custody, they've got no right to do that." He picked up a jack of hearts in full beaver and chucked the gasping Benedict under the chin with it. "You stick to your Momma there, girlie. You gonna call the fuzz?"

I looked at Bunty. "Are we going to call the fuzz?"

But we didn't have to telephone anybody, as Charlie arrived with the police just as we got back to the six yelling children, and from then on, it was nothing but questions. They finished with the other girls first. I said to Bunty, "If expressions of gratitude come into the picture, Sultry Simon ought to give you one for running after the bastard."

"Shucks," said Bunty agreeably. "I only wanted to ask him to take Grover and Sukey next time. That's our duplex, on top of the newest block there. Come and have a drink when you're off next. Tomorrow?"

We fixed it. Then she and Charlie went off, while I led the fuzz out of the park and past the notice board through which the Carl Schurz addresses its visitors.

It said:

### ENJOY

Run Hop Skip Jump Litter Skate Leap Laugh
Giggle Wiggle Jog Romp Swing Slide Frolic Climb
Bicycle Stretch Read Relax Imbibe Play Sleep.

I forbore to go back and mark in Kidnap. Who reads notice-boards?

# Chapter 4

I didn't need to wonder whether to phone Johnson on the day of the snatch: Rosamund did it for me. In one sitting, he seemed to have made quite an impression. She got on the phone as soon as the police had left us and so did I, on the upstairs extension.

Johnson's voice was sympathetic but not burning with eagerness. His advice was to phone Simon and hire a bodyguard.

My employer's tones, on the other hand, were resonant with self-pity. "Your little Joanna, you know, was hired to look after this child twenty-four hours a day. Do you suppose she's too young, or wrapped up in boyfriends or what? The Mallards' girl is a nymphomaniac."

I was interested because it was practically true. Charlotte really has the best contacts at home and abroad of any person I know. I waited to be told more about myself, but instead Rosamund went on to ask if Johnson wouldn't move in to finish painting her. She'd feel better, she said, with a man in the house.

Johnson said he couldn't, and wasn't Simon due home tomorrow and really he advised very strongly hiring a short-term bodyguard. Some people snatched babies on impulse. It might never happen again.

Rosamund rang off and so did I. I was almost as annoyed with him as Rosamund was.

Benedict cried off and on through the night and by midday had worked himself into a heat rash and got both his sleeping times and his eating times so muddled up that it wasn't worth taking him out. I cooled him off and dabbed on some lotion and surveyed him with a purely clinical satisfaction.

A new, dark stubble was joining the two patches of long silky hair over his ears and his chin was advancing. He didn't squint any longer. The previous week, he had smiled for the first time, but I hadn't mentioned it. Tradition requires that the first smile is always for the mother.

Later, preparing to take my afternoon off, I felt that somehow she wasn't going to get it today. I laid out the feeds, the written instructions, the fresh clothes, the nappies, the spare sheets and everything else that in four hours might become of urgent necessity and, leaving Rosamund and her offspring glaring at one another, departed next door to the block of luxury flats that contained Bunty Cole and the Eisenkopp duplex.


Bunty Cole's employers had thirty-two rooms in that block, and a roofgarden.

To get there, I had to pass a doorman, a speaking tube and a closed-circuit television, all of which filled me with envy. Then I got out of the lift at the Eisenkopp residence and was rendered practically speechless.

Bunty shared with the family's grandfather the whole upper floor of the duplex. Bunty had a bedroom, a bathroom, a sitting-room with color TV and a night nursery off with Sukey in it. Beyond was a day nursery, a smart room for Grover, a laundry and a miniature kitchen. The furniture was as in Abitare, and you got tired lifting your feet through the carpet.

Bunty showed me round. In the laundry was the automatic washing machine, the tumble-drier, the ironing board and the warming-cupboard full of clean diapers. In the kitchen was the cooker, the infra-red grill, the dish-washing machine, the sink with the waste-disposal unit, the electric mixer, mincer and bottle warmer, the deep freeze, and the fridge.

On the shelves were cans and cans of babyfood, instant potato, maple syrup, cereals, eggs, jam, bread and chewable vitamins in animal shapes. In the deep freeze was a stack of frozen fruit juice, waffles, pancakes, fish fingers, and whole frozen meals packed on

TV trays. In the refrigerator were ice cubes, butter, beer, sodawater, 7-up, Coca-Cola and a few lonely bottles of milk.

I said when I could speak, "Well, at least they've left you room for the milk. My lot keep the fridge full of beer packs."

"That's what Charlotte said," said Bunty placidly. "I used to share kitchens once, but you do get in a mess."

In other words, all the hard work was done by the Italian couple and the help in the family kitchen below. The hand-trimmed voile and lace ruffles on Sukey's cot were fresh as tomorrow.

I said, "Before you ask, I have one room with Benedict next to it, and there is a Brazilian daily." I had been given a gin and orange. I suppose all the world makes gin and orange with child's high-vitamin juice, but not everyone also heaps it with cut peaches and nectarines from a crate in the corner. I said, "What in God's name does Comer Eisenkopp do? Deliver doggie bags to Fort Knox?"

"He runs a business," said Bunty vaguely. Sukey, not yet unpacked from her walk, bumped the plastic butterflies bracing the hood of her pram and they revolved. Her eyes rolled together like marbles.

I said, following Charlotte's advice, "Honestly, you'll make her squint if you string things so close to her face . . . Who was the super man who kissed you as we came upstairs then?"

"With the moustache?" said Bunty, as if the crowd had been overwhelming. "Hugo Panadek, love: Father Eisenkopp's Design Director. He lives here half the time. That's who I keep the vodka for."

If that left it an open question on the matter of the other eleven bottles of spirits, I didn't pursue it. Grover, without a dummy but still wearing his lumberjack's hat, came in from the day nursery and said, "Hugo was a good boy and Bunty kissed him." He produced, absent-mindedly, a number of hacking coughs.

I had a London bus in my pocket. I said, "Grover. Look what I've got." He came over. Sukey, bored with butterflies, let out a series of squeals. With a sigh, Bunty put down her gin and orange and rising, disentangled the baby from her bedding and deposited her on the floor where she lay, her hat over her eyes. She had on an embroidered matinée jacket and a long fine wool night dress with lace, faintly tinged with orange in the nappy area.

Bunty said, "It's a lottery, ain't it? If you look after bleedin' infants you're too fagged for a love life; and if you get them able to talk then they fink on you. Grover, don't *do* that."

Grover had flung the London bus at Sukey, but missed. Sukey, breathing heavily through her hat, paid no attention. I said, "That's a bad cough, Grover. Come and open your mouth for me," and when he came, peered into his throat and took off his hat at the same time. His glands were slightly swollen but his throat, though red, wasn't spotty.

"It's only a little cough," Bunty said, in a tone which meant, "three hours at the pediatrician: not bloody likely." "Grover, go and get your new trike." She poured out more gin, and put some of the extra orange into a cup, with a splash from the waterjug. This she stirred and then, lifting the nerveless Sukey, dragged her face out of her hat and fed her a spoonful. Grover trotted across, picked up the bus, and threw it at Sukey again. It missed her, but nearly knocked over Bunty's gin.

"Don't *do* that, Grover," said Bunty again automatically. "Fetch your new trike and show Nurse Joanna."

According to College rules, every nurse expects to be called Nurse, with the Christian or surname added, as preferred. College rules are not observed by top people's parents, at whose parties I should be addressed as Nanny Booker-Readman; nor by trendy mothers or Americans, to whom I was Jo. In return I could call the Americans, but not the trendy mothers, by their Christian names also.

To the Eisenkopps, whom I had not yet encountered, I was evidently Nurse Joanna, although they were certainly American, if not dating right back to the Mayflower. Which, since they called Bunty Bunty, told you quite a lot about the Eisenkopps.

"That horrible little punk," said Bunty placidly, referring presumably to the absent Grover. "Came into my bedroom five times last night, including when I was trying out this green face pack." She finished juicing up Sukey and dumped her back on the Wilton, without apparently noticing the marks of the trade on her striped coffee nylon.

Sukey squawked and Grover came in paddling his bike and drove it straight at her face without slackening.

I stopped it with my foot. Bunty said, "Grover, be careful!" and went on telling me about the green face pack. Then she got up and went out to find one to show me, and Grover, settling violently in the saddle, backed and came once more, hard, for Sukey.

This time I stopped him with more than my foot. I lifted him off his tricycle and said, "Grover. If you do that again, I shall smack you."

Rule fifteen in the Maggie Bee book holds firmly to the belief that there is no need for spanking or smacking in the rearing of children, and indeed begs employers not to ask any Margaret Beaseford Nurse to lift a hand in anger.

The first thing a Maggie Bee nurse does in any British household is to ask the mother if she minds if the offspring get paddled from time to time, and if the mother has any sense she agrees to it. They have got, after all, to get into training for public school.

When, therefore, Grover responded to my threat in the time-honored way by mounting the trike and forcing it straight into and nearly over his sweet sister's pulsing cranium, I locked the handlebars, scoured him out of the saddle, laid him over my knee and delivered a finely judged smack on his trousers.

I might have got in another, but a broad hand gripped my arm from behind and squeezing it like a toothpaste tube, removed me from my chair so fast that the chair fell right over and my tights laddered. Grover, sliding yelling off the punishment rostrum was caught by another, solicitous hand and then enfolded, still yelling, against the stomach of what could only be his male parent. The male parent, addressing me, said, "Hit my kid again, and I'll sock you one."

Comer Eisenkopp, who ran a business which paid for the top two floors of a luxury penthouse and supported an ageing father, a wife, two children, an Italian couple and Bunty at three hundred dollars a week plus the privilege of undoing her uniform buttons, was short, stocky and healthily cleanshaven, with thickly waving dark hair and glorious teeth, which he was baring. He also had on a starched collar and tie, and a leather-trimmed alpaca cardigan.

He said, "Can the child hustle you back? You've got it made real good, haven't you, whoever you are? Pick on a kid? Pick on a poor helpless baby? What'd you do to my poor little Sukey there? Slug her jaw if she don't eat her waffles?"

His gaze shifted. "Did you bring that gin? Where's my girl? Did you bring that gin?" His voice, already powerful, swelled to appalling proportions. "Bunty! Bunty? Do you know there's a drunk foreigner in here beating my children?"

At this point, I hand it to Bunty. She could have lain doggo. She could have pretended to be out of hearing or even, at a pinch, out of the house. As it was, she appeared, if belatedly, in her doorway, with the leaf-green mud pack all over her face.

Grover, adoring every sadistic second, peeped out from his father's cardigan selvedge and went off into a paroxysm of fresh amazement and horror. Sukey, drawing breath from time to time, continued an obbligato that would have done Bishop proud. A soft voice raised in mellow alarm impinged from the direction of the doorway calling, "My babies! My babies! What are you doing to my babies!" and Mother Eisenkopp, a dead ringer for any of the Mrs. Roger Vadims, floated in, capsized over the tricycle and collapsed shrieking on top of her daughter, kicking her son in the fist as she did so.

The gin went flying. Mr. Eisenkopp, shouting "Beverley!", leaped forward and gripped his blonde and dazzling wife. Bunty, clawing mud off her face, flew in and winkled out Sukey.

I lifted the gin, bestowed a couple of stiff cleansing doubles on the glistening patch already present on Sukey's resting place, and then picked up Grover, who was standing with his eyes shut, emitting short breathy hoots with his cut paw dripping blood on the carpet.

Before he knew where he was, I had his hand under the cold tap in the bathroom, and the hoots were giving way to straight-up crying.

"Grover is a brave boy," I said. "Look. Joanna has a big white handkerchief. Now, Grover show Joanna where Bunty's bandages are."

Bandages or band-aids: they always do the trick.

"You get a bandage?" he said. He had dark hair like his father's, and maybe even his mother's; cracked lips and red patches on both bulbous cheeks.

"A very big bandage," I said. "Grover show the bandages to Joanna."

They were in the bathroom cabinet, along with a half-hearted bottle of Junior Aspirin, some plasters, some lint, some cotton wool, an obelisk of assorted make-up and Bunty's pills, all up-to-date to the minute, which tallied with Charlotte's analysis and was good news for the Mexican yam industry.

The Eisenkopps might have been hell on hygiene, but they had missed out on the First Aid Department. Or maybe that had been cornered by the Mafia. I cut out some lint, chatting, and made a beautiful bandage, with donkey's ears on it. Grover, his face smothered in half-dried tears, said, "Now Joanna give Sukey a bandage."

The fate of Sukey had been somewhat occupying my mind, not to mention the fact that if Mother Eisenkopp had broken both legs, all three of Bunty's boyfriends were in for a hard time. With three adults already on the scene, I felt the only positive contribution I could make was to keep Grover out of it. He produced a dry cough, and followed it with another. "Grover wants Bunty," he said suddenly.

I should have been more worried if he hadn't. I said, "Bunty is helping Mummy just now, then she'll come and see Grover's big bandage. Shall I tell you a secret?"

"I tell you?" he said. He continued with a phased series of croaks.

"I'll show you something that's nice for your cough. Where's the kitchen?"

He was less than eager, but he condescended to show me, and he watched while I made butter balls rolled in sugar. In the middle he said, "*That's* a topeat."

Whatever he was describing, I was being done a favor. I looked about. Bunty's English habits at once proclaimed themselves. "So it is," I said. "Some people call it a teapot."

"*You* call it a topeat," said Grover. "Again?"

I gave him another butter ball. "Grover can be a teapot," I said. "Look." I set one hand on his hip, and pulled the other out at an angle. "You're a teapot."

"You're a topeat," said Grover, and giggled. He was a quick learner, too. After a few minutes he had me by the hand and we were progressing out of the suite, bearing the plateful of butterballs with us. At the end of a passage he knocked on a door and called "Grandpa!"

It was getting like a Frank Capra film, except that the man in the bed wasn't gentle and white-haired and quizzical, but as short, black-haired and positive as his powerful son. Beside the bed was a wheelchair of the automatic kind with a mike that you talk to.

"About time, too," said Grandfather Eisenkopp. "Is Comer throwing a party out there I'm not invited to?"

"Grover's hurt his hand," I said. "Someone fell over his trike. We've brought you some butter balls."

"I'm a topeat," said Grover happily.

"I could have told you," said Grover's grandfather readily enough. He picked up a butterball, squeezed it and then put it into his mouth, wiping his hand on the sheet. Grover struck his new-found attitude and declaimed.

> *"I'm a little teapot, short and stout*
> *Here's my handle, here's my spout*
> *When the kettle boils, hear me shout*
> *Pick me up and pour me out."*

"So you are," said Grandfather. He leaned forward, picked Grover up and pouring him out, proceeded to tickle him under the arms as he lay, shrieking with joy on the bed. Over Grover's back he said, "If something needs doing, I'll keep him now."

Grandfather Eisenkopp was nobody's fool. I nodded and backed to the door. "What's your name?" he added, still tickling.

I said, "Joanna Emerson. I work for the Booker-Readmans next door. You'll make him sick after the butter."

"Go to hell," said Grandfather Eisenkopp amiably. I shut the door and went back, with reluctance, to the sitting room.

Beverley Eisenkopp was lying back on Bunty's sofa while Bunty, still green as the Frog Prince in coffee striped nylon, massaged her sprained ankle and Comer Eisenkopp held both her hands as if they were money.

I looked round for Sukey, on the carpet, in the pram, inside an arm-chair: even, if the worst had come to the worst, in the waste paper basket. Then, leaving the tableau to look after itself, I tracked her down to the curtained confection in the night nursery, where she lay fast asleep with her hat off and her fingers sticking through the same fancy shawl Charlotte and I had already deplored.

I didn't propose to wake her yelling this time in order to unbend her fingers. A silent withdrawal was on my immediate program, before any of the Eisenkopps started shouting again, or Grover was sick. As a last gesture of goodwill to the profession I bent down to the litter round the cot and, picking up a soaked nappy and a noisome Harrington square, carted them into the bathroom where the nappy pail was, and the loo.

The gentle art of loo-pan nappy-sluicing requires a stomach of iron and fingers sufficiently strong to retain hold of said nappy in the left hand while keeping your right for the flushing apparatus. According to the book, a couple of gallons of pressurized water will then cleanse the nappy and allow you to return it scoured and dripping to the nappy pail, ready for washing. At Maggie Bee's you paid for every nappy you lost down the bend, and if the plumber had to call, then you paid for that, too.

I would have backed Bunty to lose the two kids down the S bend, never mind Harrington's best. I held the square in the loo pan and flushed, and the loo rose, brimmed and stayed brimming without showing a hint of retiring. The square relieved itself of its burden. I lifted it into the pail and finding a loo brush returned to the pan for some undesirable baling and excavating.

It wasn't a Harrington square but a whole nappy, presumably Grover's, which reluctantly swam from the recess. It brought with it an assortment of unappetising debris, including a headache powder wrapper, some bits of wood and a couple of assorted sepia scrolls I identified, after a moment's brief speculation, as portions of a burst rubber dummy.

Not to let Bunty down, I wrapped the dummy remains and concealed them. The bits of wood and the paper I set aside while I dabbled the nappy. More wood floated up.

There really wasn't enough water left in the loo pan to rinse with and I wasn't going to flush it a second time. I was bringing out Grover's potty when I noticed that most of the splinters were colored. I put down the potty, fished the rest of the wood from the loo and put all the bits side by side on the vinyl. They were only fragments, but you could guess, fitted together, they might have made the whole of a very small painting. A painting on wood. A painting of eyes, nose, feet, fingers and something which could have been also a halo.

I returned, deep in thought, to the potty and held it under the bath tap, my mind still on the picture. A very old picture. One I felt I had seen before. Perhaps because Simon Booker-Readman had some very like it stored in his overflow basement.

The fact was, it wasn't a picture: it was an ikon. And Simon Booker-Readman, according to rumor, had just lost an ikon, an old one.

This one, for example?

Then, should I call Bunty?

I didn't have to. As I held it under the tap, Grover's potty burst into song. Bunty opened the door. I turned off the tap. The potty, jingling busily, completed its modest recital:

> *"Half a pound of tuppenny rice,*
> *Half a pound of treac . . . cle.*
> *Mix it up, and make it nice,*
> *Pop! goes the wea . . . sel."*

"Hullo," said Bunty. "You've found Grover's musical potty. I say, you've got the nappy out of the loo."

"And the other things," I said. "What do you do, empty your coat pockets into the lavatory pan?"

"Sometimes," said Bunty simply. "What's all that, for God's sakes?"

I spread out the fragments of unhygienic wood on some loo paper." Someone's bust up a picture. Grover?"

"Maybe", said Bunty with cursory sympathy. "Bloody kid. Wrap it up and I'll shove it down the disposal chute. Or his father'll lecture him silly. Where is he, anyway?"

"Grover's with his grandfather," I said. I gave her the bundle of chippings. "How's the scene with the parents?"

Bunty said vaguely, "Oh, I explained it all." She watched me wash my hands with a cake of Chanel No. 5 that matched the talc in the night nursery and must have tripled Bunty's aura in the Park, whatever its virtues in cases of nappy-rash.

"You explained the gin and orange?" I said.

"No problem," said Bunty. "I said you and Hugo had shared a light refreshment. Hugo'll back us both up. You must meet him some time. He practically lives here."

With difficulty, I remembered that Hugo Panadek was Eisenkopp's Design Director, and a good boy whom Bunty had kissed, according to Grover. I said, "Look, with you and Beverley Eisenkopp in the house, what that man needs is a sedative, not new introductions. What does he design anyway, apart from subterfuges?"

"Never heard of them," said Bunty, who had no pretensions.

"He's Father Eisenkopp's toy designer. Didn't I tell you Comer manufactured toys?"

"No," I said. I hadn't seen a toy in the place apart from the plastic butterflies. "You mean I'm going to be sued for criminal assault by the irate mogul of a toy empire?"

"Don't be silly," said Bunty placidly. "Come and see. I told him you'd just saved Sukey's life. Grover's always trying to do Sukey in. He tried to take off her head once with the can opener. This is where the toys are."

She had led the way back to the day nursery, which was a large over-warm room with armchairs, TV and spotless vinyl tiles patterned like games boards. Half of one wall was blackboard and the other half pinboard, covered with bits of paper scrawled on by Grover. All the other wall space, apart from the windows, was patterned with numbers, letters, animals and friezes from Disneyland. Bunty pressed a stud and the Lady and the Tramp slid aside, revealing a cavernous cupboard crammed with teddies, pandas, elephants and dogs in flare-resistant plush with safety-locked noses and eyes.

Grover's wall let down in sections to show a complete electric railway, a farm, an Apache fort and a theatre with puppets and scenery. He had dress-up clothes and plasticine and planes and board games and jigsaws. Elsewhere there was a typewriter, a record player, paper, brushes, crayons, pencils and big pots of paint.

The last cupboard revealed party games, balloon packs and masks. Also a life-sized gorilla, angularly disposed on a shelf, who climbed down and embraced Bunty with vigor. "Hugo!" said Bunty crossly. The monkey hair, I think, had caught on her earrings.

I was thinking of Scimmia and other, associated recollections when the gorilla took its head off and turning, embraced me without warning also. His head, emerging from the gorilla's neck, was bald and heavy jowled, and he had large, long-lashed eyes, a moustache and versatile eyebrows which looked, at present, pained.

"Miss Joanna is uptight!" said Hugo Panadek. "And in me reposes your reputation! Beautiful girl, you will smile; or I shall tell my friend Comer that this bottle of gin, you have brought and consumed all by yourself."

"In two glasses?" I said.

"Don't be silly, Hugo," said Bunty. She was still cross. "Comer'll bend his shape."

"Dear Bunty," said the gorilla. "Any change in Comer's shape cannot but be for the better. Miss Joanna, what are you doing with the Booker-Readmans, who are so correct, and never have any fun unless it is approved by Society?"

"I wouldn't say that," I said; though I would. "At any rate, they're not having much fun at the moment. Bunty, I've remembered something. Mr. Booker-Readman has just lost his most valuable ikon."

Nobody fainted.

"His what?" said Bunty, brightening.

"Ikon, my illiterate beauty," said Hugo Panadek. "Its absence will only damage the handsome Simon in his pocket, and perhaps in his magnificent ego." He turned to me, unzipping his gorilla. "How sad for him. I am delighted to hear it. How was it taken?"

"It wasn't," I said. "He left it in a taxi. Bunty, that thing in the loo was an ikon."

The plucked eyebrows remained arched under the brown vermicelli ball of her hair. "It wasn't," said Bunty. "That was a picture. You said so."

"Please?" said Hugo. Bunty produced the fragments, and he examined them. "This is an ikon." He gazed fondly at Bunty. "You wicked girl. You have placed Mr. Booker-Readman's ikon down the lavatory?"

"You think that's it?" said Bunty. She looked, undistressed, at the moist heap on the paper and then calmly bundled it all up again and held it out to me. "God knows who bust it, but you'd better let Sultry Simon have a look at it. If it isn't his, then forget it."

I opened my mouth to demur. It might be valuable, It might belong to the Eisenkopps, parents or grandfather. Then I thought of what it would do to Grover, and changed what I was going to say. "All right, I'll take it. I've got to leave anyway. I'm due a feed in a moment."

"Listen, Jo," Bunty said.

"You are hungry?" said Hugo Panadek.

"Benedict Booker-Readman is hungry," I said. Last time Rosamund made up the feeds, the sod. cit. tablets blocked all the holes in the teats.

"Listen," said Bunty again. "I've got a day off on Friday."

"I'm working," I said.

"I know you're working," said Bunty patiently. "But Mrs. Eisenkopp's got a sprained foot. How's she going to manage with Grover?"

I looked round the walls. "Grover needs entertaining?"

"Don't be an ass," Bunty said. "Grover'll sprint about and slaughter Sukey. I don't suppose . . .",

". . . I could let him slaughter Benedict instead?" In Hugo's presence I didn't care to say that Grover also had a personality hangup, wind-burns and a throat infection.

"Just till five. He wouldn't be jealous of Ben." Bunty's Liverpudlian wheedle was overpowering.

I had opened my mouth when a short, powerful man in a cardigan entered the room and I recognized, from our moment's sizzling clash, Grover's father once more. He said, "Do I hear you ask Nurse Joanna to look after Grover?"

"It doesn't matter," I said. "I don't think I could ask Mrs. Booker-Readman in any case."

"*I* shall ask," said Comer Eisenkopp loudly. "This evening." He held out his hand. "Nurse Joanna. You saved my kid's life. I made a big mistake about you, and I want you to know it. That's a bit of paper that says I'm sorry."

It was a check for a hundred dollars. I said, "Mrs. Booker-Readman's to be out all this evening," gazing at it.

"If you don't take it," said Comer Eisenkopp, "I'll know I've offended you. Bunty says you sterilize all your own bottles."

I had guessed Bunty bought her feeds ready-made. I said carefully, "I just like it that way. Disposable bottles are perfectly sterile, Mr. Eisenkopp. And I couldn't really . . ." I held out the check.

He ignored it. "Mrs. Eisenkopp and Bunty and I would like you to help us with Grover and Sukey. As a favor. Naturally, we should not show ourselves ungrateful."

Two jobs was all that I needed. "Mr. Eisenkopp," I said. "I'm paid to look after one baby for twenty-four hours a day, five and a half days a week. I couldn't take Sukey and be fair to both of them. I shouldn't mind an odd hour with Grover in an emergency, but you'd have to ask Mrs. Booker-Readman. And if he misbehaves, I can't promise not to smack. I don't mean beat. I mean smack, a couple of times on the bottom."

That, I reckoned, got me off the hook. He pushed the check back in my hand and stood gazing at me, more in frustration than sorrow. "You know the Germans have the worst problem of adult violence and child-to-child aggression because their kids get beat up all the time by their parents?"

Eisenkopp. I ask you.

He developed the thesis. "Mrs. Eisenkopp and I made up our minds long ago. No doctor will ever push his dirty hypodermic into this little flower or her brother. Do you believe in injections, Nurse Joanna?"

I stared at him, but he was serious. I said, "I believe child diseases can kill. I've been injected. I've also been smacked by my father when I deserved it."

He tried. His lips hung out together as he made the effort. "I want you to promise," he said, "that if you have cause to reprimand Grover, you will tell Mrs. Eisenkopp or myself?"

"Mr. Eisenkopp," I said, "Grover will tell you."

"Nurse Joanna," said Comer, "I'm real glad I met you."

"I also," said Hugo Panadek. Inside the gorilla skin he was bare to the navel, and the boundary demarcation was not all that evident either. "When you are off duty one day, you and I and Bunty will drink vodka together and play with my hypodermics. And if I am bad, you may smack me."

I left right away. I sometimes wonder which of my two trades is the riskier.

# Chapter 5

Simon was away and Rosamund was just going out when I got back to the house with my booty. I emptied my pocket on to the hall table among the air mail *Times* copies and shuffled the ikon together.

Rosamund said, "What's that? It doesn't smell very nice."

The bandeau she was wearing drew attention to her large open eyes and high cheekbones. She had the kind of fine, sallow skin that flushes easily. It began to turn red as I answered her. It became redder and redder, and then returned to being quite pale. Rosamund Booker-Readman said, "You are talking absolute rubbish. Of course that isn't the ikon my husband lost. Anyone can see it's some cheap reproduction. Give it me. You'll give us all typhoid."

And lifting the whole sopping bundle, she stalked down the basement steps and, as I watched her, thrust the lot into the boiler.

It burned like firewood. When the last chip was consumed she banged the door shut and came upstairs for some handwashing. "Well?" she said. "Hadn't you better get on with the feed? Or has Benedict lost his fascination now you've met the Eisenkopps?"

I said good night and I hoped she'd have a pleasant evening. By hook or by crook, I could see, Benedict was going to have to smile at his mother.

I fed him and he cried all the time I was trying to do my ironing. At eight-thirty I gave in and supplied him with a clean nappy and an extra five ounces, upon which he fell asleep instantly. I switched on the baby alarm and went downstairs again to my ironing.

I like being alone. Outside were the spaced lights of the street, and the lines of parked cars, and the dark space where the Carl Schurz Park was, and the blazing edifice next door in which was the Eisenkopp duplex. Distantly one heard, from time to time, the whoop of sirens, or bantering voices, or the music of a transistor. The house itself was very quiet; reproaching the central heating on occasion with a creak from the stairs or the floorboards, or the sounds of the rushbottomed chair I had used when feeding Benedict.

I had the empty bottle and teat still to wash. I remembered also that the contents of my pocket were still lying on the hall table, where I had pulled out the bundle for Rosamund. I finished the neat pile of white Viyella night gowns, the pressed matinée jackets, the feeders. I was thinking chiefly of bed as I stuck the ironing board away and went to rinse out the bottle.

Benedict's voice, crying, blared out of the baby alarm.

I stood, extremely surprised. Warm, fed, dry and exhausted, the child had no reason to wake. Nor was there pain or fright in the wailing: I knew Benedict's voice in all its limited register. Whatever had roused him, that was the grumble of boredom. It needed no urgent attention and was going to get none from me. He would be asleep before I climbed to the bedroom.

I let him get on with it, and finished cleaning the bottle and teat and shoving them into the steriliser. Benedict continued to cry. I tidied up, with the sound following me like a persistent seagull from room to room. It didn't stop.

After ten minutes, the longest I would ever leave a bored baby, I went upstairs to the bedroom I shared with him and eased the door open.

I like babies to get used to the dark, so there wasn't a light in the room. The crying, unamplified but unabated, followed me to my own bed, where I switched on my bedlamp and turned, chanting nonsense, to Benedict's corner.

It was empty. In its place was a tape recorder, crying forlornly into the baby alarm.

Then the door closed with a bang, and the main lamp came on like a searchlight.

"You took your time coming," said Johnson.

He was leaning on the wall, in shapeless corduroys, with his hands stuffed into the pockets. His voice was aggrieved.

I said, "Where's Benedict?" I didn't know it was going to come out in my nursery school bark until I saw Johnson's eyes bat behind the bifocal glasses. He looked pained.

"Asleep in his basket next door. I have put him," said Johnson virtuously, "in a draught-proof corner with the door ajar in case he wakens." He bent and did something to the tape recorder, and the crying ceased. He straightened. "And I got in by copying Rosamund's key when she came for her portrait sitting. Really, you should never trust locks."

"Or portrait painters," I said. I was reviewing, very rapidly, all that I had left lying about in my room since Rosamund's first portrait sitting. I said, "And the recording? That was ingenious."

"Thank you. I bugged the woolly ball I sent Benedict," said Johnson cheerfully. "And then got Rosamund to bring it with her to the portrait sitting. The monologue was a wow. Do nurses all chat up their infants?"

"It compensates," I said, "for the times we keep our mouths shut. What was all that about different boards and different games? And now you're bugging balls and breaking and entering. Why the big change in policy? What else have you done?"

"Well, I searched the house while you were doing the ironing," said Johnson irritatingly. "And if the woolly ball had been in Rosamund's room, I might have made a killing in blackmail. Tell me all about the Carl Schurz Park snatch."

I sat down on my bed. "Wait a bit. Blackmail? Rosamund isn't having it off with anybody. Too busy with charity luncheons."

"I know Rosamund isn't having it off," said Johnson patiently. "Although I can't say I follow your reasoning. But Simon is. That is, on the nights he tells her he's out on business, he tells the gallery people he's at home. There's a woolly ball that could have told us he wasn't."

"Here's a woolly nanny who can tell you he isn't, either," I said. "Maybe he's just feeling henpecked. Maybe someone's painting his portrait. You didn't find a small, valuable article called the Lesnovo ikon when you were hunting through your clients' house, did you?"

There was a pause. "Well, go on," said Johnson. "The paralyzed silence means you've got my attention."

"I wondered," I said. "Because I've just fished up a smashed ikon from Bunty Cole's loo, and when I brought it over here, Rosamund burned it."

"All right," said Johnson. "You win." And sitting down, said politely, "Please tell me all that happened in the Carl Schurz Park, followed by all that happened in Bunty Cole's loo." So I did, not missing out Comer or Beverley Eisenkopp, or Sukey and Grover, or Grandfather, or the gorilla-clad Hugo Panadek.

"Panadek? What nationality's that?" Johnson asked.

"Yugoslav," I said. "Claims to be an ex-Count from a long line of vampires. I have two questions to ask you. The Department set me up, you set me up, everyone set me up in this job because they hope I'm going to be approached by Mike Widdess's killers. If I'm the target, who's gunning for Benedict?"

"Coincidence," Johnson said. "He's got a rich grandmother in England. What's the other question?"

"I've asked it before. What are you doing on my board, if you're playing a different game?"

"I do apologize," Johnson said, "for intruding. But it's rather difficult not to, when you're playing with the same pieces. Can't I have access to all your splendid inside information about the family Booker-Readman and their neighbors? All you have to do is talk into the ball and I'll retrieve it."

"Why not move in?" I said. I could hear the edge in my voice. "Rosamund asked you."

"Ah," said Johnson. "But it wouldn't do, would it, for me or anyone else to take a close interest in the Booker-Readmans, or you, or the baby? Our strong point is our seeming ignorance. We don't know Mike was murdered. We don't know someone's discovered your hobby. We're simple British, weak in the boggle-cogs. What was that stuff in the hall, incidentally?"

I wondered at what stage in my ironing he had been pussyfooting up and down the stairs. I said, picking out the most controversial article, "It was Grover's dummy."

"I allow Grover the benefit of the doubt. And this?" Johnson said, holding up three torn bits of paper.

I didn't recognize them. "I emptied my pocket," I said. "Join them together and I'll try to remember, if it matters."

"It matters," he said. He was practically on the floor, lying sprawled in the nursing chair I'd been using. He leaned over and arranged the papers in sequence.

The words at the top said

MISSY'S GOLDEN AMERICAN WONDERLAND

The text down below invited him to bring the kids to spend the most wonderful day of their lives in Missy's Magical Garden, all-day tickets eight dollars inclusive: sample the Skyride, the Aqua Spectacle, the Great Wheel, the Safari Park, the Antique Car Ride.

Between the two was a map of the Wonderland, upon which had been inked in an arrow beside a thing called The Great Shoot-Out. The arrow was blurred. "Well?" said Johnson.

I said, "It's wet, but I don't remember fishing it out of the loo. I've never seen it before."

Johnson leaned forward again. This time he reversed the three pieces of paper and fitted them together once more. Facing me was the blank side of the notice, with some words typewritten across it. They said, *Shoot it out. Wear an MMA badge. Don't tell the cops or you'll never see the kid again living.*

"The kidnap note," Johnson said. "Now you tell me how it got into your pocket. And if you think what I think an MMA badge is."

I said, "It could be Metropolitan Museum of Art. The tin badge they give you instead of a ticket. Anyone can get them . . . I think I want to see that Benedict's all right," and got up.

"He's all right," said Johnson patiently. "Keep your maternal instincts out of it for a moment and think. Where did the kidnap note come from?"

"Have three guesses," I said. "The kidnapper or an accomplice slipped it into my pocket before he did the snatch. The kidnapper or an accomplice slipped it into Bunty's pocket before, during or after he did the snatch. Or one of the many denizens of the Eisenkopp household, not excluding Sukey, put it into my pocket to encourage me to go to Missy's Golden American Wonderland and get done over without telling the cops. Excuse the Bogart-nouveau vocabulary."

"I dig it," said Johnson. "You've thought, of course, that Rosamund could have put it on the hall table among the rest of the Eisenkopps' night soil. If you really can't remember having seen it before, I suppose we might as well turn it over to the police force and let them get themselves stomped at the Shoot-Out." He collected the three pieces and rising, knelt beside the tape recorder and clicked it open. There was a step on the stairs.

I shot to my feet.

Johnson said, with interest, "Would that be Simon?"

It wasn't. I knew his tread on the staircase by now: he always ran upstairs, to keep his thigh muscles firm. I made a series of signals which Johnson totally ignored. Turning his head, he trained a gaze of genial expectation on the door. It burst open, and Comer Eisenkopp skidded into the room. "Good evening," said Johnson courteously.

Comer stood, his nostrils opening and shutting. He was still in the same cashmere cardigan and striped shirt and tie he'd worn when he offered me a check for saving Sukey from Grover, or perhaps the colors were different. His black hair was still thickly oiled but a lock had escaped over his broad, beaky face and for all he didn't stand very high, you were reminded of all that swimming, and squash, and the hard muscle under that tubby waistline. He had run up the stairs but he wasn't wheezing.

Nevertheless he took a deep breath before he said, "Would you believe it I've got the wrong room? Is Mr. Booker-Readman downstairs?"

"They're both out," I said. "This is my room, Mr. Eisenkopp. And this is Mr. Johnson, who is painting the baby's portrait."

"Jeeze," said Comer Eisenkopp. He spreadeagled a broad, powerful hand and clenched Johnson's in it. "I guess you both take me for some kind of idiot. I promised Simon a name and address, and clean forgot all about it till this moment. A friend of Beverley's who wanted a blue dish."

"Majolica?" Johnson said.

Comer's black eyes narrowed in the way I had cause to remember. "No. Name of Betty Lederer," Comer said. "You wouldn't know her. So you're painting Benedict?"

"Well, sketching him at this stage," Johnson said apologetically. "I asked Mrs. Booker-Readman if I could come by now and then. Confidentially, Benedict does better with Joanna than he does in the hands of his mother. Would you care to have a look?"

I never interfere when genius is at work. I stayed dumb and watched while Johnson picked up a portfolio and drew therefrom a series of red crayon sketches of Benedict.

He must have done them, for God's sake, while I was ironing. They were so like him that my eyes filled and I went to hunt for a Kleenex, leaving a pristine dent on my virgin bed that I hoped Comer noticed. I heard his voice alter behind me as he said, "Listen. These are fan-tastic." He looked up as I came back. "Where's the baby? You could put them side by side and hardly know which from what."

I said, "I'll bring him in. We put him next door while we talked about the next sitting." I got up again, to show willing. Then I saw where our visitor's eyes were.

"You use a tape while you're painting?" Comer said. He walked across and bent down and put his thumb on the starter button of Johnson's tape recorder. I lunged to stop him. Johnson's elbow hit my ribs and I halted, gasping. There was a whirring noise and the cassette began to unreel implacably.

It wasn't the tape of Benedict crying. It was quite a different sound: a kind of regular impact of flesh against flesh, allied to the sort of noise you hear in a beer vat. Johnson had swopped the cry-tape for a Japanese womb-recording.

"Brings it home, doesn't it?" said Johnson. "I can hardly bear to eat and drink after listening to it. You might as well keep it, Joanna. I'll need it for the next sitting anyway. You have children, Mr. Eisenkopp?"

"Two," said Comer automatically. "And their Gramps there, which just about makes three. I guess we need the noise of a Bourbon distillery working overtime to put him to sleep. New York treating you well?"

"Not too badly for off-season," Johnson said. "I'm usually around for the America's Cup, but I try to steer clear of the city."

His pullover was handknitted and his spectacles a social disaster, but I could see Comer's eyes dwelling on his watch, and on the Gucci loafers. He said, "I never met a painter before who could tell one end of a boat from the other. You into racing here, Johnson?"

"I keep my hand in," Johnson said. "But I don't bring the *Dolly* over every time. I can generally find someone at the Club who'll take me on." He got up and began to pack the drawings away.

Comer said, "You know Howard Bigelow?"

Howard Bigelow was Commodore of the Senior American Yacht Club.

"I haven't seen him since August," said Johnson. "And then not really to speak to: it was a drinks party on *Britannia* and I was going on to Balmoral. Perhaps you sail yourself?"

"I was wondering," said Comer Eisenkopp, "whether you'd like a tiller in your hand for a day or two this Easter. I've a little boat, yeah, up at Cape Cod and we move up there for a week at that time. Nothing serious, you'd know: it's too soon in the season. But some loafing and a party or two and a mite of fishing. The Booker-Readmans may spend a weekend with us: if Rosamund's there, you could pack your brushes."

"Now, that's very kind of you," Johnson said. He looked surprised, and I noticed it with some misgiving, for if anyone wasn't surprised, it was Johnson.

He smiled at me and then at Comer. "I really don't know yet what my movements will be. But certainly, I shall remember. A little sailing, a little fishing: delightful." He grinned again, moving gently towards the door. And a little painting, I thought. Of Sukey and Grover, if Comer can get away with it.

Comer said, "That's settled then. I'll ring you nearer the time. Make it a weekend if you're busy, but we'll hope to have you much longer. It's been a privilege," said Comer Eisenkopp, and shook Johnson's hand.

He was still thinking about Johnson as I walked him down the stairs.

"I guess that's a genuine English gentleman. The real kind," he said. "I sure wonder what he asks for his pictures."

"About fifteen thousand dollars, they tell me; but he just paints when he feels like it. He's in *Who's Who*," I said helpfully. If Balmoral and the *Britannia* had been brought into play, I might as well lob in the rest. I added, "Do you want to leave a note about Mrs. Lederer?"

"A note?" said Comer.

"A note for Mr. Booker-Readman," I prompted. I was enjoying myself. "About the blue dish for . . ."

"Oh. Ah," said Comer Eisenkopp. "You just reminded me there. I'd gotten so taken up with meeting this painter guy that I nearly forgot. Yeah. If I might just use his desk, I'll write a line for him."

He did, downstairs, and departed, rather slowly. He was still wearing his carpet slippers. When I got back upstairs, I found Johnson had gone also, and Benedict was back, asleep in his own corner. I locked my door and went to bed.

Next morning I showed Rosamund the Wonderland note and she phoned the police. I also told her I let Johnson come in to sketch Benedict, and about Comer's visit.

Simon, it was clear, hadn't come home. I followed Rosamund into the study, where she opened Comer Eisenkopp's envelope and read his note. I said, "Mrs. Booker-Readman . . . When the police come, do I tell them about the broken ikon?"

She didn't wear much makeup as a rule, but she had put blue eyeshadow and white high-lighter all round her lids that morning. She had these handsome eyes, heavy lidded and large, and her hair had just enough weight to curl under on either side of her jaw line. She was smoking English cigarettes, hard, through her holder. She said, "If they mention it, of course you must tell them. If they don't mention it, I think you must consult your own conscience. But I warn you, it might mean real trouble for Bunty."

I looked perplexed. "You said it was a cheap reproduction?" I ventured.

"Do you think the Eisenkopps would know the difference?" Rosamund said. "I expect they paid a fortune for it, and the girl let their bloody brat splinter it. She meant it to flush down the loo, and as far as you or I are concerned, that's what happened."

"Unless the police ask," I repeated, acquiescing as a good nanny should. I thought of the Sea Monkeys and wondered if my passage through life was destined to be marked for ever with a trail of blocked loos and abused drains and musical chamber pots.

If you look after kids, one might say, you can't grumble.

The police visited The Great Shoot-out at Missy's Golden American Wonderland and reported that the stall assistant had vanished on the morning of the attempted kidnapping of Benedict. The stall-holder, a Greek by the name of Alexei had not seen him since, and knew nothing of him except for an address in the Bronx which turned out to be a false one. The police department did, however, turn up a set of fingerprints in the stall that tallied with prints on the trash cart in the Carl Schurz Park, proving that the assistant and the kidnapper were one and the same person. The name he had gone by was Rudi Klapper.

By common consent, neither Bunty nor I told the police anything about the broken ikon. Bunty, questioned by a goodlooking detective, was almost sure that the card had been in her pocket when she emptied its contents into the loo.

The day after the police investigation Charlotte phoned and said they were all going to take the kids down to Missy's Golden American Wonderland to see what it was all about, and why didn't I come for the hell of it.

"*All*" proved to mean herself and Bunty and Donovan with the Eisenkopp and Mallard offspring, together with Johnson, who had offered to drive them.

"In a Porsche?" I said. That is, I admire sports cars, but there would be five adults and six children on this outing.

"No. Apparently," Charlie said, "he needs a Mercedes-Benz to carry his canvases. What about it? Tomorrow?"

I was off tomorrow. I agreed. I couldn't make out whose idea it had been, except that it probably started with Bunty and Charlotte, and spread from there to Donovan.

If Johnson thought Benedict's kidnapping had nothing to do with Mike Widdess, then his share in this trip was pure mischief. On the other hand . . .

I thought about the other hand all morning.

I switched the tape recorder on for the feed. Benedict took two spoonfuls of oat gruel and his formula, and went to sleep to the glug of Japanese intestines digesting their bamboo chop suey.

I wrote home to mother: a long, newsy letter that could have been broadcast coast-to-coast without wakening anything, never mind a suspicion. As I wrote it, I saw in my mind's eye Comer Eisenkopp in his carpet slippers, staring at Johnson as he stood in my doorway.

You could say he looked thunderstruck. So should we have been.

We hadn't asked him the obvious question. If the house was locked, and it was, how had *Comer* got inside that evening?

# Chapter 6

Missy's Golden American Wonderland is one hour due west from Manhattan for adults. For carsick children it stretches to an hour and a half or even two hours away.

Johnson's hired Mercedes-Benz was the size of a bus and had everything: child-proof locks, automatic windows and compulsory seatbelts without which the dashboard apostrophized you in green but wouldn't start up the engine. It arrived at the brownstone with Denny Donovan sitting grinning by Johnson, which left me to get into the back, along with the four junior Mallards, the two junior Eisenkopps, Charlotte and Bunty.

It was a foregone conclusion that Bunty would bring the baby on an all-day fun fair excursion: if she didn't it would rank as a day off. Sukey, in a carrycot with the hood and the apron both clipped, was asleep in a dark, satisfactory fug, and long might she remain so.

Grover, full of Tootsie Rolls, grits and tinned apricot, was wearing a pattern-matched shirt and sweater from Sandpiper, while the four Ducklings, predictably, were full of Freakies and dressed by Marks and Sparks from their skins to their anoraks.

I asked Donovan if he was a plant doctor and he said Sure, he thought everyone knew, and did I need any help.

Charlotte asked Johnson what he had for breakfast and he said Hanky-Panky, the Nifty Goodie (*A little Hanky-Panky will Brighten your Day*).

Donovan slapped him on the back and the Mercedes shot across three lanes and back again, causing the youngest Mallard to belch. There followed the first of our many stops by the wayside.

Nothing got out of hand, because Charlotte and I were there, moving into the accustomed routine with Kleenex and sick bags and damp sponges and towels and barley sugar. We sang the usual songs and played the usual games and, in the intervals of coping with the four little Mallards and Grover, listened to Bunty's mesmerising account of Comer's plastic sprayed teeth and the Chow Chow's flea collar, and the poodle's doggy bootees, and Beverley's Wig'n Lift, the hairpiece for hitching the chins up.

Hygiene and after-care in the Eisenkopp household seemed to embrace just about everything except Bunty, who reeked of Balenciaga's Ho Hang and wore platform shoes this time with her uniform gaberdine trench coat. Donovan was attired in a fairway cap with his Alaskan Timberwolf which made Charlie, sitting behind him, look like a gas inspector.

She was the only one in Maggie Bee uniform, since I wasn't on duty. I think she rather enjoyed it, even when we plunged in among the flags and the lights of the Wonderland and the parking attendants converged, dressed as animals. We bought a ticket from one, with *Saggy Baggy Elephant* written out under his trunk. Julia, the youngest Mallard, burst into tears. We all got out of the car and Charlotte opened her bag and began handing out little blue badges.

There were a score in her bag, made of thin pale blue tin with a clip, and the letters MMA printed on them. I said, "What's the idea?" as she started pinning them on coats and jerseys. Julia stopped crying and Grover got two.

"Reconstruction," said Charlotte succinctly. She handed one to Bunty, who had unbuttoned Sukey's pram apron to check that she was breathing, and was buttoning it up again. "Remember the kidnap note you found in your pocket? *Shoot it out* and *Wear an MMA badge*? And an arrow next to The Great Shoot-Out?"

"Vaguely," I said. I was incensed. I knew they knew all about it, but they needn't have taken it over. I said, "I don't really see the point. The kidnap failed. The note was never acted on. The kidnapper didn't come back to the stall. Rudi Klapper. The man we saw in the Carl Schurz Park. The police told us that. After he tried the snatch, he didn't come back to the Shoot-out."

"Then it won't do any good," said Bunty cheerfully. She had fitted Sukey's carrycot on to its wheels and was leaning on it. "But it can't do any harm either. Come on. You're at your auntie's. God, who'd like a hot dog? I'm famished."

Johnson locked the car and we set off.

Missy's Golden American Wonderland is a large wooded park, set out as a pleasureland for kids of all sizes squired as needed by friends, parents and sometimes the Haitian help, down at heel on seventy dollars a week because behind every Haitian help is a Haitian lady on a percentage.

It is not a place haunted by English nannies with toddlers. It gives that sense of illicit excitement one gets parking a pram outside Woolworth's, when one is meant to be out for a health-giving bash through the common.

Not that we saw all that much to begin with. Flinging down dollar bills, we were sucked through the entrance and propelled past stalls, bandstands, pavilions, big wheel, roller coaster, arena and an assortment of aerial networks by Bunty's sixth sense for hot dogs, which would be worth a fortune in Perigord. Then full of chippolata sausage and mustard the nine of us, pushing Sukey, proceeded to test our digestions.

You'd expect an ice hockey buff to go for speed, but it wasn't till I saw Johnson upside down on the Great Whirling Moon Ride or with his spectacles glued to his face in the Amazing Centrifugal Saucer that I remembered that yachtsmen have strong stomachs also. Bunty went on everything as well. Side by side, Charlotte and I pushed Sukey and carried Grover and led the four little Mallards through the train rides and into the mouse circus and in and out of the distorting mirrors while engines of death hurtle above us, full of Alaskan fur and Afro hair-do and spectacles.

Neither of us, I suppose, really minded. I liked Charlie's four little girls and so did Grover, who had a nice healthy scar where his hand had been cut but the same cough, along with incipient dandruff. He moved up while I was toting a Mallard and said, "You need to walk aside Jonah," meaning me, and stayed firmly attached until Charlie took over the Mallard and I acquired Sukey's vehicle, whereupon he tried to climb in, kicking Sukey sharply.

It had struck me he might. I whisked him out before his feet hit the blankets and jacked him instead on my shoulders. "And so," said Charlie, "they leave home and land at a head-shrinker's. What should we advise Bunty to do?"

"Shoot either or both of the parents," I said. We were halfway between the Kremlin and the Amsterdam waterfront in the Garden of Miniature Masterpieces. A bald head, stirring, rose like a harvest moon from behind the onion domes of the Cathedral of the Annunciation, and the owner, stepping carefully, crossed the Red Square and stood, gazing through his long-lashed soft eyes, directly in front of us.

Booted, dimpled and inconvenient, it was Hugo Panadek, Comer Eisenkopp's Design Director. He had gold rings in both ears and a wolf-smile under the bush on his lip. Indeed, he looked quite different out of gorilla-skin. He said, "So. You would shoot either or both of the parents!"

"To Hugo!" screamed Grover. I set him down and he rushed straight off the path and into the Adriatic. It only came to his ankles and he was out of earshot, so I left him.

"Of course," I said to Hugo. I kept my voice mild. "Don't you know it's every trained nurse's dream, a world full of well-mannered kids and no adults? Do you know Charlotte Medleycott?"

One soft eye turned to Charlie, who was grinning. "You have been to Data-Mate again," said Hugo Panadek accusingly. "Every time she comes to the Eisenkopps, it is to say that she has run through another eight boy friends. Who is it this time?"

I looked up in the air, in all directions. "Over there," I said. "Inside the Alaskan Timberwolf. I've got him second-hand, actually, at the moment. What is it that compels bachelors to jump into fur suits this season?"

"The company," said Hugo. "Sometimes the company, alas, is too chilly. Nurse Joanna, what do you do in the evenings?"

I said, "Lift bachelors out of their furry suits and unpin their diapers. Do you come here a lot?" Grover was attempting to scale a papier mâché range of mountains. I rescued him. The castle on the top, of the Mad Ludwig variety, had its windows lit and a plastic dragon endlessly breasting the waterfilled ring of the moat.

A discarded banana stick impeded its progress and Hugo, reaching over, removed it tenderly, and inspected its working parts. "The real dragon," he said, "is ten feet long."

"And fire," said Grover.

"And has fire in its mouth. The real moat . . ."

"Is a whimming place," Grover said. "Hugo whim there."

"In his fur monkey suit?" I said. I could feel my bland slipping.

"In my part of the world," said Hugo Panadek, "you don't need a suit to go swimming in. Read the notice. It is a real castle. The fortress of Kalk, Yugoslavia. Owner, Hugo Panadek."

I wouldn't have believed Hugo, but I believed Grover all right. Grover knew all about Hugo's castle, and so I suppose did Bunty, corkscrewing presently round a sloping platform in Johnson's arms. I said, "Well, congratulations. It must be famous, to appear in Missy's Golden American Wonderland, yet. Did you have to supply the blueprints?"

"This is no trouble," said Hugo. "I design for a living." He waved a hand. "I design the Wonderland."

Charlie scraped a couple of Mallards off the Acropolis. "You mean you're *Missy*?" She stood, her arms full of kids and her end-curls sticking out at the side like demented butterfly wings, showing him thirty-two perfect teeth in her ecstasy. "You're Missy, Hugo?"

"You want proof?" Hugo said, his lashes descending. "Well, I have enough shares of Missy to be able to show friends a good time, let us say. Where is Bunty? What do you all wish to see?"

That was when I remembered the time, and what we were all supposed to be there for. "The Great Shoot-Out," I said. "We're supposed to be doing a reconstruction of Benedict's kidnapping, or at least of what the kidnapper planned to do afterwards. He'd been working beforehand at The Great Shoot-Out."

"Oh, I remember all that," said Hugo. "The Carl Schurz Park. The police came and grilled Bunty and did a conducted tour of the johns. It sounded like the worst-organized heist of all time. No wonder The Great Shoot-Out has been losing money. If you pardon my curiosity, what do you think you will find that the cops didn't?"

"Ask Bunty," said Charlie. "Here she comes. Bunty, what are we hoping to find that the cops couldn't?"

"I believe," said Bunty weakly, "in P.P.S. Holy Jesus, that was a bitch." She lurched, and the Data-Mate hitched her under the arm, without speaking.

"E.S.P.," said Johnson kindly. "You shouldn't go on these things if you haven't a strong stomach. Ask the gentleman with the earrings where the powder room is."

"Johnson," I said, "let me introduce the designer of Missy's Golden American Wonderland. His name's Hugo Panadek. That's his castle over there."

Johnson turned. The dragon droned round the moat. He watched it critically. "You can't," he said, "do much entertaining?"

"I get it," said Hugo. "You're Charlie's newest Data-Mate. Jeeze, that computer's a bum."

They stared amiably at one another. With no change of tone Hugo added, "Glad to meetya. I hear Rosamund's psyched out of her skull with the oilpainting. What's the slumming for?"

"It seems to be a benefit for the Metropolitan Museum of Art. I'm not complaining," said Johnson. "We've finished, really, except for watching Bunty's P.P.S. operate."

Hugo Panadek grinned. The flashing teeth, the lashes, the dimples all confirmed the first, magnetic impact he'd made at Bunty's flat. He surveyed the kids and flung out his arms. "The Great Shoot-Out," he said. "And then steak'n French fries and ice cream all round. Fudge ice cream. Maple walnut ice cream. Butter brickle ice cream. Chocnut and pineapple and mint and chocolate chips . . ."

The Mallard girls were all squealing with joy and I saw in Charlie's eye a reflection of my own simple juvenile greed. It was Bunty who said, "Do you mind? My stomach's still wrapped round my tonsils," and led the way, behind Hugo, to the shooting stall.

Having no sons, my father taught me to shoot. I brought down my first pheasant at twelve, and parted from blood sports at fifteen, but I've always kept a soft spot for fun fairs. You could say I'd shot all over the world, from target practice at a pound for two bullets in Russia, to flying monsters in Paris, to activated comedy popups in Tivoli. Lead me to Madame Tussaud's and there I'll be in the fun parlor, mowing down planes in an airfield.

The Great Shoot-Out had none of that kid stuff. Four guns were trained on four cut-out Midwestern town backdrops through which, on an endless belt, cattle rustlers appeared and vanished. You got a second to shoot and reload. Six out of six rustlers got you a free replay. Three free replays, if your loading arm hadn't broken, got you a woolly bear to take back to mother. There was another twist.

If you shot a rustler and missed, he shot back at you. With a bang and a little red light. I kid you not.

Charlie tried first, and it shocked her at any rate. At the first burst of counterfeit counter-fire, she flung herself back on the pram and woke Sukey, who started to yell, in competition with the stallholder, a large Greek with black curly hair, who was explaining tetchily that all the explosions were totally harmless. But Charlie's nerve had expired, and she fired her five other shots without winging a rustler; though they didn't get her actually, either.

The Data-Mate, stepping up casually, killed all the rustlers, got a free reload, killed them again, and then got overconfident and missed the one that dodged out through the bar-flaps.

Johnson shot and made a hash of it.

I had an unfair advantage, through standing there watching the sequences. I got the one on the jail roof, the one through the bar flaps, the one through the hotel window and the one who jumped out the waterbutt. I waited, and got the one who peeked out of the stable door. The last one jumped from a Wells Fargo van and I got him right through the heart.

Hugo kissed me with fervor and Grover said, "*You* bang the guns this time." I offered the rifle to Bunty, who turned it back.

"Don't be mad, you've got a free shot. Go on. Hell, we only shot policemen in Liverpool."

They all said go on, so I did it again.

This time Donovan, Hugo and Grover all kissed me, while the stall-owner snatched back the gun and broke it as if he planned never to use it again. Then he handed me over my bear.

It wasn't quite as massive as Panadek in his gorilla suit, but it was a fairly near miss. I could see why takings might be low if they had to pass these things over too often. The cramp in my left arm explained why they didn't run very much risk.

Silence fell on the Mallards, Sukey and Grover as six pairs of eyes switched hopefully back and forth between my face and the bruin's. Grover said, "The men died. Jonah died them."

"They were just pretend men," I said, and knelt. "Everyone is to hold Joanna's bear for a little. Grover hold it first."

It was as big as Grover. He put it on its feet in the dirt, seized a ring on its chest and looking at us expectantly, tugged it.

"My name," said a thick, oily voice next to Grover, "is dear old Brownbelly Bruin, your Lover Bear. Stroke your Lover Bear. Kiss your Lover Bear. Take your Lover Bear home to bed with you. And remember. Only Love beats Milk, baby."

There was an assorted silence. Grover looked smug. Charlie and Bunty both looked queasy, for different reasons. Donovan, Johnson and Hugo all looked at one another, after which Johnson turned to the Greek and broke the silence by saying, "I want to buy all your bears. What'll you take for them?"

For, of course, that was how the absent Rudi Klapper had meant to arrange for his ransom for Benedict. By ensuring that the right talking bear and the guy with the MMA badge got together.

I said, "Why didn't the police think of that, then?"

"They didn't have Grover with them," said Johnson. He was still looking at Alexei the Grecian.

"No sale," said Alexei. "I need them bears to run the stall with. They've stopped making them."

"O.K." said Johnson agreeably. He took out his wallet and flipped twenty dollars on to the counter. "We won't take them away. That's just for letting us pull all their talk-strings."

"Are you a weirdo?" asked Alexei. "What good will them bears do with their strings broke? You cats piss off. You're violating my privacy."

In silence Johnson licked off another ten-dollar bill. Alexei let it lie. He said, "The law says you win them bears by shooting. You win 'em by shooting and you got the law on your side. You try to force me to sell them and I'll get a patrolman down on your neck and I mean it, man."

There were twenty-four bears on that stall. I'd been counting them.

"There is no call to argue," said Hugo. "We summon the police. It is their business."

It was, of course. But meanwhile the Mallard kids had set upon Grover, and Sukey was yelling for sustenance. I said, "Suppose you all take the kids off for a feed, and Donovan and I will shoot till you're finished? It's worth a try. The police'll keep us for ever."

"You're going to shoot?" said Alexei. He looked flustered.

"Two rifles, brother," said Donovan.

"Three," said Hugo. "You two mommas go feed the family while Daddy goes hunting. There's a card that says guest of the management."

Charlotte took it, and she and Bunty pushed off with the children.

"Three rifles?" said Alexei cautiously.

"Four," said Johnson stoically. He picked up a bill from the heap and pushed it over the counter. "You won't reconsider?"

Alexei shook his head, and he was probably right. This way he couldn't lose, anyway.

Although my back and left arm and elbows have never been quite the same since, I have sterling recollections of that competition.

We settled down side by side, Donovan and I, and started to shoot. So did Johnson. After a chain of disasters that threatened to shiver his glasses, Johnson dropped regretfully out while Donovan and I, with the occasional black, began winning bears slowly.

Hugo Panadek watched for two rounds, then took off his long leather tunic, revealing a silk jersey shirt with balloon sleeves over his fine shrink-wrapped gaberdine trousers. He picked up a gun, leaned over, sighted, and killed eighteen rustlers, pausing only to reload in a blur between corpses.

He received a bear, pulled its cord, and left it to talk while he loaded and fired a fresh volley. "My name," began the bear, "is dear old Brownbelly Bruin. Stroke your Lover Bear. Kiss . . ."

"Jesus," said Donovan. "You train under John Wayne?"

Bald head gleaming, Hugo pooped the hood in the butt and dispatched the fifth and the sixth with a flourish. "At home," he said, "we shoot chamois on mountain tops. These are for children."

Half an hour from that moment he had ten Brownbelly Bruins beside him. I had four and Donovan five, and around us was the biggest crowd in the park, with the up-tight faces of all the other stallholders behind them. Johnson did a great job pulling the strings in a kind of canon effect. They all said the same thing: it was the best mass advertisement for love and milk since Cleopatra.

It was not, however, serving any other purpose whatever. It began to seem depressingly clear that the four of us had outsmarted ourselves. The Shoot-Out, no doubt, was the rendezvous. But whatever the plan, Brownbelly Bruins could have played no part in it.

My fractured right arm agreed. The spring in my rifle deserved to go into Mrs. Eisenkopp's Wig 'n Lift hairpiece. At the end of the next round, I proposed to retire, lock, stock and barrel.

I was still shooting when Hugo claimed his next bear. I saw Alexei stretch up to lift one, and heard Johnson walk up and stop him. "No. Not that one. Not the shelf this time."

I potted the rustler in the hotel window. Alexei said, "What?"

Johnson said, "What about the bear on the ground over there? Let's take that fellow next."

I potted the stooge through the bar flaps.

Donovan fired his last shot and craned, with Hugo, over the counter. He said, "*I* didn't see any bears on the goddam . . ."

I couldn't help it. My eye followed theirs down to the floor instead of watching my target.

Alexei, stooping, lifted a bear from the ground. It had a badge on its bosom. I shot, and missed the guy in the waterbutt.

Alexei straightened, holding the bear in both arms like a parcel. With a bang and a flash, the little tin guy in the waterbutt shot back with a red light, and missed me.

He got Alexei, though. Alexei bellowed.

We all looked at him. There was blood all over his arm, and even more on the bear, which he had dropped on the counter in a blizzard of guaranteed sterilised kapok. Alexei had only been winged. But the Brownbellied Bruin would speak no more; for it had been drilled cleanly through the brown belly.

We taught those rustlers a lesson. The waterbutt killer had gone. But the next little tin hoodlum got three pellets bang in the stomach and went offstage bent like a hairpin, while Hugo managed to hammer the Wells Fargo hatchetman twice. Then he said, "For Chrissakes, what are we doing!" and flung the rifle down and dashed to where Johnson had already plunged through the scattering crowd, towards the distant form of a man whose black, curly hair I had seen retreating like this once before, just after he'd thrust Benedict into a trash bucket.

The smoking tin cutouts were guiltless. It was Rudi Klapper, of the Carl Schurz Park, who had shot Alexei, and shot also the one bear which had been hidden from casual custom. Set aside with an MMA badge in its fur to await another MMA badge to claim it. Because recorded inside, of course, was the kidnap message.

I scooped up the wreck of the bear and took to my heels after Johnson.

I lost him. I couldn't see Donovan. A red wooden buggy appeared flying a streamer saying "Missy's Wonderland" and with three familiar heads crammed into it. I took a flying leap and landed in Donovan's lap just as it rocketed off at top speed through the Park, with Hugo's bald head lowered over the wheel. I said, "It was Rudi Klapper. Where is he?" One wheel ran up a tree root and down again.

Donovan said, "Will you take your bloody bear out of . . . Thanks. He jumped on the Transcontinental Adventure Train."

"What?" I said.

"He's crossed the pond on the train to the parking lot. We have to get round fast, if we're to catch him," said Johnson. "*Christ*, watch the . . ."

He didn't bother to finish. Behind us, a twenty-foot cluster of balloons rose in the air, over a blaspheming and recumbent balloon man. An ice cream and pretzel stall rocked and there was a small crunch as we went over a set of low railings. There was a smell of fish, and a sound of squealing and splashing. Hugo turned abruptly left, missing two shining grey shapes lumbering out of a swimming pool, grinning.

A rubber ring, descending, pinned our Missy flag to its mast, stinking of dolphin. Donovan uncovered his eyes and covered them again as a chain of antique cars approached, full of children. Hugo spun the wheel and the buggy plunged into a garden of sheep, angora rabbits and llamas, which spat before bolting.

Hugo drove between trees in hysterical lunges. We came out into the open and there ahead was the parking lot, with Johnson's Mercedes in it. And far beyond it, near the entrance, a low grey Dodge pulling out slowly, with its near front-door open and Rudi Klapper racing towards it. We fell out beside the Merc. Johnson said, "Joanna, come with me. You two, get up the Sky Ride and watch."

He had the doors open already. He flung the bear in and switched on the ignition. I dived in behind him. I slammed the door.

Rudi Klapper jumped into the Dodge.

Johnson switched on the ignition again.

Rudi Klapper slammed his door. The Dodge revved up and began to move, fast.

Johnson switched on the ignition again. The dashboard glowed green in his glasses. Without a word, he grabbed and fastened his seatbelt.

The Dodge, accelerating, shot to the gates of the park.

Johnson tried the ignition again and then, his hands on the wheel, turned and looked at me.

I said, "I think you need to fasten the bear into its safety-belt."

With infinite care, my father's friend Johnson leaned over and ripping out both ends of the belt, clipped them round the sagging fur paunch of the Brownbelly Bruin. Then with equal care he switched on the ignition.

With a roar, the engine fired. The tires squealed as the car hurtled forward. They squealed again as it stopped with a jolt at the feet of a Saggy Baggy Elephant standing placidly in mid-road, demanding our parking-ticket.

I yelled out of the window while Johnson jerked backwards and sideways to get round the obstacle. The Saggy Baggy sidestepped thoughtfully and leaning its elbow on the window, began to make a long, muffled statement in Brooklynese.

Johnson reversed again, nearly taking its rubber trunk with him, and this time scraped round and down the road to the highway.

There was no sign of the Dodge, and there were fifteen container trucks passing. We got out on the tail of the last one, and weaving from lane to lane raced for five or six miles before being flagged down for good, by the State troopers. Johnson's explanation, with the burst teddy bear tidily strapped into the pullman beside him, was a miracle of courteous forbearance in the face of raucous incredulity.

We drove under escort back to Missy's American Wonderland and found a lot of screaming coming down from the Sky Ride. Investigation disclosed that Hugo and Donovan had been up in the cable cars for twenty minutes plotting the Dodge's itinerary, in aid of which Hugo had cut off the power.

We introduced him to the police as the designer of Missy's Golden American Wonderland, and the police became suddenly interested. We all repaired to Hugo's office, having sent word to Bunty and

Charlotte and visited both The Great Shoot-Out and Alexei in the First Aid Room. All the bears had disappeared from the ground by the stall where we had left them. The State trooper who had asked the most questions said, "And you think this was the bear you were meant to win, if the kidnap had really taken place?"

I said, "I suppose so. Or at least, Klapper thought so."

"Then," said the trooper with impeccable deduction, "the message inside must have contained something he thought would give him away?"

"Who can tell?" Johnson said. His glasses looked soulful.

"Well, I can," said Hugo Panadek. "If you'll give me a while with a tool or two. He's smashed the spindle, but the rest is mostly all right, I shouldn't wonder."

We made our statements while Hugo worked, and then Bunty and Charlotte arrived, with six kids and three new boyfriends, and Missy's catering staff sent in a stack of hamburgers.

I was on my fourth when Hugo said, "Well. I think that does it," and set something in motion.

From inside the last Brownbelly Bear a new voice spoke: a guttural voice, quite unlike that of the Lover Bear we all knew and were sick of.

The voice said, *"Mr. and Mrs. Booker-Readman, I have your son. He is nailed in a box, without food and drink and with enough air to last him until midnight tomorrow.*

*"At eight o'clock tomorrow night, you will come to the tree nearest this stall, and leave beside it a paper carrier bag containing four million dollars in old bills. If you tell the police, no one will collect the money and your son's box will never be found. He'll starve and suffocate, Mr. and Mrs. Booker-Readman, if I am arrested, or if I even suspect you have set a trap for me.*

*"So bring the money. Do as you're told. And you'll have your son back. He's very upset, Mrs. Booker-Readman, and very cold and very hungry. And he's going to stay that way, till he's paid for. Remember—no police."*

Someone, I don't know who, put an arm briefly round my crumb-strewn sweater. The patrolman said, "Well, that's freaky. Why should he stick his ass out to smash up that message? It don't tell us nothing!"

"It does," I said. "The accent. It tells us the accent is Russian.

And that goes with the man in the car. The man who had the Dodge ready and out in the parking lot. I thought I recognized him, but I couldn't be sure. I'm sure now."

"So am I," Johnson said, "I was wondering if you'd seen him. The man waiting for Rudi was Vladimir, your laundrette Ukrainian from Winnipeg."

# Chapter 7

Whatever they did to the Booker-Readmans, the kidnap demands got me into a tangle.

Arriving home from Missy's Golden American Wonderland I wasn't interested in anything or anybody but checking to see if Ben was in good running order. I lurched creaking up the stairs like a blackcurrant straddle harvester and barely noticed that Simon and Rosamund were engaged in the preliminary bouts of a magnificent spat. The words "Your pathetic Kraut" rose to the surface several times, and after I had checked that my brat was safely asleep I slung my things off and went and had a good listen.

If I thought it was going to be about my call from Hugo's office about the threat to their son, I was out in my reckoning. They were discussing Comer Eisenkopp's invitation to spend Easter with them at Cape Cod.

Simon saw no harm in going and Rosamund thought he was out of his tiny mind, to put himself under an obligation to these people. Simon said it was pathetic Krauts like that who kept her mother going, and Rosamund said that if Comer and Beverley Eisenkopp thought they were going to get an invitation to the gala at Venice, they were going to be bloody disappointed. To which Simon replied that invitations to Warr Beckenstaff galas were Warr Beckenstaff business, and since when had her mother paid the slightest attention to anything her darling daughter said or did except to do her level best to keep her from marrying anything less than a duke, until she had to get herself in pig.

"Well put," said Rosamund bitterly. "I bloody nearly did have to do it myself. And now look what's happening. Some hoodlum snatches her grandson, and there's Grandmother's fortune, gone for nothing."

"She won't pay, darling," said Simon. "You're quite safe. They'll kill the boy next time and you can take Joanna on as your social secretary. However will they get their jollies at the Long Island Cerebral Palsy Fair without you?"

"Don't knock it. It does wonders for your image, Simon, if you'll forgive the expression," Rosamund said. "On the other hand, helping the underprivileged has never been your thing, has it? If someone destroyed your looks tomorrow, what would you do? What *would* you do? Do you ever think of it?"

"You mean you'd stop loving me?" Simon said, and laughed. "My word, I can't think what I'd do, darling. Or yes, I can. I think I'd have to run to Grandma for help."

There was a little silence. Then Rosamund, in a voice drawling with rage said, "Of course you must do as you like. Don't fail to explain, while you're about it, how the Lesnovo ikon came to be smashed in the Eisenkopps' bog."

"What?" said Simon.

"You're so quick, darling," Rosamund said. "Joanna the paragon found it, along with Bunty Cole and God knows who else. Joanna brought it here because they thought it might be the lost ikon."

"And?" said Simon. His voice had weakened.

"And I said it wasn't, and burned it. It was a rotten copy, even for you. I shan't ask the obvious question."

"You might as well. You'll get the obvious answer," said Simon Booker-Readman. "I've no idea how it got there. Probably one of the children."

"Benedict?" said Rosamund scathingly.

It couldn't have been telepathy. But as Rosamund mentioned his name Benedict woke, and finding himself wet and unhappy and hungry, broadcast the fact, without delay, through the baby alarm. The sitting room door opened and Rosamund came out.

I was three steps back, on the last tread of the stair when she saw me. I said, "I'll see to it, Mrs. Booker-Readman. I was just coming down to tell you I was in."

Rosamund stood perfectly still. Below her long face and incurving hair everything was in the severest good taste: her cardigan, her ombre striped silk blouse, her wrap-around skirt and good shoes.

She said, "I should rather like you to come and see me the moment you get in, Joanna. One likes to know just how many people are in one's house at any moment."

"I'm sorry," I said. "I just wanted to make sure Benedict was all right."

"I'm sure I don't know how we manage without you," Rosamund said. "But he seems to have survived. We had a call from the police. Thanks to Mr. Panadek, they found the getaway cars."

The crying intensified. I had one foot on the upper step, but I took it down. "Cars? In the plural?" I said. Hugo's vigil with Donovan in the Sky Ride had paid off.

"A Dodge, and another car with some sort of fancy elephant costume in it. They assumed a third car was waiting to take the three men away. The police think it was another kidnapping attempt which didn't come off, since you didn't take Benedict with you."

"Take Benedict to a fun fair? They must be crazy," I said. "But economical, at that. They could use the bear message twice."

"Sukey was taken," Rosamund pointed out. There was no sign of Simon. If she wondered what I'd heard of their conversation, it didn't show in her manner, which was coolly non-affable, as usual. She said, "The police have advised us to get a bodyguard, and this we shall probably have to do. In the meantime, Benedict is not to go out. Do you understand?"

I understood. I was not to gossip in parks with other interested elements of the network. And Grandmother's money was to be preserved as well as might be for better ends than paying Benedict's blackmailers. I ran upstairs and picked up Benedict, who was crying real, glistening tears. Then he saw it was me, and delivered a chinless smile and I said, "Benedict Booker-Readman, you represent unpleasant, menial work with unsocial hours, and I am not going to get hooked on someone else's incontinent bastard."

He lay on my lap by the wash basin, his head turned to watch all my movements, and smiled, and cooed like a pigeon. It isn't fair. It's my last brat. I'm going to leave the profession. I'm going to turn into an old, unmarried lady who keeps retired cart horses.

The next day, Simon appointed his personal strongman for Benedict. It turned out to be Denny Donovan, which wasn't too surprising, since he knew the job was going, I suppose, before most people. They gave him a room in the attic, and he moved in from his digs with a sleeping-bag, a moisture gauge, a light meter, some insecticide, an old army revolver and a can of liquid banana. I remember thinking that I wouldn't have employed him. But he was hefty, and willing, and cheap, and no doubt was expected to keep my mind off everything that wasn't business.

Certainly, he was a revelation on the subject of plant doctoring. He had, he said, majored in fiddle leaf figs and was now fully qualified to make house to house calls including treatment and surgery. He could hold discussion groups for troubled plants and open clinics and sell records to grow them by. He was saving for a sunray lamp for a sick Mottled Bigleaf Periwinkle. It was so fascinating I was quite surprised when he mentioned the Wonderland, and observed that one of the getaway cars had been traced to a private parking lot belonging to Madison Square Garden.

It had been stolen, he said, the previous day, and from an area virtually inaccessible to the public. Which made it look as if Rudi Klapper, or the man I knew as Vladimir, or the unknown inside the elephant outfit, or even all three, may have had showbiz connections beyond the scope of Missy's Golden American Wonderland.

It seemed weak-minded to me, to steal a car from your own car park instead of a public one. But on the other hand, but for Hugo and Donovan's sky spotting, the getaway cars would probably never have been found.

"Don't tell me," I said. "There's to be a parade of Madison Square Garden employees wearing Saggy Baggy Elephant suits and pushing trash cans."

"Nope," said my ice hockey king, continuing with his current task, which was erecting illicit shelving. "They reckon that someone's still hoping to entice Benedict out of the house, and that some time, you'll be sent a couple of tickets for a kids' show. Meanwhile, the fuzz are making like they know nothing of it."

"Wait a minute," I said. "Denny, Benedict is *nine weeks old*."

"Well," said Donovan. "It's not all boxing at the Garden. They put on other things."

"No?" I said. "He won't stir out of his pram unless it's a strip show."

Donovan thought. "Well, if I don't know what a kid that age wants, I guess they don't know either. Hey, d'you know Mrs. Booker-Readman's Busy Lizzie's got greenfly?"

I let it pass. As far as I was concerned, it was just a redress of the Balance of Nature. But two days later, I remembered that conversation when the Brazilian daily came in with a note from the Eisenkopps.

It was for me, from Grandfather Eisenkopp. In it, he said that he and Grover thought I would like one of the great American experiences. Enclosed therefore were four tickets for the forthcoming Okmulgee World Championship Rodeo at Madison Square Garden, and he hoped I would use them, whether to take kids or my own friends on an evening off. Yours truly, Elijah Eisenkopp.

"There you are," I said to Donovan. "The Eisenkopp fortune has nothing to do with their toy empire. It is founded on kidnapping. A Prussian branch of Mafia. Grandpa Eisenkopp is only bedridden because he got a low sabre-cut at a christening. He could have planned it. He knew how and when I was going with Bunty to Missy's Golden American Wonderland."

"If he did, he also knew you were going without the baby," remarked my plant doctor.

He was not stupid, that fellow. Not entirely stupid, anyway. He phoned the police, and then he phoned Charlotte, who broke the news to Mrs. Mallard that two nights hence she was expected to look after her own four kids and Benedict Booker-Readman for an entire evening.

No one told her the reason. On police advice, the Booker-Readmans and I were all going to the Okmulgee World Championship Rodeo with Benedict's carrycot and a dummy inside.

I had heard of more original and even more sensible suggestions, but I was far from objecting to any device which might lead to nabbing our elephant friend or Klapper, or Vladimir. Or at the very least, a bareback Texas cowpoke for Charlotte.

I wondered, after his burst of participation at the Wonderland, if Johnson would phone me in the next couple of days, if only to say he was glad to have known me. He didn't. A boyfriend of Charlotte's knew someone who'd been to a dinner party he'd given at the New York Yacht Club, and someone else's employer came home stoned from another at the Harvard Club at which Johnson had been principal guest. He had at least one sitting from Rosamund and two others that I knew of from Philly socialites. He was playing hard to get. So I went to the Rodeo on the strength of the only real piece of advice the Department had bothered to give me: *agree to everything*.


There are nineteen thousand raked seats round the big bran ring in Madison Square Garden, and the first person I saw down by the barrier was Gramps Eisenkopp in his sonic wheelchair. He was waving. An eighteen-year-old redhead in an Indian browband and braids sitting on the arm of his chair waved as well, giggling, and half the stadium waved back, hoping to make her neckline move half an inch to the right. Rosamund said, "My God."

Simon said, "I think you should sympathize, darling. Imagine living in the same house as Comer with nothing but backnumbers of Rogue and Dude and Nugget to keep you going." He pulled down his shirt cuffs under the Dunhill hopsack blazer and leaned back in his orange seat. Rosamund was also dressed for the wananchi in a jersey print with a tie-hankie on her hair, and kept knocking the carrycot with her elbow.

Eventually I transferred it to my other side, next to the passageway, where it could be attacked more easily. Denny Donovan, who came in a bit later with Charlotte, leaned over the loge steps and cooed winningly at the wrapped shape of the china doll, before settling down across the passage. Charlotte, in cheesecloth with oasis-green eyeshadow, peered under the hood and gave an even more realistic flinch. "I'm sorry to tell you, he needs changing, Jo. Want me to do it?"

Surrounded by hate from the adjoining spectators I said, "You won't notice it when the cattle come on."

There were two detectives behind us. I supposed there might be others, watching. I wondered if any of the Department's men were about. In all the recent upheavals, I had never come across any. And tonight I wanted support, for I didn't know what to expect. Nothing was going according to expectations. No one had attacked me. No one had laid a finger on me, even at Missy's American Wonderland, with three accredited villains in the offing. Only Benedict had been threatened, in terms I couldn't forget:

*Mr. and Mrs. Booker-Readman, I have your son. He is nailed in a box, without food and drink . . .*

I had said to Simon in the cab, with the china doll in its box on my knees, "What if it's a trick? What if it's a plot to get Benedict out of the way while Donovan and the rest of us are sitting like fools at the Rodeo?"

"Really, Joanna," had said Rosamund. "The police did think of that. They'll leave a plain-clothes man with Mrs. Mallard. Obviously, we have to have Donovan here, to convince people we're bringing the baby."

Obviously. Down in the front, Gramps Eisenkopp turned round again, flapping a Stetson, which he rammed on his head, grinning. His black wig, shifting a little, peered over his brow, but his broad, thin-lipped grin stayed unaltered. Charlotte, leaning over her Data-Mate, said, "He used to ride in the Cow Palace rodeos when he was young. Would you believe it? Bunty told me."

"Jeeze. Hence the Buckle Bunnies," said Donovan, interested. Pocahontas had been joined by two girls in curled hats and pointed lizard-skin boots and pink slip-ware faces. Rodeo groupies usually hung about behind the scenes, waiting for the best-looking bull riders. No one could call Grandpa Eisenkopp good-looking, but who cared, with those financial resources? I wondered what the socially sensitive Comer and his gorgeous Beverley thought of Grandpa's hick past. If you believed Hugo, the brainstorm which removed him from active life had reached his relatives as one of the minor blessings from Providence.

I also understood why no one had been allowed to bring Grover.

Below us, the band struck up, the lights dimmed and the Grand Parade poured into the dazzling well of the ring. There were a lot of cowgirls, in hats and feathers and fringes and sequins, and quite a lot of nice looking cowboys and Indians, and some clowns. A Red Indian sang. I was aware of my confidence sinking as I looked at those clowns. Saggy Baggy Elephants and clowns: they have one thing in common. You can't recognize them.

Then the Parade juddered out through the red wooden corrals, and the rodeo started.

A rodeo is like a circus in which every other act is an open contest, for money. There was a total of eighty-five thousand dollars riding that night on six competitions, and even Rosamund and Simon, exuding well-brought-up and faintly ginned-up boredom, began to sit up slightly as the five-thousand dollar bucking broncos shot out with their yipping, one-handed riders from Tx, Fl, Ok, Nev, Mich, Wash and even wilder cow country such as Bronx, N.Y.

Each rider has to stay on his horse for eight seconds, and to swing his heels up on the horse's neck at every jump, which is why it looks and sounds like an octopus beating a rug in a hurricane. I remembered, halfway through, to turn and pat the frilled quilt on the carrycot, being conscious that Benedict, had he been present, would have been adding to the perceived Noise Decibels in no uncertain way by this time. Fortunately, such was the pandemonium, it was impossible to tell he wasn't. A man called Clint got seventy-five marks and won ten thousand dollars. We applauded him. No one attacked us.

The Mexican trick roping came on, and the calf roping contest, which showed how hard it is to knock down anything with a leg at each corner. Simon laughed all through that one, and Rosamund smiled twice. I patted the blankets.

A cowboy sang hill-billy songs with a guitar, and Donovan roared out the choruses. Rosamund looked at her watch and one of the detectives bent forward and said, "I think your baby's crying, ma'am."

It was a bloody charade. I bent forward and patted it hard enough to crack its china buttocks. The last bronco bucked and the winner was announced: Chuck Loos from Tecumseh, nine thousand dollars. Clowns and cowgirls and pickup men poured on to the pitch while the band played, and the voices of the beer and Coca-Cola men shrieked through the noise of the audience. Down below, Gramps Eisenkopp was showing off his wheelchair to the Buckle Bunnies, giving it orders to run right and left along the passageway and grinning and waving at intervals in our general direction. A piercing squeal behind me proved to be the Coke-summoning call of a six-year-old black girl in a shirred bodice, colored bows and a topknot.

An orange-shirted vendor with a shoulder-high board of candy-floss sticks walked past the wheelchair and started climbing the staircase towards us.

Donovan got up and began buying beer for himself and Charlotte. The candyfloss merchant, arriving on the step above us, unslotted a pink stick and proceeded to flog it to the six-year-old who wanted a Coke. The large glistening wand of spun sugar, waving in argument, stuck successively on the hair of the first detective and the coat of the second, both of whom twisted round, snapping. The candyfloss, jolted, left the vendor's grasp and nosedived straight under the hood of Ben's carrycot.

Surprised and aggrieved, the vendor turned on both detectives. "Hey, you gonna pay for that? Who'll buy that, now? You buy it for the baby? The baby's got it anyhow, man, ain't he?"

He hadn't, because I had snatched the stick up the moment it landed on the coverlet and was holding it out. But as he spoke, the vendor hooked one thick finger under the hood of the carrycot and jerked. The hood folded back, revealing the silent hatted cocoon of the china doll, sunk motionless under its blankets.

"Ain't that a dog?" said the vendor. "Is he human, that baby? You land a big piece of candy in his lap and he just goes on sleepin'?"

"You land Jane Fonda in his lap and he'll just go on sleeping as well," I said. "At two months he's got no discrimination. Push off, will you? I don't want him wakened." A woman in white sequins had begun to sing with the band. Shouts of *Hey, sit down, willya!* and *Push off!* added themselves to the invitation of the two detectives and the yowls of the six-year-old Coke-hunter. Donovan had turned round, a beer can in either hand. I pulled up the hood of the carrycot.

"O.K." said the vendor. "O lousy K. I get it. You don't want the effing stick. The poor man always pays. You take it an' shut your mouth." And thrusting the candyfloss into the child's nerveless black hand, he stumped off down the steps with his tray.

The two detectives looked at one another. Donovan slowly sat down and had one of the beers removed by Charlotte. Simon said, "Listen."

Rosamund took a pair of dark glasses out of her handbag and put them on. "What?" she said.

"He's put his cap on backwards," said Simon.

"Well?" said Rosamund. One of the detectives stood up.

Simon said, "None of them wears his cap backwards. He had the peak in front a moment ago. Joanna, what did he see?"

I was in no doubt. I said, "He saw all there was to see: I think it was deliberate. In which case . . ."

"It was a signal," said the second detective, and jumped out into the passage just as the vendor, below us, looked over his shoulder. The soprano hit a loaded B flat. Donovan, also jumping into the passage, shouted "Stop that man" and began racing down steps after the plain clothes man. Grandpa Eisenkopp, twisting round, gave his chair a fast order and sat, blocking the left-hand passage along the barrier. The right-hand passage, before the vendor could turn, was closed off by the quicker detective. The vendor threw his tray in the face of the slower one, and vaulted up on to the barrier.

Both detectives made a grab, but Donovan was quicker still. He took a gun from his pocket, aimed and fired. In a flash of orange the vendor fell, rolling into the arena, to be lost to sight for a moment in a ground-swell of clowns and horses and cowgirls. Charlotte squeaked, and so did three or four other people—not more—who had seen him. The ice hockey plant doctor's visage was a cherry rectangle of pleasure. "Oh boy, I got him," he said, and tugged the sleeve of one of the detectives. "Did you see that? I got him?"

"Got who? What's that?" snapped the lieutenant, tearing his gaze from the crowd in the ring.

"It's a dart gun. It fires tipped darts. They induce unconsciousness in thirty seconds. Clear the ring," said Donovan joyously. "Clear the ring. The bastard'll be lying hyped in a heap of cow-flop. All you have to do is heave him and charge him."

Simon had joined the rest of us, staring into the ring for a glimpse of a bright orange tunic. "What with?" he said. "Wearing his vending cap backwards?"

Donovan gazed back at him, his ruddy face paling. "Well . . ." he said.

"You do realize," the first detective said, his hard gaze still on the arena, "that if this cat presses charges, we can put you behind bars for unprovoked assault with a weapon?"

"What?" said Donovan.

"So you've got to hope," said the second detective, "that he's into somethin' real big, like recycling heroin balloons in a bubblegum factory. How soon d'you say that stuff knocks them out?"

"Thirty seconds," said Donovan. He said it in a much quieter voice.

"All righty," said the first detective. "Where is he? He didn't have time to cross the ring and there it is, just about clear. There's no candyfloss vendor lying hyped out on that bran. Look at it."

There wasn't. The Indians had gone, and the cowboys, and the clowns. Nothing was left but the announcer and a mounted cowgirl in blue satin with a riding crop in her mouth, waiting for the barrel horse racing. Donovan said, "I hit him. I tell you, I hit him. He must be about some place."

The detectives exchanged glances. "We'll look," one of them said. "Listen, man. Assuming you hit him, and assuming this kooky stuff works, how long is it till he wakes up?"

"Ten minutes," Donovan said. "I'll come and help you. He'll be lying . . ."

The sound of Grandpa Eisenkopp's voice talking to his wheelchair intruded on the discussion. "Listen boys," said Grandpa Eisenkopp. "I kin identify the bastard. You all get along home. I don't mind staying."

"It's all right, Mr. Eisenkopp," I said. "We'd better stay. The baby's at home, you know. This is just a doll in the basket. It was a kind of decoy."

"You don't say," said Grandpa Eisenkopp. There was a quantity of shushing, which he ignored. The Booker-Readmans, repressively, had resumed their seats.

The old man looked up at me. "What made them think the kid would be snatched at a rodeo? Damn fool place to bring a squeaker."

"It was just a theory," I said. "And I had the tickets you sent, so we thought we'd go along with it. The police ought to thank you. You took a risk, blocking the passageway."

"Of course I did," said Grandpa Eisenkopp. "And what do they do? Hot-damn, they let the guy over the barrier. You should have told me what was going to happen. It annoys the hell outa me to be treated as ga-ga. I coulda tied a rope to the chair and lassoed him." He turned round and swore, mildly, at the barrage of complaint rising behind him.

I said, "I'd better go to my seat. See you later."

I found when I climbed up that someone had shoved the carrycot under the seat and Charlotte was there in its place. She tucked my hand under her arm and squeezed it, and gradually, I began to see what I was looking at. One by one, twelve cowgirls in stetsons and tight-fitting clobber shot into the ring to race a cloverleaf course round three barrels.

It was right up Grandpa's street, this one.

It was spectacular. The hooves drummed. The bran flew. The

girls galloped over and heeled, close-hauled as a yacht round the barrel, with the reins sheeted far out in one hand. Behind me, someone said "Excuse me," tapping my shoulder.

I turned to face the indignant pouched eyes of a lady with deep chestnut hair like a wasp's nest, and earrings. She said, "You will excuse me, but I must tell you that it is against the principles of accepted hygiene to lay any young child on this floor."

Behind me, everyone gasped as a horse kicked a barrel. Beside me, her dark glasses trained straight ahead, Rosamund was ignoring the visitation. To the head at my shoulder I said, "It's all right. The cot's empty. But thank you." The rider had recovered and made a good exit: there was a round of applause, and a platinum blonde with a pigtail stood waiting for the flag to come down.

The lady behind me said, "Excuse me. I must tell you that I saw you talking to your little girl."

"Little boy," I said automatically, and caught myself up. "That is . . . Really, don't worry. He's not here; he's at home." The pouched eyes, puzzled and resentful, stared back into my smile. The pigtailed rider threw her horse into the ring in a shower of chocolate peat and I noticed that they hadn't had time to fix the barrels in position again after the previous rider. One of them was several inches to one side of its buried marker.

Just then, the nearest judge saw it, and flagged the race to a stop. The platinum pigtail looked furious, with reason. The next time the flag came down, she was out like a shell from a cannon.

She was so angry in fact that she nearly crashed the first barrel. The horse skidded round with nothing to spare, found its feet and stampeded across to the next drum.

It was the one the judge had just corrected, and it should have been firmly centered, but wasn't. It was four inches off, and as the horse exploded up to its side it moved four inches further, straight into the horse's powerful shoulder.

There was a horrific noise, made up of a bang and a howl. As in the slow-motion frame of a popcorn-chomping oldie, the horse and the barrel climbed up one another, hesitated, and then languidly parted company. The horse slid sideways, mane flowing, and ejected its rider before sinking into the peat, rolling and kicking. The girl fell face first into the flaccid brown mould. The drum, moving as if on an ice rink, performed several drunken parabolas. It then assumed the vertical, rose three inches and, moving on dirty white sneakers, swam toddling off like the Queen of the Wilis.

We all sat, mouths open, and watched it. It was Grandpa Eisenkopp, down there in his chair, who screeched to the men at his side, "Well, go on! Hog-tie it! Get the crittur! Where's your pigging-string? Get him down, boys! Throw him! Brand him!"

Rosamund said, "He'll have another stroke," but she snatched her glasses off to see better. Both the pick-up men had their ropes in their hands. The drum, running in diagonals, clanged into one yellow barrier, paused to recharge and, lifting its tin skirts, proceeded to recross the peat to a swelling back-up of clapping and catcalls and laughter. Then a rope spun through the air and the white noose drooped and tightened and tugged.

For part of a second the barrel ran frantically backwards. It toppled. It jumped backwards, tugged like a bull-calf. It rose into the air, leaving behind it its contents: a candyfloss vendor in orange.

Donovan's dart had done all he claimed it would. It had dropped the vendor in the ring, with just enough strength to crawl under a barrel. And it had wakened him up again, after ten minutes. He had enough sense restored to recognize the way out, as well.

There were horses waiting in the corrals, and cattle behind in the compound, but the candyfloss merchant went through them like a hooked marlin. One of the judges trotted after. The pickup men didn't bother, and everyone else was laughing too much to think of following.

Except Charlotte and me. Running headlong down the steps, we found neither Donovan nor the detectives.

What we did see was Grandpa Eisenkopp whooping off in his chair to a doorway. It was double-leaved, and marked "This is not an accredited egress". He cascaded through as if flipping a card deck, and Charlotte and I and the Booker-Readmans went rampaging after. Somewhere to the right there was a bellow of taurian challenge and a screech, and a flash of retreating orange. Grandpa yelled to his chair and we all changed feet, running.

Grandpa shot into the street, first of all of us.

First in the flesh, that is, but not in the spirit. Donovan got there before him, with his liquid banana. Grandpa Eisenkopp was next on the pavement. He shot out, waving his stetson, and made a dramatic right turn, to halt blocking the exit.

He went on turning. He flashed before us like an old fashioned shilling, in a blur of spinning chromium, and was joined almost immediately by the two detectives and the candyfloss vendor who came out on one foot, performed three arabesques and slid by on his shoulder, ending up at Simon's handsewn footgear. Simon stood, brushing his hopsack distastefully, and then unexpectedly fell on him. Beside me, Rosamund gave a sharp laugh.

"Excuse me," said a voice. An accusing, ruched face thrust between us, its earrings swinging. Below the large chestnut head and pouched eyes was a thin, trousered body with many brooches. In the reedy and braceletted hands hung, carefully preserved, Benedict's carrycot.

"I cannot believe," said the guardian of health and hygiene, "that you would willingly abandon this little child. I have not called the state troopers. I wish you to take this second chance. Put yourself in the hands of your welfare officer. You will never regret it."

She got to the liquid banana at that point and we all watched as she revolved and let fly with the carrycot.

I caught her as she fell, and sat down myself in the same moment as the cot descended to earth, upside down.

There was a tinkling crash, as if a tray had been dropped at a tea party. A cheek, attached to a long-lashed and lidless blue eyeball, hurried past and coasted to rest near the gutter. With a grunt, the earringed lady closed her own eyes and lay, her lips glossily mumbling.

Can in hand, Denny Donovan confided, over ten feet of ruin, in Rosamund. "Well, whadda you know? The darts worked, and the can worked and you know what? I bet that new spray has got the red spider on your begonia all laid out cold too."

"Denny," I said. "Tell me the truth. There are fools who play ice hockey *against* you?"

He grinned at me, and at Charlotte, and at the recurring front view of Grandpa Eisenkopp. The Freud of the plant world. The bodyguard with the most bodies, as of this evening.

# Chapter 8

There was no trouble getting the candyfloss vendor to talk. The pity was that he had nothing that mattered to say. Someone had paid someone who had paid someone who had paid him to find out whether or not there was a live baby in Benedict's carrycot, and flip his cap if there wasn't. End of episode.

In the six hours Benedict had spent at the Mallards', he had laughed for the very first time, at a stranger. This is commonplace.

There passed an edgy week. There was no word from Johnson. Simon went off, on unexplained business.

The plant trade remained brisk and the only time I had Denny Donovan's undivided attention was on pram-walking afternoons in Central Park, when he stalked beside me in a baggy golfing jacket with a banana can in one pocket and a dart gun in the other, eyeing everybody. Since we couldn't, naturally, have our evenings off together any more, Charlotte had retrieved him, and was giving him lessons in riding.

He was also invited to spend an evening with Grandpa Eisenkopp, who had taken a fancy to him. He went there straight from his riding lesson and returned stoned with a plastic aspidistra: Grandpa Eisenkopp had a sense of humor.

Rosamund attended three committee meetings for various charities and spent the rest of the time locked in the utility room making her dress for the Warr Beckenstaff gala in Venice.

My own evenings off I spent at the English Speaking Union: I was in a mood to play safe. It was seven weeks since, on the advice of the Department, I had got myself attached to the Booker-

Readmans because it seemed as if someone wanted me very badly to do just that thing. For seven weeks I had led a life made eventful only by the continual assaults on my poor baby Benedict.

It occurred to me that I had been picked to look after my poor baby Benedict for my incompetence. Except that it was the baby's own grandmother who had picked me.

It further occurred to me that everyone in the Department was round the twist and Mike Widdess's death which closed my last job was really an accident. In which case I had landed merely into a standard kidnapping situation which could happen to any kid with rich relatives.

Bunty, whom I bumped into, surprisingly, coming out of the E.S.U., was in no doubt. "Look, ducky: ask around and get yourself another job. I wouldn't stay with that kid if you paid me. You're going to get a bullethole through your apron one of these days."

"What, with Donovan there?" I said. "You only want to get me out so that you can move in with the security guard. I can tell you it's no snip. I've crossed the TV camera in my underwear twice already."

"You're fond of the kid, that's it, isn't it?" said Bunty. "I warn you. You'll still be there three generations later, darning their socks and making the drop scones for Rosamund's tea in the Dower House. The mean bastards might have let you come to Cape Cod."

I had had an idea that Rosamund would win that particular fight. I said, "No. I gather both Booker-Readmans are spending Easter in Florida. I'm to stay behind in New York with the baby and Donovan."

The sources of Bunty's training were the only subjects she was ever reticent about, but on one score she was an expert. She knew her rights.

"Soft, aren't you?" said Bunty. "You're supposed to have forty-eight hours off every month, aren't you? Ever get it?"

I hadn't. I wouldn't, either, when they came back. Both Simon and Rosamund were flying instanter to the family gala in Venice. In no one's debt and therefore without the family Eisenkopp. I said, "I wish someone would tell me what's happening in Venice. It's not that I want to go there, just to know why everyone else wants to."

Bunty sighed. "What it is to be secure in your employment. When you go through the mill like the rest of us, love, you learn to read your boss's correspondence. It's Ingmar's party, for the fifty years she's been in the face-painting business."

I thought of the Booker-Readmans whose combined makeup, even counting in Benedict, was minimal, and Beverley Eisenkopp, who could support the whaling industry singlehanded and probably did. The Ingmar cosmetic range may not be the biggest seller in the world, but it's by far the most exclusive, and the most expensive. I said, "I should have thought Mrs. Eisenkopp would rate a free invitation, printed in twenty-four-carat lipstick."

Bunty halted under a street-lamp, beside an open red coupé that looked astonishingly like one I had seen Comer drive now and then. "Oh, come on," she said. "Nouveau-riche; in trade; no title? A Warr Beckenstaff party is strictly for those and such as those. I'm surprised they even invite Simon and Rosamund. I expect she's making her own dress?" She got into the coupé.

I said, trying it out, "Mrs. Warr Beckenstaff is Rosamund's mother . . ."

"Mrs. Warr-Beckenstaff is Ingmar," said Bunty patiently. "Face-muck. Cosmetics. Rosamund was heiress to the Ingmar fortune until she decided to marry Simon, and now the kid will inherit. If he survives. Will you get in?" said Bunty plaintively. "I'm not supposed to have this bloody car, and I don't want any of Comer's friends exactly to see me around in it."

I got in. Encounters with Bunty always had their own brand of astonishment.

The next day Johnson arrived in the Mercedes with his painting-case, his portable easel and a large canvas on which, half-finished, appeared an entirely beautiful portrait of Rosamund Booker-Readman cradling the upper half of a charming, sleeping Benedict.

No one had told me he was coming. I had just spent a concentrated two hours giving Benedict his bath, his Farex and his bottle, and was making up feeds while he lay peacefully sleeping under the eye of the closed circuit camera. I didn't want to be interrupted and I wasn't going to waken Benedict for anybody.

I said so, repelling with firmness any other emotion I might have felt at his unlooked-for appearance.

In return, he was soothing. "It doesn't honestly matter. My fault. When does he have his next bottle?"

He had it at 12:30, because he missed his early feed now. It wasn't Johnson's fault that the routine was now different. I said, "I can lift him later, if you want to paint Mrs. Booker-Readman in the meantime. You can fold the christening-robe round him. He wouldn't get into it anyway."

"I meant to tell you to stop feeding him," Johnson said. Above the spectacles his black hair was flat as an off-color Labrador's. He looked more than a trifle the way my Data-Mate Donovan looked after the evening with Grandpa Eisenkopp.

Rosamund smiled. Naturally, she was on the whole pleased to have her portrait sitting unencumbered with Benedict. I, of course, was going to be required to hold Benedict to be painted later that morning.

Which—it belatedly came to me—was precisely what Johnson intended. Two hours later, he had finished with Rosamund, and I took her place, carrying Benedict, for thirty minutes of unexceptionable privacy with my father's friend Johnson.

He worked as we talked, his eyes on Benedict's face. I had never seen an artist painting before. If I had thought at all, I had expected something static, like sight-reading from music. Instead he strolled backwards and forwards, palette and brushes in hand. He seemed to spend more time leaning on the walls, chatting, than he did brushing paint on the picture. I interrupted myself, describing the rodeo in detail, to say, "You paint really from memory, don't you?"

"Type of short-term memory, yes. I like a broad effect. As many methods as painters," Johnson said. He was also extraordinarily neat. For a man whose clothes were a shambles, he coped with tubes, oil, turpentine, sticky brushes, rags and palette without spill, drip or smear marring the various worn and/or antique surfaces of Simon Booker-Readman's sitting room, and without a mark on himself either. I said, "You must have had a bloody good nurse."

"I had those feeders with bags in them," Johnson said. "If I dropped a crumb, a mailed fist shot up and socked me one. You don't know, therefore, which of the nineteen thousand people at the rodeo was watching for the candyfloss vendor's signal? It was unlikely, I should think, to be Rudi, who tried the original snatch in the park, whom you might see and recognize again. Also unlikely to be Vladimir from Winnipeg, who helped him escape from the Wonderland, for the same reason. The man inside the Saggy Baggy

Elephant who delayed us at the Wonderland is probably the best bet, if we assume these three are the prime team against Benedict. And we don't know what he looks like. That's their strong point."

My arm had gone numb. I looked down and found Benedict's eyes were open. I smiled and he smiled, and I shifted my arm. He shut his eyes again. I said, "The tickets for the rodeo came from the Eisenkopp grandfather. He gets them every year. There's no reason to think he's involved. But if he isn't, how did anyone know we'd be there?"

"The nanny network," Johnson said. "Bunty. Charlotte. Grandpa's Buckle-Bunnies, if you like. The same means by which it became known that we were all going to Missy's American Wonderland. The great inter-staff grapevine. The alternative is even weirder."

It was the alternative that was bothering me. I said, "I thought of that. The whole thing could have been phoney. The police could have been induced to stage that stupid trap which was bound to lead nowhere. Who in their right minds would try to kidnap a baby among all those witnesses? But why go to that trouble? If they want Benedict," I said, trying to keep my voice as even as his was, "why don't they shoot me and Donovan and take him?"

"Because he's too young," Johnson said. "They know that now. If they're to keep him alive they need you, Joanna, as well as the baby."

I swallowed. I said, "Then—"

He stepped back, brush in hand, and moved his eyes from Benedict's face to mine. He wasn't smiling. He said, "Then the nonsense at the American Wonderland and the nonsense at the Rodeo had no meaning at all except as a careful preliminary. They were meant to frighten. They were meant to frighten you, and Benedict's parents. Especially Benedict's parents. So that when the real snatch comes, they don't tell the police."

Benedict stirred. His mouth made eating movements and he opened his eyes again. His arm, untucked, moved about vaguely and I collected it and turned his head into my arm with the warm palm of my hand. Then I said, "The Booker-Readmans are going away. To Florida, and then on to Venice . . . I'm sorry. I forgot not to move him."

"It doesn't matter. I've nearly finished," Johnson said. "It's lucky, in a way, I've got so far with Rosamund. I was surprised myself when she said they were leaving for Easter. I'd hoped to finish the thing at Cape Cod."

Benedict grizzled, but this time I paid no attention to him. I said, "You're going to Cape Cod?"

"I thought you knew?" Johnson said. Above the glasses, his black eyebrows arched in surprise. "Comer Eisenkopp invited me. A bit of sailing, a bit of loafing. You remember. You can let go now, he won't settle. Come and look, if you like."

He was sweeping up paint with his palette knife as if nothing had happened. I said, my hand under Benedict, "You're going to Cape Cod for Easter? Leaving me here alone?" I got up.

"With Donovan," said Johnson reprovingly. I had used the same tone myself to Bunty. But this was different.

He folded his scrapings into a rag, dunked and wiped his brushes; wiped his palette. I walked round and stood over him and then, as he didn't jump to attention, glanced at the canvas.

There was the likeness of Benedict, with the quarter-inch of dark fuzz, and the sucking-blister, and the cleft chin, and the line across the broad, sunken bridge of his nose. I said, "Oh bloody hell," and upended the live, wet, reeking, grumbling Benedict so that my eyes lay against his round forehead and cheek, which is a very bad thing to do, since they just suck off your makeup, thereby adding to the Warr Beckenstaff fortune. It is, however, comforting to the upholder.

Johnson said, after a pause, "It's all right. I have eighteen sleepless nights in a row which say that nothing will happen to Benedict. Otherwise, of course, I might not get paid for the portrait. Ah, there you are," said Johnson as Rosamund Booker-Readman, without preliminary, pushed open the door. "Come and see. We've just finished."

I took the baby away, and changed and fed him.


The next day, a Sunday, Donovan went riding with Charlotte, fell off his horse and returned with his right arm in plaster.

Despite a vivid demonstration with a can of liquid banana in his armpit the Booker-Readmans were not impressed, and informed him, with extreme irritation on Rosamund's part, that they were not prepared to entrust their son's life to a cripple. He was in the nursery, telling me about it and asking me to mind a bad case of leaf curl, when Comer Eisenkopp phoned.

He had heard from Bunty who had heard from Mrs. Mallard's girl that we were in trouble. Why didn't Nurse Joanna bring that nice little kid up to stay with them at Cape Cod for Easter? It'd be great for Bunty, and the kids could all play together.

Play together, I ask you. You could put a hand grenade into Benedict's hand and he wouldn't even know he was holding something. And all the playing together Grover did was steer tricycles over his sister. Great for Bunty, it would be. All the time off she wanted, and someone else—me—to take all the trouble. And great for Comer who wanted—who so much wanted—to attend the Warr Beckenstaff gala.

But when Rosamund called me down to tell me about it, I didn't make any objections—quite the contrary. For in other ways it was the most promising news I'd been offered since February.

# Chapter 9

Cape Cod is a peninsula shaped like the foot of a jester. It lies on the eastern seaboard of the United States just below Boston, and sticks its thin curling toe seventy miles into the Atlantic ocean. On its instep is the gulf called Wabash Bay, on one headland of which lies the Eisenkopps' summer residence. On the day before Good Friday, Ben and I flew there accompanied by Bunty Cole and the whole of the Eisenkopp family with the exception of Gramps, who was to spend the weekend, I understood, at the Playboy Club.

I thought we should fly Eastern Shuttle to Logan. We didn't. We flew in Comer Eisenkopp's personal seaplane, made a perfect landing in Wabash Bay and chugged to the jetty, where the garden buggy was waiting to save us the long, difficult walk up to the house. The two principal cars had arrived the night before, bringing the houseboy and the Italian couple. Benedict's pram was waiting on the garden patio and his cot and luggage were already in the night nursery when I got there. He was to share it with Sukey.

I had the other twin bed in Bunty's room. I set Ben to kick in his cot and then, walking through, opened Bunty's French windows and stepped out on to the balcony.

The Eisenkopp house was architect-built in the Hollywood hacienda tradition, all white marble and wrought iron and potted geraniums. Below me was a paved terrace edged with creeper-hung rail and equipped with lights and with flowertubs, and white and red tables and chairs for breakfast, or Sundowners. Sunk below the terrace was a walled garden, and beyond that, lawns which appeared to stretch to the beach. You could just see the tops of upturned dinghies and what looked like a speedboat. On either side, beyond the walled garden, were glimpses of stables and tennis courts. I wondered if there were horses, and thought it a pity Donovan wasn't here to break his other arm.

Beyond the beach was the flat April blue of Wabash bay, with a number of small boats already out sailing. And beyond that, the curving line of the Cape Cod jester's sole, disappearing round to the north. The air smelt mild and salty and fresh, with the slightest touch of roast duck and orange. An Italian voice said, "You no need to unpack, miss. We do this. Miss Bunty to say to tell you lunch is in one-half hour, and there is brandy and vodka in the refrigerator."

Here, also. I was standing holding the vodka and wondering, in a mild haze of wellbeing, where Hugo Panadek was when the door opened a second time and a brown, bald, earringed figure strolled through and paused, clicking its tongue.

"Well, darling," said Hugo Panadek. He walked forward, removed the vodka, kissed me warmly, replaced the vodka and stretched himself full length on Bunty's bed. After a moment he extended a hand and, removing Bunty's Ho Hang from the dressing table, sprayed his naked chest liberally and lay back again, breathing deeply. His eyes shut, "Really, darling," he said, "I am not intending to abduct your poor Warr Beckenstaff infant. Was it not I, Hugo, who shot all your bears for you?"

"So what?" I said, sitting down on the windowsill. He had short Central European legs in flared velvet trousers and a striped silk Charvet shirt, open to the waist, and an assortment of chains and medallions. The bald head, of course was ridiculous, but the skin, though sallow, was smooth, and he had a torso the same size and shape as a rodeo barrel. I added, "That doesn't prove anything, does it? You might be deeply in debt and suffering a total toy-invention block which threatens to throw you into the hands of your creditors. I haven't noticed you invent anything recently."

"Heartless!" said Hugo Panadek comfortably. "But I have, darling. Ask Comer." He lifted one finger, with his eyes closed, and pressed a white button on the bed head. There was a cautious creak, a groan, a buzz, and the mattress beneath him began to vibrate. His medals ringingly started to clatter on one another. "They're called massage-boys," I said. "They have them all over France. Try again."

"Darling," said Hugo Panadek. "I had no need to invent the massage-boy. Of that I assure you. I am merely throwing off the weight of your disapproval. I am also postponing the time when I have to go downstairs to lunch and witness the appetite-destroying spectacle of Comer swimming thirty-two lengths of the pool before every mealtime. You know there is a swimming pool in the sitting room?"

"I wondered where it was," I said.

"One part water to three thousand parts disinfectant. The only known mix that kills both the germs and the antibodies," Hugo said. "Then there is the Health Room, with the Rowing Machine, the Electronic Bucking Horse, the Electric Camel and the Traxatou Massage Couch with Vacumatic Suction. You must admire Comer. He persists."

"What at? His weight?" I said. It was fascinating.

"That, too. A major counter-offensive in the general battle against varicose veins, thrombosis, diabetes, dental caries, arteriosclerosis, peptic ulcers and appendicitis," Hugo said. "Obesity enters somewhere but that is more Beverley's field. She would so dislike you to know that she is thirty-five years of age. Myself," said Hugo, "I prefer European women. Every civilized person should spend at least one third of the year in Europe. Even in England. I have had some commissions of great interest in England."

I made the sort of reply he was asking for, but I was really thinking of Beverley. That made her two years older than Comer, when I had put her down as an easy twenty-five. Not that I'd had the chance to make a study in depth on the two occasions I'd met her: once when falling flat over Sukey, and today sitting with Comer on the lounge seats of the seaplane, well away from the regurgitating kids and their staff in the rear. A mink jacket, what else, over a russet suede pants suit and striped yellow shirt; bouncing blond hair like satin and a Barbarella profile with eight different shades of under-cream, and the nostrils oiled. And that, I can tell you, is a trick that only one nose in ten thousand can use and end up looking like Dewi Sukarno and not Bella the Cook. "She doesn't have to worry," I said.

"Ah," said Hugo. "But she is a perfectionist. Do you imagine she would have had her two children if Comer had not finally insisted?"

Something caught his eyes and infuriatingly, he broke off. Rolling on to one elbow, he examined the row of aerosol cans on Bunty's dressingtable. "You know, you could kill a woman, making her dress in the dark. Foot refresher spray, makeup spray, toilet water spray, fly spray, hair spray, deodorant spray, all insulting the ozone layer and for what?"

"Putting money into inventors' pockets, when they wear any," I said. A thought struck me. "She's had a nose job?"

"Beverley?" said Hugo lazily. He lay down again. "Beverley, darling, has had everything lifted. Chins, chest, eyelids, haunches, everything. She hasn't tried Bucharest to date, but you can be sure that as soon as the Warr Beckenstaff gala is over, she will be in the pits for an overhaul at the Radoslav. Bunty tells me she booked in a month ago."

Everyone who has worked in a rich woman's household has heard of the Radoslav Clinic in Dubrovnik. Cosmetic surgery in Yugoslavia has been in the news since the first nose-bob doctor thought of advertising a combined ten-day holiday offer and was knocked down in the rush of misshapen tourists. "Don't tell me," I said. "It's Missy's Radoslav Clinic?"

"Is every science to be laid at my door? I had nothing to do with it," said Hugo Panadek. "Merely, the first time Beverley answered an advertisement and went by herself. Perhaps to escape from her father-in-law, who deserved a stroke but had not yet had it. A lady friend of mine introduced us. That is how I got to know Comer. I owe my fortune to the Yugoslav National Health Service. Now you tell me something. Why is the daughter of Professor Sir Bernard Emerson performing menial services for punks like Simon and Rosamund?"

I knew now why the Eisenkopps called me Nurse Joanna. Indeed, it was surprising that, unlike Hugo, they hadn't tried pumping me earlier. I said, "Charlotte's father is actually better off than mine. But, you know, we're big expensive girls with big, expensive tastes. We have to earn a living."

"But in this fashion?" said Hugo. "With jumping beans in your pockets and the mouth full of nappy pins? You swim. You shoot.

The Tiffany Brides' Register is not, I suspect, your immediate goal. Did no other career commend itself? You are meticulous: precise as an engineer, a scientist. Did you never wish to pursue such a calling?"

Shrewd Mr. Panadek. I grinned and said, "Are you making a cross-cultural sociological study or offering me a job? I don't need to change my work. I'm a social engineer as it is. And I do try hard, I promise you, not to neglect my potential."

"According to Mr. Donovan," Hugo said, "not hard enough. What is the appeal of other people's children?"

"Very little," I said. "But it grows on you. Some people can't even stand their own children. Hence the market. You might say that punks give their kids a punk childhood which leads to the next generation of punks."

"And every Margaret Beaseford nurse is dedicated to breaking this chain?"

He had impudent eyebrows. "Wouldn't do much good if we were," I said. "You can't fight heredity. Keep 'em healthy, teach 'em manners, and give the kids and their parents a break from one another. Bearing in mind that a bad parent is better than a bad nurse any day. Do you suppose that's a summons for lunch?"

Hugo swung his neat feet to the floor. "It is. And I am lunching over the Bay with the Princess. I expect, since she is our local celebrity, to find our Brownbelly colleague Mr. Johnson staying with her. Comer tells me he is coming to visit here next, and moreover has been invited on Wednesday week to the Warr Beckenstaff gala. What it is to be simple, and shortsighted, and popular."

He slid off after I made a sufficiently flippant rejoinder. Conversation with Hugo Panadek had some aspects in common with hang gliding. Afterwards, I allowed myself to dwell on Johnson's shortcomings. His interest in Mike Widdess, it seemed to me, was as erratic as his interest in Benedict. And now he was going to Venice.

It wasn't that I had come to depend on him. But it was hard to look around, and find neither the board nor the player.

He came to stay two days later, and was immediately sucked into the vortex of the Eisenkopp routine, which began with a swim, a ride or some tennis or squash before breakfast and proceeded with several rounds of competitive sport culminating in Comer's thirty-two lengths of the pool. Some of his guests got in and swam with him. The rest sat about drinking martinis. The pool was cleaned by a pool bug called Percy, who ran about at the end of a cable and ate all the dead leaves and popcorn. Sometimes it tried to eat Comer.

After lunch, everyone slept, and there would be a sail, a race or a fishing expedition before the evening drinking began, either at home or in one of the neighboring mansions.

After dinner, there were games. Both Comer and Beverley were taking backgammon lessons.

Bunty and I had our meals in our room with the children. While the others were out, Bunty showed me the rest of the house. Beverley's suite was done in shell-pink taffeta and had a mirrored ceiling and frilled zip-linked beds: *Separate in a Jiff for a Sniff or a Tiff.* Automatic switches opened the curtains and put on the lights and the TV and radio and controlled the record player. Bunty pressed a button and a rich voice started intoning behind the heaped pillows. *"Relax. You are going to lose weight. You will not be able to overeat. Sometimes you will not be able to finish a meal . . ."*

I listened fascinated for a bit, and then Bunty switched it off and led the way out, scooping up a boxful of Bissinger's Nut Balls from under the bed before, she said, the dogs got it.

There were two dogs and they each got three Panteric and four Vitamin E tablets a day and their own beef-flavored Doggy Dent toothpaste. Grover liked the taste too, and ate it until Bunty found it all squashed up in the pocket of his Tooth Fairy pillow and threw it away.

I made him some dough and he wrung out a dirty grey flower and a fish, and the Mafia let us put them in the oven. We had them quickly for tea, the plague in every mouthful, before Comer could see us. Then I boiled colored eggs and we rolled them down the chute, what else, which at least took Grover's mind (and Bunty's) off the chocolate kind, which arrived by every post from the expense accounts of Comer's business colleagues.

Not that there was any shortage of means by which the Wabash community could get shot of their Special Little Princes and Princesses as and when it seemed desirable. There were films for children and play groups and puppets and Punch and Judy and musicals.

You could have your Little People taught to swim, play tennis, speak French, ride, play an instrument, dance, fish and play simple card games. Left to Bunty, Grover would have spent in a play group all the waking moments he wasn't already spending in his high chair, his cot or his playpen.

I begged him off after a day and whipped him out when I'd finished with Ben to the shore or the swings or the chute. We had a bucket with starfish in it, and a wheelbarrow for pebbles. I taught him eight more nursery songs and started a big Easter mural of cotton wool rabbits and crêpe paper trees.

Johnson arrived to stay while I was working on it and escaped a whole afternoon's riding by devoting himself to equipping the bunnies with large-eyed, smiling and flattering likenesses of all Grover's immediate circle, including Sukey and Benedict. Grover watched, building bricks in an absent-minded way, quite entranced, and unaware that with exceptional sleight of hand, Johnson was sketching him at the same time.

The sketch was quite brilliant, as well. After Grover had returned to his sand-pit I said, "The guest for whom every door is open. Did you draw the Princess as well?"

He looked no trendier, but a little less like a lush from a quilting bee. He was also unmoved by sarcasm. "That's how I do it," he said. "Swiss quality at Hong Kong prices. Have you seen Comer's computerized bar? It served three Virgin Marys into my pocket, and a pack of Sun Giant Almonds the Adult Nut zing into the automatic shoe cleaner. It was like Bad Day at Black Rock." He stuck some black cotton wool on his upper lip, looked at himself in the nursery mirror and then peeled it off.". . . But I will say they've got the War on Want licked. No further bloodcurdling incidents?"

"Not so far," I said. "But Bunty wants danger money." She was in the next room, not quite within earshot, trying to persuade half a pound of tuppenny rice out of Grover.

"Nonsense," said Johnson abstractedly. "The house is wired, and the garden is full of Alsatians. You'll be better off here than you would in New York, with Donovan changing you into a bottle garden. It was the nearest thing to the rats and the pumpkins that I ever saw outside Cinderella."

"But in ten days' time, you're going to Venice?" I made it pointed.

I daren't embark on anything less than ambiguous. "A free suite at the Gritti and you're painting the manager?"

His glasses flashed. "You forget," said Johnson. "I've worked my passage already, commissioned by Benedict's grandmother Ingmar. My costume's all fixed: too exciting. Then after the bash, I may drift on to Malta."

"To paint Mabel?" I said. I was not amused. I didn't know, either, that it was a fancy dress party.

"To pick up *Dolly*. She's wintered at Sliema," said Johnson.

His yacht. I had forgotten. The one he brought over the Atlantic, sometimes; and painted on, and lived aboard, and used from time to time as a means of exit. I said, "And what about Benedict's portrait? He's going to look a bit odd in collar and tie and a christening robe."

The riding party was back. The dulcimer chimed. It was time for the plunge pool with the hydrojet massage. Johnson said, "You let me worry about that and everything else. Just put your mind to being polite to itinerant painters and doing everything that everyone tells you to. That way you won't get the sack."

But I did.

Easter Monday was the Eisenkopps' ninth wedding anniversary, and the house was full of florists, electricians and caterers and six-foot vats full of crushed ice. Dr. Gibbings arrived in the morning to check Benedict's vaccination and to give one to Sukey and Grover. This represented a triumph of Maggie Bee diplomacy over an army of Eisenkopp prejudices. I didn't know until later that—anything for a quiet life—Bunty had agreed to have her charges vaccinated, but hadn't actually mentioned it to her employers.

While Dr. Gibbings was there, I got him to look at Grover's throat also. He advised a waiting game over his tonsils and was prevailed upon, without difficulty, to remain for the party.

The party was attended by two hundred guests and had as its main feature a surprise neon sign from Mrs. Eisenkopp to Mr. Eisenkopp which said, COMER I LOVE YOU. The Wabash Bay Musical Society rendered a selection of Great American Love Songs in harmony after the buffet.

The only conversation which came within our range of hearing as we sat, Bunty and I, out of sight at the top of the stairs, was about the lethal properties of maraschino cherries. An argument broke out, as I remember, to do with fruit salad, in the purest of senses, during which Bunty broke into weeping.

Next morning, Grover had a field day throwing building bricks, tiddley-winks and bits of paper from his mother's bedroom into the pool, finishing up with the entire contents of his bottle of Giant Little Folks' Bubble Bath. When Comer came in for his thirty-two lengths the water looked like the effluent stream of a soda pop factory with the pool bug lurching wheezing about like a hand whisk.

The scene that followed is only relevant insofar as it ended with Comer, swollen with rage, gouging Percy out on to the wall-to-wall carpet and prising open its glutted mouth-trap from which emerged a stream of small toys, cigarette butts, Adult Nuts, dirty tissues, crumpled paper and rejected maraschino cherries. It was what I might have expected to find in Bunty's loo, for example, if the party had been held there.

There were other parallels. One of the pieces of paper, uncurling itself in Johnson's careless hand, proved to be a fragment of writing, much chewed and washed out by bubble bath, which said nevertheless quite distinctly, "Look out for me then, darling, on Tuesday."

"Why, he's torn Gwenny's letter," said Beverley quickly. "You bad, bad boy, Grover."

I saw Comer Eisenkopp's hand rise quivering to waist height and then, disappointingly, drop again. He knelt. "Son. What you've done today has made your Momma and Dad very unhappy. Are you glad you made your Momma unhappy, Grover?"

"Yes," said Grover.

Bunty smoothed out her coffee striped nylon and kneeling also, laid her hand on Grover's forehead. "Oh, dear," she said. "We've got a little temperature, haven't we? Mr. Eisenkopp, you'll have to let me take him away to lie down. It's all come as a shock, poor little baby. Mrs. Eisenkopp, you know you have a very sensitive son."

She looked reproachfully at Beverley who had already switched expressions and was saying, her hand on Comer's naked shoulder, "He didn't mean it, I know. Easter always upsets him, darling. Why don't we just go and have a sauna instead?"

They retired. Grover got the flat of Bunty's hand three times, cried, was given half an Italian Easter egg and was sick in the sandpit. His parents, clean, pink and restored to calm, knelt on either side of his bed and promised to take him sailing on Dadda's yacht in the morning.

Or Comer did. Beverley never boarded the thing, it was common knowlege, since she got sick to her stomach, in the colorful phrase, if she walked on wet grass. And by arrangement, it was Bunty's day off.

I remember saying, in an attempt to stem the flood of reconciliation, "Mr. Eisenkopp . . . He'll have to have someone with him in case he falls in. And I'm looking after Ben and Sukey."

Grover burst into tears. Beverley looked up. Her nose in profile was high-bred and slender as a humming-bird feeder, and if there were any tucks, I couldn't see them. Her skin was flawless. She said. "He is so sensitive. Nurse Joanna, you go with Grover. No problem. I'll stay at home and look after the babies."

Even bearing in mind Bunty's serial horror story of precisely how Mrs. Eisenkopp looked after the babies on her weekends off, I was tempted. Then common sense took over and I said, "It would be simply splendid, but I did promise I'd stick with Ben. His parents are so upset about these rotten kidnappings."

It was the wrong line to take. The enormous eyes opened and Beverley said, "But honey, have you *seen* the security precautions? Why, there are two men patrolling the grounds right at this minute and of course I shan't be alone: Paolo and his wife are there in the kitchen. You run along tomorrow and have yourself a good time."

The clincher came with Johnson's assenting voice. "Yes. Why don't you?" he said.

If he was convinced that neither Beverley nor the Italian couple wanted to kidnap Benedict, then it was all right by me. I wanted to see the yacht, and to sail again. My father used to race, once. I agreed.

The third week of April is too early for Squibnocket Beach, but the mild, sunny weather had brought quite a few cruising boats out next morning, as Comer collected his crew along with Grover and myself on the terrace. The crew consisted, it appeared, of one or two stockbroking neighbors and their polite sons. Then Johnson came downstairs in a stained yellow nylon kagool and promptly outraged both the Eisenkopps by ripping undone and taking off the tasteful Little Mermaid life jacket in which Grover had been dressed by his father.

"Burn it," said Johnson.

"My kids wear these," someone said. "Hey, they're all right. They float."

"Of course they float," Johnson said. "It's finding out whether they've floated face up or face down that's the exciting bit."

We boarded the boat: a handsome Australian-built auxiliary sloop my father would have approved of.

Grover objected to his orange cork lifesaver, his harness and his running leash, to the sound of the anchor coming up and the noise the engine made when it started. Then they got a sail up and the engine went off and he saw the house with Sukey in it falling behind and other beaches coming up, and gardens, and houses; and Johnson asked him to get the frozen octopus out of the ice box. And he stopped crying.

I won't say there was much to do. Comer held the tiller and issued the orders, and the boat was so full of tanned, husky weekend sailors that there were three people to every sheet and the winches were whipped incandescent. Grover and I went and sat on the foredeck and watched Johnson baiting lines and waved at all the people we knew on their jetties or gardens or putting lawns.

Wabash Bay is a private community and the beachside properties are expensive and large: anyone from the Third Crusade would have felt instantly at home. And because the morning was wearing on by this time, a good many of the patios and terraces were occupied with neighbors having their pre-lunch stingers in company. I spotted at least a dozen of the Eisenkopps' guests from the other night outside three different houses.

We drifted on, fairly close inshore and were passing the last house in the bay before sailing out into the Sound towards Chappy when someone onshore hailed us.

Among the knits and tight denims and jumpsuits, there was no trouble in identifying the one bald and volatile head. It was Hugo Panadek, in yellow fringed poncho and boots, and waving a drink in his hand.

What he heard could not be said, even though we could see him put down his drink, embrace his hostess and stride, calling, down to the boatless jetty. I said to Johnson, "Do you know he does all Mr. Eisenkopp's automation? Heat-sensitive burglar precautions, sit-up beds, garden sprinklers, dust extraction and humidity, robot snack-servers and squash players, magnetic door locks, movable wall dividers. The garage opens if you walk towards it with the key in your pocket. And the safe won't open unless you put your gloves in the 'fridge before touching it. It's your name he's calling."

Johnson went on fixing bait. "So it seems. My guess is that he wants a lift back to the house and is dying to spill a good joke he's just heard about Comer."

"It'll be a long lift," I said. "We haven't started fishing yet."

"We haven't even started drinking yet," Johnson said. "My other guess is that he has noticed there's a girl on board, and who she is. Do you want him, or not?"

"If you mean on board, I have no strong views either way," I said. "Provided he brings his refrigerated gloves . . . Are you going?"

The glasses looked pained. "What else? You've just sent me, haven't you?" said Johnson, and disappeared aft. Grover put some bait in his mouth. "One for Grover," he said. "What did Josso want?"

I reckoned that, without the hook, the bait could do no permanent harm. "He's gone to get Hugo," I said. "Look, the wind is blowing towards Grover now, and the boat has stopped. That's to let Mr. Johnson get into the dinghy."

He did, too, without any fuss and also without any company: a fact accounted for by the unmistakable clink and splash of drinks being served in Comer's saloon.

I went to find out if there was any juice for Grover, and didn't even see the collision.

One moment there was a narrow strip of blue bay water, with Johnson's dinghy and sundry small craft in it, and Hugo waiting, arms akimbo under his poncho.

The next, there was a shout and a crash, and the belting roar of a strong speedboat engine.

I swung up the companionway: the others jumped to the rail, or the portholes.

Where Johnson's boat had been was the overturned wreck of the dinghy: a mess of curved and sprung wood with planks, rags and litter wagging about in the shearing wake of a white ocean racer. Of Johnson, there was no vestige. "Oh Great Christ," said Comer, and seizing the helm, put it down.

Someone said, "You've only got eight feet, and shoaling."

Comer said, "I know. Jake, take Clem and unlash the speedboat. Marty, the lifebelts. Ready to anchor. Who swims best? Stewart?"

No sweat. I was down to my bra and bikini pants by then, with Grover screaming beside me. "No. I do," I said; and as she came round to anchor, I dived.

It was freezing. Who swims best? Comer, you'd think, with his thirty-two bloody lengths daily. But he was handling the yacht. Of course. I shook my head in the air, got a line on the wreckage and put my head down again, with my arms turning like ships' propellers. There are two things I can do, apart from the jobs I am paid for. One is swimming. The other, as it happens, is sailing.

I thought, a speedboat from the local boatyard would have had to stop. So that was a stranger. An accident? A diversion? An effort by the kidnappers to get rid of Johnson? Hardly. Even at the Golden Wonderland, Johnson had scarcely made an impression as Benedict's most dangerous ally. And anyway, no one could have known that Johnson would be alone in a boat in Wabash Bay at this moment.

Except, of course, Hugo.

I was close now, but there was no movement ahead in the water.

Behind, I heard the splash as the yacht's speedboat was lowered. I heard Hugo's voice shouting and realized that he, too, was swimming towards the overturned dinghy, from the opposite direction. I couldn't move any faster.

He had been under for four minutes.

If he was thrown in the path of the keel, he could be broken in two. Not pretty. A lot nastier than the things you saw in a maternity hospital.

My mother's voice: *Johnson is coming over. He's painting the duchess.*

Painting was all he'd done, really. And play jokes with the Eskimos and the baby alarm. And shoot badly. And forget to belt in the Brownbelly Bruin.

I had got to the wreckage. I was tired. and my breath was sobbing anyway. There was nothing on top, so I dived.

There was air under the hull of the boat, and something solid encased in slippery nylon. "I remember when you got a gold medal for doing that," said Johnson appreciatively. "Get me back in the launch. I've concussion."

I made a mad sort of sound. Before I'd bitten it off, he had grinned, shut his eyes in the gloom, and slid off his perch into the water. I hung there, stupidly watching him sink. His hair waved up, black in the green, and his yellow nylon swelled out and his hand, white and limp, gave a couple of testy twitches and became white and limp once again. With the start, I let go the boat and went headlong after him, before he drowned.

I met Hugo halfway with Johnson's clothes in his hands, already shoving him up to the air. The gagging and choking he did when he got there had the stamp of true authenticity and won no sympathy from me. It was agreed, as we heaved him into the speed launch, that he'd had a bang on the head and was in a state of concussion. As a nurse, I got the job of getting his lungs clear of water, and I enjoyed that as well, I can tell you.

While I was pummelling, the speedboat got back to the yacht, and the anxious Comer and his craning son.

I wondered how in the last few minutes I could have forgotten Grover. Then he saw Johnson and started to wail again.

I didn't need to persuade anyone to send Johnson back in the launch: it was the obvious thing to do. It was also obvious that Hugo and I, who were cold and wet, should go with him and that Grover might as well come with us too, and give me rather than his dinghyless father the benefit of his hysterics.

Concern for the health of his favorite international portrait painter had given way, already, to a blast of fury directed against the invisible and unknown hoodlum in the speedboat. The stockbrokers climbed back aboard the yacht. I could hear them all having stiff drinks as Hugo took the wheel of the launch and I sat behind him in a large borrowed sweater with Grover, our feet on Johnson's motionless torso. We began with a sweep to pick up the sad, floating Ophelia of Hugo's mad poncho, and in five minutes arrived at the Eisenkopps'.

You could hear the screaming babes from the jetty. Obligingly, Johnson recovered enough to paddle his feet up the garden, an arm round each of our necks. I left Hugo to cart him to his bedroom and, dragging Grover, made for the nursery. Sukey and Benedict, lunchless and reeking, screamed each in his or her cot: our suite was otherwise empty.

The sitting room was empty, and so, literally, was the pool.

There was no one on the patio, or in the garden, or in the Health Room, the card room, the diningroom, the breakfast room or the sauna. I managed to convey to Grover, who was yelling for her, that Bunty was still off for the day. He then wanted his mother.

In the kitchen, I found the Mafia, having its luncheon with the door firmly closed. No, they had not heard any sounds from the nursery. The Signora came when she required heated food for the babies. The Signora had not come so far. Perhaps the Signora was still asleep.

True enough, the door to the pink silk bedroom had been closed. An odd silence reminded me that I was still wearing a chest 44 cableknit sweater and little else, so I explained quickly about Johnson and tacked on a bit about hot soup and brandy and hot water bottles, which fell somewhat flat as they had only just put the lasagne, I could see, on the table. Then I hared off, with Grover, to Beverley's bedroom.

The door was shut, and when I tapped, no one answered.

I tapped again. Grover said, "Are you there, Momma? Come out to Grover?" The sight of the Mafia had settled him.

I had almost turned away when I heard the voice talking. When I pressed my ear to the door, I could just make out what it was saying. *Relax. You are going to lose weight. You will not be able to overeat. Sometimes you will not be able to finish a meal . . .*

It figured. After all those Easter eggs, a quick weight therapy session with her Lady Schick Face Sauna, her bio rhythm machine, enzyme peeler and even perhaps oral wormer were just what anyone might have predicted. I said, "Mummy can't hear, Grover: she's got her weight record playing."

"Open the door," Grover said.

"It's locked. We'll see her later," I said.

"Key," said Grover. In both hands, he held something I recognized as Beverley's new blonde crocodile handbag.

"No," I said. "Lunchtime, Grover. Let's go and have lunch. Would you like chicken sandwiches?" Distantly, the hoarse squeals from the two cots redoubled.

"Key," said Grover, undisturbed. He walked up to his mother's bedroom door, still bearing her handbag. And with a click and a whine, the bedroom door opened.

As I have said, I had been there before. The pink taffeta I knew to expect, and the white and gold paintwork, and the bright mirrored ceiling. I expected the console of switches, and the soothing voice from the record player, assuring Beverley she would gag over cream cakes. But gazing wildly around, I was at a loss to locate Grover's mother. On the bed with a Danish pastry? Upside down on the Porta-Yoga with a headache? In the Jacuzzi jet bath for two with a loofah?

Wherever she was, she was entitled to privacy. It wasn't her fault that a combination of Grover and her magnetic locks had given us entry.

I had my hand on Grover's head and had already switched him round to march out of the room when I saw her. Not in front of my eyes but reflected out of the pink mirrors set in the ceiling.

The angle was too high for Grover. But I saw her, and she saw me before I shut the door firmly and left her.

In the Jacuzzi jet bath for two, with Simon Booker-Readman.

# Chapter 10

I got the sack later that evening.

That is, with Grover, Sukey, Benedict and Johnson to look after, the afternoon passed in an orderly frenzy, and the only other people I saw were Comer, come to enquire after the invalid, and Hugo, who had taken a liking to Johnson and outfitted him, while he was still officially semi-conscious, in a green quilted kimono with a copper rheumatism bracelet.

Almost immediately after, making a brilliant recovery, Johnson pointed out that he had his own dressing gown, but Hugo insisted and went off, busily, to search in the kitchen for calvesfoot jelly. Johnson said, "Well?"

On his nose, the bifocals or their substitutes rested, glinting once more. I said, "I shall sue you. I swear it. For a full nurse's uniform, and my hospital bills, if I come down with pleurisy."

"Well," Johnson said. "I wondered why Beverley wanted us out of the way. Did you find out?"

I must admit, I gaped before I remembered how cross I was. I remembered something else. I said, "Good lord. What day is it?"

"Tuesday," said Johnson. He looked, sitting up in Hugo's caftan, once more like a lush from a quilting bee. He added, "Who was she with? Simon Booker-Readman?"

"Yes," I said. I didn't add where.

"I thought so," said Johnson. "Remember how Comer came bursting in one evening? He thought they were together then. He had certainly supplied himself somehow with a key. But he still isn't quite sure, I fancy . . . It makes you think, doesn't it?"

I said, "Why were you run down? Was that an accident?"

"I'm not sure," Johnson said. "Someone may be tired of seeing me hang about Benedict, except that I have been rather carefully refraining from hanging about Benedict. Or perhaps it had nothing to do with Benedict at all. Perhaps someone wanted an excuse to send Comer or his friends back to the house to discover exactly what you did discover. Except that if that was it, they were unlucky. Neither you nor I is going to make Simon's visit public . . . What did they say to you?"

"Nothing, yet," I said. "I wonder if Rosamund knows. Was that why she was so upset . . ."

". . . when you told her about the broken ikon in Bunty's loo? Yes, of course. If it was a copy Simon was hoping to pass off as the real thing, and if it got itself broken during a visit by Simon to the Eisenkopp house, then it explains both why Simon had to pretend he had lost it, and why Rosamund was so furious. We don't know why it was broken, but we can speculate. Perhaps Simon told Beverley he was going to defraud her loving Comer as well as cuckold him, and Beverley didn't think it was funny and smashed up the copy. I can imagine that possessions mean a lot to that well-pleated lady. But why put the pieces in Bunty's loo?"

"On Bunty's day off," I said. "It was Beverley's bad luck that Bunty came back and promptly jammed a nappy down after it . . . Where are you staying in Venice?"

"In luxury," said Johnson with satisfaction. He was worse than Hugo. "The Warr Beckenstaff Corporation have chartered a cruising ship for the party. We fly to Venice to board her. Hugo is going to row us all out."

Hugo came in as he spoke, bearing a vase of arum lilies, which he placed with a flourish at Johnson's bedside. A steaming trolley made its appearance. Napkins were unfolded. Hugo bent over the flowers, and selecting a stem, presented a branch of lilies to me.

"We are staying, dear heart, on board the *Glycera*, and do not tell me you don't know of her. She is chartered for every extravagant party afloat. You will find her half the summer off Monte Carlo and the rest of the time in the Aegean. A seagoing millionaires' pleasure club. It is a great pity, Joanna, that you are not to be with us."

"With Benedict, Sukey and Grover?" I said.

"I should create a robot nursemaid to look after them. By the way, do you know, darling, that your employer has arrived? One at least of the Booker-Readmans has returned from Florida. Rosamund remains to attend the latest charity fash-thrash in Palm Beach, and Simon has flown up to persuade my dear Comer to allow you to stay here next week. Will you like that?"

"Nothing better. When did Mr. Booker-Readman arrive?" I asked. I avoided Johnson's glittering glass.

"Just five minutes since. In a taxi from Logan. You like the soup I arrange?" said Hugo to Johnson.

"It tastes," said Johnson, "as if they've boiled your poncho in it. Why did you get me into this mess anyway? Anyone could have rowed you across."

"Ah," said Hugo. "But I was going to tip you into the bay and row myself across to spend the morning sailing with Nurse Joanna. As it was, we both did better. Have you any idea, darling, what you looked like? From Nantucket to Newport, the boys were out with their binoculars. The legs! The waist! What the apron-bib has been concealing from us! The . . ."

"The children," I said, "will be yelling for tea. Excuse me."

In fact, the children were asleep, and Simon Booker-Readman was waiting in the empty day nursery.

He still looked like Apollo, but with an acid tinge under his tan; and he was jingling the coins in one pocket. He said, "Please sit down. I hope you won't mind if I shut the door for a moment."

It sounded like the moment Charlotte had always been hoping for, but I knew it wasn't. I shook my head and sat down at a desk chair while he picked at a toy on a shelf. There was a tinkling burst of mechanical music and he put it down as if stung. He said, "I am not prepared to say a great deal about what has happened. I'm sure you feel it is none of your business anyway. But you must understand that it makes the whole situation quite impossible for Mrs. Eisenkopp as well as myself however much we know . . . I am sure . . . we may count on your discretion. You are, after all, one of us. I understand that perfectly."

I said, "You mean you think because my father is a knight and a professor, I shan't tell Mr. Eisenkopp what is happening under his roof?"

I was sorry after I had said it. He had education, he had social ease, he had style. But for all his looks, he didn't possess the brain of Comer Eisenkopp, or his father. He did have intuition, however, and it pulled him out of that one. He said, "I am quite sure, for Grover and Sukey and Benedict's sake, that you won't tell him. But I don't expect you to stay on here or in New York knowing what has happened, even though it has only happened once, and will naturally never happen again. You are fond of Benedict?"

"He'll do," I said. "He won't give you much trouble now, if you can keep to his routine."

"Yes." He bent to pick up a fire engine and straightened, his face rather flushed. "Well. I shouldn't expect you to work the usual notice: I fancy you'd like to be gone by the end of the week. We'll take the child ourselves to Ingmar's party. It would mean your concocting some story about a recall to London, or being offered a glamorous post . . . I should leave it to you. But in consideration of the upset, and the lack of notice and your discretion and . . . of course . . . your care of Benedict, I should like you to accept this from . . . from us both."

None of your hundred dollars for preserving Sukey. This was a check for ten thousand dollars. Signed, of course, by Beverley Eisenkopp.

I told him to make it out for one month's salary instead, and gave it back to him. He tried to argue, but was cut short by the sugar-sweet call of the dulcimer. I made no demur about accepting my dismissal: the Department had been explicit. Agree with everything.

I went where I was led. But I recognized at the same time that one of Johnson's theories was correct. Someone had arranged this morning's collision with this very issue in mind.

He was only wrong in one thing. He had said it had nothing to do with Benedict.

But of course, it had. It had resulted in my dismissal. And now, without me, without Donovan, Benedict was going to Mrs. Warr Beckenstaff's party in Europe, alone with his parents. And, of course, with Comer and Beverley Eisenkopp, and their Design Director, Hugo Panadek.

# Chapter 11

For the last three days of my stay in Wabash Bay, I was never alone with Beverley Eisenkopp, although I caught her sometimes watching me, with sheer fright in her eyes. I didn't see all that much of Grover, either.

Johnson I told of my interview and dismissal. There was no time for much comment. I gathered he thought I was right to agree, and that it might have set their minds more at rest had I accepted the ten thousand dollars. Then I saw the glasses flash, and knew he was less than serious. Simon had left without staying the night.

I told Bunty on the flight back to New York that I was leaving the Booker-Readmans because of a cable to tell me my aunt Lily in Toronto was ill. I had sent the cable to myself, and knew half the household had seen it. The Eisenkopps, father and mother, were casually sympathetic but not over-concerned. Beverley's face cleared as if swept by a snowplow, and Comer's mind was on other things.

It wasn't until we had almost landed that he turned and called back to me. "Say . . . You won't be staying in Wabash with Benedict then?"

"No, Mr. Eisenkopp. I think Mrs. Booker-Readman will be taking the baby to Venice."

"Well, that settles it." He was pleased, for whatever reason. He turned to his wife. "Hey, Beverley, baby. We don't need to leave you alone, all those days after the party. Bunty can bring the kids right over to Venice, and fly down to Dubrovnik. They can come and visit you. Cheer you up while that nice little derrière is being taken care of."

He grinned and from the jump she gave, I thought he probably pinched her. But alarm had something to do with it as well, and maybe even real consternation. I wondered how much of her time would have been spent alone at the Radoslav Clinic. And I remembered Johnson's remark. When Comer Eisenkopp had burst into my room in New York that evening, he might well have believed that his wife and Simon were there together. I wondered how much he really knew.

Bunty flung her arms round my shoulders and hugged me. "Did you hear that! Oh Jo, love. I'm bloody sad about Auntie, but yippie! I'm going to Venice!"

I didn't remind her: with Sukey and Grover. It seemed a pity to spoil it.

I didn't know until I got back to New York that Rosamund hadn't come back from Florida yet. When I arrived, with Benedict and the luggage, Simon was at the gallery and the house was empty, but the drop-side cot I had ordered before we left had arrived, and I unwrapped it and put it up in the nursery, with its mattress and new sheets and blankets, and then sat down and moped until recalled by Benedict, evincing a desire for his tea.

That meal, he took a spoonful of coddled egg for the first time without fussing. After, when I laid him in the new cot, he pumped with both legs in his excitement, and lay for a bit after that, cooing and lacing his fingers. He was sixteen pounds, and his eyes were blue-grey, and he would laugh if you were witty enough merely to shake your head at him. I spent a couple of minutes morning and night brushing his downy head with a baby brush, to encourage a parting, which I would never see.

I had been blowing my nose hard again when Donovan rang to ask about the Swiss cheese plant with white fly, and I had to tell him that all its leaves had dropped off. He came round for an hour just to look at it, and I was glad of his company. I think too, his arm being out of plaster, that he had a hope of being taken back on to the strength, but Simon, finding him there, had nothing of moment to say and I could see why.

In a few days they would be abroad with the baby, and if Benedict needed any protection, presumably Mrs. Warr Beckenstaff was the lady to fix it. And in any case, for the opposite reasons from Comer, Simon had no desire for a friendly neighborhood bodyguard in a neighborhood which was to include Mrs. Beverley Eisenkopp.

Rosamund returned on my last day, when Bunty had asked the Eisenkopps to let her put on a small party for me in her rooms. The Eisenkopp parents were out, but Charlotte was there, and half a dozen other Maggie Bee girls, and Donovan and three other boys and two of the original Huskies who flew down from Toronto.

In fact, most of the talent was Charlotte's. I once asked Bunty if she collected pen-friends like our Charlie and she said no, most of her mail came through answering nanny ads. I suppose it gets to be a habit, however cushy your current posting. The ones she liked were the ads the Maggie Bee told you not to touch with a barge-pole, such as *Casper, Amanda and Dominic and all the dogs want a young, cheerful nanny to take Mummy's place. Must have sense of humor and a driving license.* The kind, perhaps, I ought to be perusing.

The fact that she had her eye on her next few posts didn't inhibit Bunty from exploiting the present one to the full, to my benefit. We had a buffet supper, accompanied by wine and spirits from her never-failing resources, and some dancing to her quadruple stereo record player. At their own request Hugo and Gramps Eisenkopp arrived and joined in, and a little later Hugo phoned Simon and invited him over.

Whether or not because of a guilty conscience, my late employer did his best to be sociable, throwing himself into the dancing and even more into the spirits department, egged on by Hugo. By the time his wife Rosamund had arrived at her empty home, found the scrawled note and walked round to ring the bell of the Eisenkopp duplex, Simon had kissed all the girls in the room several times and was trying to get Charlotte to take his temperature while they were dancing; and with the kind of profile he had, he wasn't getting much resistance at that.

Then the door opened and like the traditional figure of doom, Rosamund stood in the doorway.

Grandpa Eisenkopp ordered his wheelchair to right turn and

run up to her, which it did, bringing his neat black hairpiece just under the fisher lapels of her coat. "Well ma'am, you've come to the right place. It wouldn't be a send-off without Benedict's mother. Come and tell Joanna how sad we all are that she's going."

*"Going!"* said Rosamund Booker-Readman. And I realized then, as Simon turned, that he hadn't told her.

I went forward, fast. "I'm afraid it's true. It is my last day, and I hate to tell you. But my aunt in Toronto is really ill, and they're going to need someone to nurse her. I said I'd come this weekend. It's going to be a long business, I'm afraid, and there's no one else."

"There is," said Rosamund, "your second cousin in Winnipeg. Isn't there?"

Simon pulled his shirt down and stepping forward, cleared his throat. I said, "She can't travel, and they can't leave Government House. I'm afraid there's no way out. Believe me, I'd have taken it if there was. I'm going to miss Benedict more than I can tell you. I'm so sorry. But at three months at least . . ."

She wasn't listening. She said to Simon, "When did this happen?"

"When I was at Wabash. On Tuesday," he said.

"And you didn't think of telling me?" She turned to me. "This is not a month's notice?"

The record had ended and the conversation had dwindled, too, into an embarrassed silence. Charlotte, rounding up the nearest group of guests, took them over to the drinks table and started a fevered conversation. Donovan hung nearer, listening. I said, "I was needed by the weekend. Mr. Booker-Readman did say it would be all right." I didn't see why I should have to play Simon's game for him.

"Mr. Booker-Readman," Rosamund said, "has nothing to do with the upbringing of Benedict, in a sense either moral or monetary. You were hired by myself and my mother. If you wish to leave, it is to us you must make your case. I have yet to hear one."

"Look, Rosamund," Simon said. He was sweating, and his lips and tongue and breath had got out of step with one another. "Look, Rosamund. The girl made a perfly reas'able case and I said right. Can't go back on it now."

"If you committed yourself, then that is Joanna's misfortune. You had no authority to do so. You came to us, Joanna, on the understanding that a month's notice on either side was obligatory.

There was also a clear understanding that your employment would endure far beyond the span of three months. Why therefore should we release you?"

I looked at Simon. I was beginning, very faintly, to enjoy myself. "My aunt," I said.

Rosamund surveyed me, and I was glad to be wearing, on this occasion, more than bikini underwear. "Your aunt in Toronto, I think you said. She cannot afford help?"

"She can't get it," I said.

"What help does she require?" Rosamund said. "Nursing? Cleaning-women? A housekeeper?"

"It's . . . She needs a housekeeper and a little regular nursing by someone who is strong and willing," I said. I kept my face straight. My aunt Lily is a lawyer and shares a large, well-run house with her brother, who is a retired cabinet minister. Charlotte opened her mouth and then shut it again.

Rosamund said, "Are you perfectly sure that without you, no such help would be forthcoming?"

She was a shrewd lady. I said, "So her doctors said on the phone. But of course . . ."

"Of course, you only had their word for it. And what could be easier from their point of view than to phone up a niece and have her drop everything and come north. I applaud," said Rosamund bleakly, "your sense of family duty, but I really think all this self-sacrifice is unnecessary. If you are really concerned about the wellbeing of Benedict—"

"Oh, I am," I said. I didn't dare look at Simon.

"Then I shall phone my lawyer. You shall fly north with him tomorrow, sort this whole business out, get your aunt settled and return here on Monday. Have you any objection?"

I looked this time at Simon. He looked alarmingly sobered. He said, "There must be other nurses in New York. We can't bulldoshe, doze, the poor girl, Rosamund. Anyway, the Eis'nkopps are taking their children to Europe. No good, leaving Ben'dict behind in New York. Take him with us."

"To the ball?" said Rosamund sarcastically. She took the dry martini Bunty held silently out to her. "Or on board the *Glycera*? I'm sure three-month old babies will make their own welcome."

The sarcasm worked. He straightened, got his tongue under

control and made a distinct effort, looking round, to put the impossible scene at last into some kind of accepted framework. "How boring for everyone. We're spoiling poor Joanna's party with all this nonsense. A drink, Mr. Eis'nkopp."

"Hardly," Rosamund said scathingly. "The point is, if you remember, whether Joanna has cause for a party. You were going to suggest, I hope, where our happy family party, without nanny, might put up in Venice?"

"Not in Venice. In Dubro ... Dubrovnik," Simon said. He sat down, and remained there looking up at her. "Your mother's manager cabled today. No berth for the *Glycera* at Venice. They're having the gala instead in Dubrovnik. And Johnson Johnson says why don't we stay on his ketch. You know her. The *Dolly*. He's having her brought round from Malta."

There was a crackling silence. Then Hugo crowed like a cock. "You mean this nice cosmetics lady, your mother, is to hold her party on the *Glycera* in Dubrovnik?"

"Of course," said Donovan. Below his rectangular pink face, he had a primula in his buttonhole. "You live there."

"I am Yugoslav. I," said Hugo, "shall be your interpreter. And Joanna will stay, and will come to Dubrovnik with her little Ben, and will live on board the *Dolly*, where no one can kidnap him, with perhaps—why not with Donovan, who can grow vines up the rigging: grapes on the coach roof and muscatels filling the hatches? We shall tread them in the autumn. *Premier cruise! Entre Deux Mères! The Dolly vignoble!* Does it not intoxicate, merely to think of it?"

The Booker-Readmans, facing one another, paid no attention. Rosamund said, "My mother is pleased with Joanna, and wishes to meet her. There is no question of the girl resigning."

"Suppose," said Grandpa Eisenkopp's hoarse, amused voice from the wheelchair. "Suppose you put it to the girl. Joanna. You wanna go to Dubrovnik and stay on this yacht with the baby?"

Agree to everything. I said, "I'd like nothing better. But ..."

"There are no buts," Rosamund said. "You fly to Toronto tomorrow and arrange things. If there is any trouble at all, telephone me. Either my mother or her business associates will arrange things. Is that clear?"

It was. I turned to Simon. For a moment I saw pure, wild-eyed frustration laid over something else much more threatening. Then it was gone and he raised his eyebrows in a resigned way at me. "You heard. You fix things, and come back to the baby," he said. "Remembering that you've had an extra month's salary and a party . . . Mr. Eisenkopp? This parcel's for Comer. Can I leave it with you?"

Fortunately, for my ego, everyone forgot about me and my undeserved salary and fixed their eyes on the thing he was holding.

It was a flat, square package in heavy brown paper: he'd had it with him when he arrived. Grandpa Eisenkopp, taking it, turned it round eagerly. "The other ikon? The new one, to replace the Lesnovo thing that went missing?"

Looking at the interest in Hugo's face, I remembered the quantity of Byzantine paintings in Yugoslav churches. Of course he knew all about it. He said, "What can you sell him to replace the Lesnovo?"

"Wait and see," Simon said. He was smiling. "It's not quite as good, of course. Nothing could be. But I think he will like it."

Hugo's large, liquid eyes and those of Gramps Eisenkopp met. The old man grinned. "Shall I open it?"

The record player had started again, softly, and three or four couples were dancing smoochily at the end of the room, Charlotte and Donovan with them. Rosamund had finished her drink and without being asked was helping herself, her brow corrugated, to another. Simon stood, his hands in his pockets, and said, "It's up to you. Open it if you don't think Comer would mind."

"He won't mind," said Comer's father, and digging in his small, blunt-fingered hands, tore off the wrapping and sat, the light on the painting.

We all moved to the wheelchair to look.

No one said anything. Then Hugo said, "But that *is* the Lesnovo ikon."

At the table Rosamund turned round, spilling her drink. Beside the chair, Simon had turned the color of self-blanching celery and Hugo, leaning forward, was whistling between his teeth. Grandpa Eisenkopp said, on a long drawl, "Well, if that don't beat all! Simon, you sly crittur! You got the Lesnovo back. And this is how you planned to surprise Comer. And boy! Is he going to be surprised!"

He wasn't the only one. I was thunderstruck, in my own way, behind him. Even Bunty, struck by the sound of our exclamations, came drifting over and stood beside me, glass in hand, to peer at the painting.

I saw her eyebrows lift right up into the unravelled wool ball of her hair. I was even ready for the dig in the ribs when it came.

"Will you look at that?" said Bunty in a whisper which nearly blew out the windows. "It's the bloody image of the picture you took from the . . ."

Then she broke off gasping because I stood on her toe cap.

None the less, she was right. The picture Simon was selling to Comer was not, clearly, the picture he had thought he was selling to Comer. Instead it was the perfect twin, in its aged cracked beauty, of the ikon stuff in the loo pan, which Rosamund had rushed to get rid of.

It was even better. That had been an illegal copy. This, no one could have any doubt, was the original.

# Chapter 12

I flew to Toronto next day. Aunt Lily was surprised to see me, and even more surprised to learn that I had come to hire her a geriatric nurse-housekeeper.

She phoned my uncle Tom to come home early for lunch, and then listened, perched among the briefs on her desk, while I told her the essence of Simon's dilemma. "You mean I'll have to give up my Gojukai karate classes?" she said plaintively as I finished. "Hell's bells, we were to get into eye gouging on Thursday."

I reassured her. The Booker-Readmans would never check her condition. I'd persuaded Rosamund that I'd fix it without even needing her lawyer, although I should have trusted Aunt Lily, sufficiently primed, to deceive anybody. And Charlotte I had taken aside and persuaded that Simon had paid me to leave from motives of private expediency.

In nanny terms, that had only one meaning: he had his eye on a girl for the vacancy. I had left Charlotte plunged into rapt speculation.

Then Uncle Tom arrived home, to my aunt's extreme annoyance, with company, whom he installed in his study before coming upstairs to greet me.

In fact, he hardly greeted me at all. He said, "Hi. Thanks for phoning, Lily; but I knew she was coming before you did. Honey, there's someone waiting in my room to see you."

That was to me, and from the way he said it, I knew it wasn't a Husky, or one of the party at Winnipeg, or anyone, indeed, who was connected with the lighter side of this our pilgrimage through the life cycle. I looked at Aunt Lily, whose expression told me she didn't know either, and then left the room without speaking and ran down to the three thousand books lightly mounted on wallpaper that Tom calls his study. I opened the door. It was midday and the sun was shining, but the door opened on darkness. The curtains had been drawn. I could just see the man who had pulled them together: a tall man in a shapeless overcoat and dark glasses, who crossed the room as I watched, peeling his coat off, and bending down, switched on the table lamp. Then, lifting his hand, he took off the concealing dark glasses.

"I'm sorry, darling," he said. "Shut the door and come in. We've not much time, and a good deal to talk about."

It was my father.


My father's side of the family are all big. Tom and Lily are tall and stringy and, like my father, their muscles and bones show up like basket-weave when they are tired.

My father was tired, with that enthralling combination of rigor mortis and indigestion that comes from long, cramped time-saving journeys by jet plane. He held my shoulders hard and kissed me in the way he always did, and then we both sat down on different sides of Uncle Tom's desk.

I crossed my ankles and folded my hands in my lap and said, "You've just flown in from London? To see me?"

"To see you," he said. "I'm going back this evening. In fact, I've never been. I know everything that's happened to you. Not very jolly, in spite of all the low comedy."

"It hasn't happened to me," I said. "It's happened to the baby I was looking after. Your friend Johnson has a theory that all the kidnap attempts have been pure coincidence."

"My friend Johnson," said my father with some asperity, "had no call to begin that portrait in the first place and is taking too damned long to finish it." Someone tapped on the door and he raised his voice. "Who is it?"

"Your friend Johnson," said Johnson peaceably, coming in. He looked just as he always did.

I said, "I left you in New York."

"I came by the same plane you did," Johnson said. "I was the hostess with the blue and white sash and the wiggle. Sir?"

"And you've been a bloody nuisance," said my father testily, addressing the world's best known international portrait painter. "Sit down. I haven't told her anything yet."

Johnson sat down and, seeking permission, proceeded to fill his pipe. The top of his head gave nothing away. My father said, "You've been a good girl, Joanna, and it really isn't fair to go on without letting you know what you're in for. Because everything that's happened to date has just been a plastic mock-up for what's going to start now. And this time, if you want to go on with it, you'll have to play more than a passive role."

I had been playing a passive role. I wondered what big executive in Mike's Department had fed my father that story and induced him to come across instead of confronting me personally. I let it pass.

Johnson was having no trouble at all lighting his pipe. Clouds of grit began to move past the lamplight. My father said, "You were told that Mike Widdess's death was not the accident it appeared. You were also told that your share in his work had come to light, and an attempt might therefore be made to exploit you.

"That was to put you on your guard, and to explain why the Department wanted you to accept this job with the Booker-Readmans. Two pieces of information were kept from you. One was the fact that Mike Widdess, when he died, had just finished coding some top secret lists known by the stupid name of the Malted Milk Folio. He had no papers connected with this in his house. There was no reason to believe that his murderers knew of it. Until this week, when it was found that the Folio lists had been photographed."

"It wasn't in a self-destruct acid container with three triple locks?" I said rashly.

"It wasn't," said my father. "Because it was entirely in code. Your code which, as we all have cause to know, is virtually unbreakable."

There was a reverent silence, due on Johnson's part possibly more to boredom.

I had a bizarre mathematical brain even at school. Since I wanted to nurse, I might never have found any use for it if my father hadn't suggested Mike Widdess. Mike Widdess worked for Intelligence. And my peculiarities, even before they were trained, were exactly those needed for code making.

It isn't a job which need take up much time. Much of the heavy work is done by computers. The application of the code is someone else's affair. I devise it and I provide the key. I am given someone else's code and I break it down and, again, supply the key. When I do my coding and my nursing for the same employer, life is even more simple.

Until your employer is killed and his papers searched. Including the papers which tell his killers that you, Joanna Emerson, can unlock any code they happen to light on.

"I see," I said after a pause. "Oh, I do see. That's why I haven't been attacked until now? They didn't need me until they had these particular papers. And now they have them, they'll try to force me to decode them?"

"That's part of it," said my father.

I looked at Johnson. "And you were right then. The attempts to kidnap the baby had nothing to do with me or my coding? It was just a plain, simple heist by someone gunning for grandmother's bank account?"

The two half moons stared at me through the grey cloud of smoke, but he didn't answer. It was my father who said, "Johnson knew it wasn't a coincidence. He had to say something to satisfy you. I told you you didn't know everything. You haven't asked, for example, how Mike Widdess's killer knew about the coded Folio."

I hadn't asked anything because I was still assimilating, furiously, the fact that Johnson knew more about this than I did. When I had achieved some aplomb I said tartly, "The killer knew Mike worked for the Department. The same man could have had other information as well. He could have been a double agent."

"He wasn't," my father said. "At the time he was killed, only Mike and one other person knew about this group of papers. If someone else found out, it was because Mike was forced to tell him. There are ways."

There are, of course, ways. And a car crash is as good a way as any of disguising them. My father went on, "Everything that Mike knew of value is now being checked over by his people to prevent any misuse. That's called locking the stable door. His killer got away, however, with three things that mattered. The information about you. A description of the set of papers I've called the Malted Milk Folio. And the name of Widdess's chief, in whose house the papers were kept."

"Don't tell me," I said warmly. "I might give it away under drugs or duress or kindness or something. I don't suppose I dare ask, either, what was in the Folio?"

My father is used to dealing with student sarcasm. His hands in his pockets, he lay back and looked at me. "Those, indeed, were the reasons why you weren't told," he said calmly. "Now it's necessary you should run the same risks as the others in the field, and you have a right to know.

"The name Widdess gave to his killer was mine. The Malted Milk Folio contains, in alphabetical order, the names and addresses of every British agent working internationally with me or under me. One of whom, as you may have guessed, is the perverse gentleman on your right."

At school, I should have been dazzled. Even before I worked with Michael Widdess I became aware that people of balance and status might expect, from time to time to be co-opted by their country for help or advice in this area. I knew my father sometimes was.

That he or anyone I valued should elect to make this his whole employment now filled me only with fear, and a dull kind of puzzlement. Life in the Department had not been gay or gallant for Widdess. Just humdrum and painstaking and sordid. And he had worked—and so had I—for my father.

With Johnson there, I couldn't say "Why?" With my father there, I couldn't say what I wanted to Johnson. I looked, no doubt, quite moronic. It occurred to me to wonder if my father had become a crack shot before or after he had taken the Department. I said to Johnson, lightly, "How good a shot are you?" and he shook his head behind the smokescreen. But he didn't answer.

My father said, "Some day you'll want to ask questions. Just now we must hurry. For you see, as my daughter, how important a hostage you are. You can decode the list of agents, and provide the key to all existing government codes. And you can be used as a stick against me.

"That, we guess, is why the baby has been threatened so often. No one will be surprised when he is kidnapped at last and you, his nurse, are kidnapped as it happens along with him. The Booker-Readmans will receive the normal ransom demand. They may keep it quiet from the police. Certainly this time there will be nothing facile or public about the arrangements. This kidnapping will be planned to succeed, and as far away from a sophisticated police system as the kidnappers are able to manage."

"Italy, for example," I said. "Or no. Now the gig has been moved to Dubrovnik. But why the baby? Now they've got the Folio photos, why don't they go ahead and simply snatch me?"

"To make it easy for me," said my father. "Don't you see? If my daughter is openly kidnapped, immediately it is a matter for Government intervention. Even if I wished to negotiate privately I should never be allowed to. But who in Government is to know, when the Booker-Readman baby is kidnapped, that I am the target and not the Booker-Readman parents? That all the time the baby is held, and the ransom for its release is being negotiated, I am in secret negotiation also for the release of my daughter? Whatever secrets I choose to trade, my reputation, if I'm careful, needn't suffer. And your kidnappers have a hold over me for the future." He failed to read my face and added, "I'm sorry, Joanna."

I said, "Apologize to Benedict. I take it therefore that I am being asked to allow myself to be kidnapped?"

My father said, "We have no other way of finding Mike's killers. They have the Folio, or its photo-copy. You have the key to decode it. They will never rest, whatever happens, until they have you. We have the advantage of surprise. They think we know nothing. Let them take you."

"You mean," I said sarcastically, "I've got to arrange to sneak them past Donovan?"

I went on because of the silence. "Or am I being naive?"

My father turned his head. "Never naive. Say stupid," said Johnson kindly. "Donovan is one of mine. Your genuine back-up, substituted for the Data-Mate Charlotte thought she was getting."

"You might," I said coldly, "have ruined her chances. Suppose the real Donovan had been an elderly millionaire with no dependants?" I thought of all those hearty ice hockey embraces and turned hotter scarlet.

"If he has to use Data-Mate," said Johnson mildly, "then he must suffer from drawbacks even I can't quite imagine. As it was, I am led to believe that Charlotte did all right. Forget Charlotte."

I did, with my teeth clenched. I said, "All right. You tell me. What's going to happen?"

There was a pause. Then Johnson answered me. "To get it straight: we think the snatch will be made during the three days the baby will be in Yugoslavia. We don't know yet who the principals are, but we're prepared to treat as hostile any member of your immediate circle included in the Yugoslav party. To keep up our hard-won appearances, I shall stay with the Warr Beckenstaff guests on the *Glycera.* We board on a Wednesday, go to bed at breakfast-time Thursday and fly back out with you on Friday. From Wednesday to Friday you will be on *Dolly* with the baby and Donovan. There will be a skipper of mine aboard, and a hi-ho chorus of twenty inconspicuous staffmen all over the Yugoslav coast line.

"Within these three days, we have to let them snatch you. We have to let them show you their copy of the Malted Milk Folio. We have to discover who they are and who runs them. In a foreign country, complete surveillance isn't easy. But you and the baby will both be safe as we can make you."

My hands were cold. *We are prepared to treat as hostile any member of your immediate circle . . .* I said, "Hugo Panadek belongs to Yugoslavia."

"And for that reason," Johnson said amiably, "is probably the least likely candidate. He also mended the Vladimir Brownbelly tape, when he could just as easily have destroyed it. And got you the sack, which nearly wrecked the whole villainous plot, I imagine. With help, of course, from Simon and Beverley."

I found it hard to believe that Simon and Beverley were innocent parties merely because they had been found in a Jacuzzi bath. If you started to work out motivation, I shouldn't have gone to Cape Cod at all if Charlotte's horses hadn't thrown Donovan. And if I hadn't gone to Cape Cod, the Eisenkopps would never have been invited to Dubrovnik. Also, of course, there was the fact that without

Rosamund, I shouldn't have been going to Dubrovnik either. I thought of something else. "You must have some suspicions. What about Comer and his key to the Booker-Readmans?"

Johnson said, "He used one belonging to Beverley. Donovan found it in her room."

Donovan, I noted, had been visiting Bunty. A special agent's life clearly isn't all Busy Lizzie and thorns. I said acidly, "If you've been getting into their houses, then presumably you've discovered something worth knowing."

I caught the tail end of my father's smile. He said, "We've done a bit on telephone calls. Comer Eisenkopp has been phoning Italy, but then he has business interests everywhere. The same applies to Panadek, who has made a number of calls to Europe recently: Lübeck as well as Yugoslavia. The only other item of note has rather mystified us. Donovan was given a plant by old Mr. Eisenkopp."

After the rodeo. I remembered. "It was poisoned?" I ventured. Hopefully.

I wouldn't have been surprised if my father had nodded. Instead he said merely, "It was bugged. Everything said in Donovan's room was supposed to be relayed somewhere. Anyone in the Eisenkopp household could have fixed up that plant with a microphone. Or anyone in the Booker-Readmans', for that matter. We were worried for a while that someone had spotted Donovan. We think now it was merely an attempt to plot Benedict's movements. Donovan has been feeding it assiduously with mixed information. And he checks your rooms every day with a bug-alert."

I must admit I relaxed. I said, "I have a favorite theory. The villain is Mrs. Warr Beckenstaff herself, in the market for all the stuff in the Folio. By herself, or with Simon, or Rosamund. They could blackmail themselves quietly for weeks while they tried to pump you or me or the Department at leisure. And, of course, they'd be sure nothing happened to Benedict."

Whatever passed between the two men, it wasn't a murmur of awestruck agreement. Johnson said, "It's possible, yes. Someone made quite strenuous efforts to have you employed by the Booker-Readman family, but it mightn't have been Rosamund or her mother. Vladimir threw you together at Winnipeg. Another parent or nanny could have recommended you to Ingmar. Any one of your colleagues, knowing you to be somewhere in Canada, could have encouraged the Booker-Readmans to call at that shindig at Winnipeg. Such as Charlotte."

His pipe had gone out. He drew an ashtray towards him and tapped it. "I give you an interesting thought. There was no kidnapping attempt at Cape Cod. Charlotte, Grandpa Eisenkopp and Rosamund Booker-Readman were not at Cape Cod, alone of all those we've mentioned."

"That," I said, "is ridiculous. You might as well say it wasn't Charlotte who ran a launch over you. There might not have been a kidnapping but there was bloody nearly a murder, as I remember it."

"You mean," my father said, "the episode involving Panadek and the dinghy? We considered it, but thought it was harmless. If Panadek had wanted Johnson dead, he would have been dead, and not rescued."

I said, "No one knows who you are, then?" to Johnson.

He rolled on one hip, hunting with concentration for tobacco. "That," he said, "is the general notion. They think you know nothing. All the same, they're bound to keep their eyes open for any obvious bulldogs. Excluding, one hopes, dead-ass limeys who can't fasten seat-belts. On the other hand . . ." He broke off what he was going to say. He had found the tobacco.

"On the other hand," my father said, "this idiot painter is our barometer. He's alive. And that's how we know they haven't decoded the Malted Milk Folio. Anything else?"

I folded my hands together again. "The ikon. The Lesnovo ikon: what about that? Simon was flogging copies to Comer, and both his wife and Beverley seem to know; but so far neither has split on him."

My father looked at Johnson, and Johnson fielded it for me. It was like bloody Pinky and Perky. He said, "If you remember, your laundrette acquaintance Vladimir was an ikon painter, as well as being one of the three men you chased in the Wonderland. Poor Simon doesn't really seem much of a conspirator. A clever man playing for very high stakes would never have got involved with Beverley, or with a doubtful trade in spurious ikons; but because of all these things, he might have made a reasonable tool. I wondered if Vladimir could be blackmailing him."

"So?" I said. I knew my father was watching my face.

"So I copied the Lesnovo ikon myself. Eighteen double night-trips to that basement for nothing, as it turned out. I put the genuine ikon into the parcel Simon took to the Eisenkopps and hung my own copy in its place in the basement. It was the first thing Simon went to look at, of course, when he got back to his house. Naturally, he thought he had been double-crossed by the painter who did his copies, and phoned him. I hoped it would be Vladimir, but it wasn't."

"So you are no further on," I said. "Vladimir could still be blackmailing him."

"So I'm no further on," he agreed. "Except that I have a name or two for the New York city police when all this is over, and the Eisenkopps have the ikon they paid for. The Robin Hood of the paint box." He got up unexpectedly, leaving his pipe where it was, and strolling to the end of the desk, stood with his hands on either side of his seat, surveying my father. There were worn leather squares on his elbows and his cavalry twills, planked a little apart, were undeniably bagged at the knees.

"All right. Don't be impatient," my father said. "I've had your plan, and I approve of it. Now you've stopped smoking that bloody thing, in fact, we might as well settle down and get on with it. The drinks cupboard is behind you and if it's rye, I don't want it."

I thought of the Eskimos and opened my mouth, it must be told, to comment on any plan made by Johnson Johnson. Then, although he wasn't looking at me, I shut it again.

The Eskimo episode had placed me firmly where the Department wanted me to be: in the Booker-Readmans' household. And it had flushed out for inspection all those who might be interested in Benedict and in me: such as, for example, Vladimir. Behind the continuous floor-show existed a gentleman who was no slouch and never had been, even when I was seventeen.

The discussion only took ten more minutes and Johnson and I had perhaps three more together after my father had gone and before he also slipped out by a back door, to make his way back to New York. I said, "I should have guessed. About you, I mean."

"I know. It's annoying, isn' t it?" said Johnson. "Like not getting the solution to yesterday's crossword. You probably don't realize it, but both your parents have put quite a lot of time and energy into keeping you out of the muddier bits of the field."

Mother too, then. I said, "What brought you into it? Or were you always in from the beginning, and the portraits came after?"

He had stopped on his way to the door and looked as if he might continue to drift out at any second, though the pipe in his hand had been lit again. He said, "Oh, the painting came first. The rest, through Naval Intelligence: a popular way of recruiting legalized conmen. They expect you to tie all your victims in reef knots . . . . Does this whole scheme appear fairly nerve-wracking? I'm sorry there's no other way. But they won't kidnap you without the baby, or the baby without you. We have to let them have the matched set or nothing."

"Well, let's put it this way," I said. "If it had been anyone else I'd have said no. Do I see you again before Yugoslavia?"

"Not unless anything goes wrong. I'll be on the flight, of course, and I'd like to have the pleasure of showing you *Dolly*. Lenny Milligan, who looks after it, is a very good sort of gent."

He put his pipe in his mouth and had been walking to the door as he was speaking, but when he got there he turned, his hand still on the knob. "Joanna?"

"What?" I said.

He was looking at me through the top halves of the bifocals. "If it comes to a shoot-out, Benedict is my affair. Look after yourself and leave the baby to me. It isn't what I told your father I'd do, but that way, he'll live even if you don't. Check?"

No slouch, and a bloody psychologist into the bargain. I did say "Check," after a moment, but he had gone by that time.

I spent the afternoon very, very privately, at the dentist's.

Three days later, Bunty and I flew to Dubrovnik in a Warr Beckenstaff charter plane, ankle-deep in orchids and Bollinger. Since we had the three kids with us, both were necessary.

Along with us flew all Ingmar's guests who were not already in Europe. They included both Booker-Readmans, the Eisenkopps, Hugo Panadek and Joshua Gibbings, the family doctor. And, of course, Johnson and Donovan, with his arm in a sling. I didn't know who had rehired Donovan, but I strongly suspected Rosamund.

I was glad to see him, if unable to show it. However well organized you may be, it is a well known truth that eight hours in the air with a child can drive all thoughts from your mind except possibly those of public suicide. Benedict's cot swung hammock-wise from the ceiling, and there wasn't one of the crew or the passengers who failed to chuck him under the chin whenever passing. When he flaked out after three hours of crying it was probably because he was punch-drunk.

Sukey, also clipped to the ceiling with her Lolo Boochie Soft Camel, fared rather better, through her preference for wearing her hat on her face, which produced a knitted landscape not conducive to chucking. Every now and then Bunty cleared the pattern with cotton wool buds in the nose area. Sukey, who was teething, was in trouble at both ends and kept Bunty busy while I inherited the problem of Grover, who could sit on a potty, musical or otherwise, until kingdom come, and still have an emergency as soon as the lunch trays were with us.

Around me, concealing a murderer, was the Yugoslav party Johnson said must be treated as hostile. No doubt. I was busy. And avoiding, if it must be known, the bright, steam-cleaned glances of Donovan. Our forthcoming three days together on *Dolly* I was looking forward to with some ambivalence.

But for Bunty and her two kids, everyone else on the plane would be living on board Ingmar's *Glycera*. Bunty, her hair newly frizzed, was off to a seaside hotel thirty miles south of Dubrovnik with Sukey and Grover and an envelopeful of addresses from Charlotte. I couldn't see Bunty getting to Zagreb or Sarajevo, but there were a couple of boyfriends in the Dubrovnik/Herceg-Novi vicinity whom she'd marked with two stars and a question mark. One was called Jesus Krysztof and the other Lazar Dogíc. I'd been offered my pick, but had pointed out that I'd be bloody well immured on *Dolly*. With Donovan.

What Bunty did was obviously not weighing too much on her happy employers. Ever since their hospitality to the baby and me had wrung an invitation from the reluctant Warr Beckenstaffs, they had been lying about producing alphas like fortune cookies. Bunty said they'd had four hundred special cards printed, headed *As from the MS Glycera,* and had found out how to spell Omar, Ira, Merle and Bianca. She thought they could manage Sammy, Peter, Grace, Cary, the Aga, the Bedfords and Jackie O already, or were prepared to risk it.

I hoped her list was accurate. *Glycera* habitués tend to have a short season, like cauliflowers. I also remembered with interest that according to Hugo, Beverley Eisenkopp had booked her bed at the Radoslav clinic four weeks before Ingmar invited her. So sure had she been, clearly, of wangling it.

I wished I could have asked her how. This wasn't the first time I'd seen Beverley since I came back from Toronto, bearing the glad news that I had found a nurse-housekeeper for my ailing aunt Lily. Bunty had hardly left for her day off before her employer sent me a message. Would I bring Ben to spend the afternoon with Grover and Sukey, who had been missing me.

Considering that their mother had been willing to pay ten thousand dollars to arrange my permanent absence, I might be forgiven for receiving that sourly. But I took some routine precautions, and went. Donovan, as I remember, volunteered to stand outside the door.

The principal Eisenkopp sitting room is forty feet long and apart from Grover and Sukey contained only Mrs. Eisenkopp herself, looking teenage and vulnerable in levis and a lumberjack shirt, with thick blond hair falling down to her shoulderblades, and smelling of Sukey's lamb dinner.

She said, "I wanted to talk to you," and did, eventually, with both of us locked in the bathroom, this being the only place within earshot in which we could discuss the topic of adultery with any assurance of privacy.

The opening gambit, delivered with her incredible lashes down-turned in her exquisite profile, was that she supposed I found it a pretty strange scene, someone with a nice home and two fine kids and a wonderful husband like Mr. Eisenkopp even thinking of dating another man. The development, which was slightly confused, had, I finally worked out, something to do with Mr. and Mrs. Richard Burton. The conclusion was predictable.

"It happens once in a hundred years to a girl, and you can't say no," said Beverley Eisenkopp, raising her voice a little above the noise of Grover kicking the door in. "I love my husband, Nurse Joanna, but Simon Booker-Readman is my prince. We were made for one another."

They had certainly fitted very well into the Jacuzzi bath. I said, "You aren't thinking of a divorce?"

She put the lid on the lavatory seat and sat on it. "Have I done any God-damned thing but think?" she said peevishly. "Of course all I ask is a golden future with Simon—but what would be the cost? Two fine homes destroyed, my husband's peace of mind gone, the mental health of three little children damaged for ever. I wouldn't do that to my children, Joanna."

I took it as a good sign that I had become Joanna, and said, "It's none of my business anyway, Mrs. Eisenkopp. You can be quite sure that no one among your family or friends will hear about it through me."

She lifted her lashes and there were beautiful tears in them. "Do you mean that?" she said. "Do you really mean it? But you hardly know me. Is it for the sake of those lovely children?"

To the sound of Grover's feet and Grover's voice, hoarse with rage, was added the rattle of the doorknob, violently turned from outside. I said, "Well, they've got Bunty, of course. But certainly, it means a great deal to both of the children to have you there as much as possible. Grover is doing all this because he wants you to love him, you know."

Her eyes were bright, pellucid hazel, with the whites clear as boiled eggs. She said, "Then if Comer were to ask you a question that threatened our marriage, could I count on you, Joanna, to be a real friend?"

I wondered how many files her romance with Simon Booker-Readman already occupied in British Intelligence and tried to look well-disposed but unbending. "We are trained, Mrs. Eisenkopp, never to interfere in the personal affairs of the family. If awkward questions are asked, the rule is to answer that we know nothing about it."

Beverley Eisenkopp got up and snatched at a tissue, dislodging a shower of Bunty's personal James Bond plastic frogmen into the empty bath. "But that's not enough," she said pettishly.

"I'm sorry. I did try to leave. Don't you think, if Mr. Eisenkopp finds out from anyone, it will be from Mrs. Booker-Readman?"

Her face relaxed. If the discussion had been less fraught, I think she might even have laughed. "No," she said. "Oh, no. There's no danger of that."

The doorhandle fell inwards on to the carpet. She said, her voice melodious still, "Grover! What are you doing? You bad boy, leave Momma's handle alone!"

He did, too. We could hear his shouts receding into the playroom and a series of crashes, such as bricks being thrown at a television set.

I undid a pin from my bib and set to work on the door while Mrs. Eisenkopp wheedled through it. Bathos. I tell you, my private life and my career both sure as death were designed by a plumber.

We arrived at Čilipi, a little south of Dubrovnik, just before lunchtime.

You could see, looking out of the plane, how the Magistrala, the Adriatic Highway, ran down the west coast of Yugoslavia, on the green strip between mountains and sea. And on the sea, opposite Italy's heel, stood this ancient walled town of Dubrovnik.

From the plane, it looked pretty well preserved, considering. The Balkans have changed hands so often that they're a kedgeree of names and religions and languages. Yugoslavia has Austro-Hungarians in the north and there are negroes in the south, descended from slaves of the Barbary corsairs. Occupied in the last world war by the Germans, the place liberated itself in a fearsome upheaval, complicated by the fact that there were two opposing Resistance movements. The Partisans, under Marshal Tito, ended by ruling the country, but the men of some regions, such as the Croats, have never really accepted the outcome.

So in his briefing Johnson had told me. The country was Communist, but its mixture of public and private enterprise was unlike that of Russia. It was still poor, and vulnerable to recession and trade barriers, but helped by the new tourist industry. For the tourist industry they needed Adriatic Highways, and Beverley Eisenkopp and places like Dubrovnik.

Its harbor town lay to the north. We saw, as we circled to land, the white banded flanks of the *Glycera*, lying there at the quay under the confetti-like swags of her bunting.

There were cars waiting for us all at the airport, with Warr Beckenstaff escorts in pink silk rosettes and makeup. The Eisenkopps went off first, on Comer's insistence, to install their little prince and princess with Bunty at Herceg-Novi.

Our car came next, to take us with the baby to Johnson's yacht *Dolly*. With us, not to be outdone in conscientious parenthood, came the Booker-Readmans and Johnson himself, to see the child safely aboard before going on to the *Glycera*.

It was all going according to plan. I believe I heard, as we drove away, the boom of some announcement behind, being made over the airport's tannoy. But I paid no attention.

I remember that drive up the coast towards the harbor because Benedict was asleep, and I was able to relax, too, for perhaps the last time. For one thing, the car was a hired one and driven not by a member of the Warr Beckenstaff Corporation but by the little man called Lenny Milligan who looked after the *Dolly*, and had brought her round from Malta. And beyond his smart navy uniform and suntanned neck I had my first, and what might be my only close look at Yugoslavia.

It was more dramatic than I had expected: the high lilac mountains clothed with green almost to the top, and full, they said, of both Venetian fortresses and houses weekendica. The coast showed the same contradictions: the pink and white stucco buildings and the stone ones, with door rings and carved lintels and flanking pilasters.

The highway was international. There were green and yellow pumps of Jugopetrol, and snackbars, and autocamps and a notice *Top Strip Tease* by the roadside. We shared the route with Peugeots and Skodas and Opels, Fiats and Volkswagens, Zastavas and Trunus with thick hairy upholstery. There were also a herd of white goats, and donkeys with panniers of green stuff, and a man leading a horse with a wooden saddle. A Tam lorry full of Valencian oranges passed by a grove of citrus trees.

One third of these people were farmers. There were orange and lemon trees everywhere, and vines, just putting out their new leaves, and the pale trunks of fig trees, with the fruit small and firm as green light bulbs. There were flowers everywhere too, in beds and parks and balconies: phlox and tulips and begonias and low thick spidery succulents; geraniums and irises and bushes of small full pink roses. Wistaria and mimosa, and palms with great sprays of bright orange dates. We passed a window full of pot plants and I saw Donovan's lips moving, silently.

Of course the summer was hot. Today it was merely mild, and

the sky was overcast, although we passed men in the fields working stripped to the waist: tall brown-skinned men with an easy walk, as had the girls. Dressed, they wore in the country the Mediterranean uniform you see on older people everywhere: the long or short black cotton skirts, the headscarf, the black beret worn with faded blue denims. The old men with bad teeth and thick unwashed grey hair, each with his brimmed hat tipped over one narrowed eye, rakishly. They played cards in the sidestreets we passed, on small tables littered with glasses and coffee cups. It reminded me of those other men playing cards in the Carl Schurz Park in America.

It reminded me of everything. How did twenty strangers expect to blend into a countryside such as this? How did you walk the hills in your good British clothes, avoid the dogs and the cats, produce the smart walkie-talkies from under your jacket; explain the use of your binoculars?

On the other hand, Mike Widdess had done it. So could other people, if driven hard enough. If driven, of course, by my father.

Then I saw Donovan watching me, and thought about nothing for the rest of the journey.

Johnson Johnson's yacht the *Dolly* lay with six others at the Orsan, the yacht club on the opposite side of the basin from where the *Glycera* was berthed, and I heard Simon draw in his breath when he saw her. I thought I knew what to expect, but it wasn't the elegant sheer of fifty-six feet of white topside; the tailored teak of the deck with its brass sparkling; the pale soaring poles of her masts. Graceful, orderly and implicitly workmanlike. I should have checked my suppositions against the experience I already had, of Johnson painting. Denny Donovan, his arms full of baby luggage, said, "Wow!!!"

Rosamund followed Johnson into the cockpit and looking around said, "Why the *Dolly*? She's a beautiful boat."

Her tone was critical, but he smiled at her.

"Crummy name, I agree. It's really the *Doiley*," he said. "Once belonged to a fancy paper goods manufacturer." A door leading aft had swung open under his fingers, disclosing a double stateroom, brightly and impeccably furnished. "Suppose you come in here while Lenny and Donovan take the luggage through for Joanna and the baby, and Donovan gets his stuff settled. I've given Joanna the forward stateroom with Lenny on one side of her in the fo'c'sle cot and Donovan on the other, next to the galley. I'll show you in a minute. There's a place for lashing Ben's basket and no one can possibly get at them there."

"Your bedroom?" said Simon, looking curiously around. I dumped Ben's cot on one of the beds and sat beside him. Rosamund sank on the other side. The boy was sleeping, his new lashes stuck out like bristles.

"It's the master bedroom," Johnson said. "Bathroom off. Fittings as you see. Place for wet canvases here. I can get to the cockpit in one second if need be, and there's a plastic cockpit cover I use when I'm painting. All the dials you see through the door are the usual things—radar, echo sounder and what-not. And radio telephone, so you can speak from the *Glycera*. You'll have a drink I hope with me here, and then as soon as you feel happy about the baby, we can push off round the quay to your mother. You said Mrs. Warr Beckenstaff wanted to see Joanna?"

That was an understatement. The command had come, by transatlantic telephone, the night before we left New York. She wanted to see me, and her grandson. I had said she could see me with pleasure, but not her grandson at the end of a long day of air travel. There had been a three-cornered argument which by remote control I had won. Benedict's health came first, it was agreed. Eventually.

Now Rosamund said, "We've been asked to take Joanna aboard for half an hour. May we leave the baby here with you until she comes back?"

The saloon was clear. Johnson moved from the cockpit down into it and waited while we all filed after, taking Ben with us. From a bar just behind him there came a pleasant chinking sound as Lenny laid out the drinks. "You can leave him with Lenny and Donovan," Johnson said. "He'll be quite safe. They're moving *Dolly* out from the jetty as soon as we've gone, and then no one can get aboard without warning. We carry a pram and a launch; we'll send the launch to fetch Joanna whenever she's ready."

Behind us, Lenny coughed and Johnson turned. His face behind the glasses was as bland as if he really didn't know exactly what Lenny was about to remark. Johnson said, "A problem?"

Lenny's accent was Cockney, and his ears stuck out. He had exchanged his blue jacket for a white steward's coat, spotlessly laundered. He said, "I'm sorry, sir. The Avenger's out of action. Temporarily. They're fixing her in the repair shop."

Neither of my employers displayed any interest. Donovan, coming through the door forward said, "You can't leave shore then, can you, sir?"

The *sir* was a new phenomenon, due perhaps to the owner of such an evident piece of floating capital. Johnson said, "We've got the dinghy. For that matter, Lenny can bring the yacht over to take Joanna off. After that, we meant to move round to Dubrovnik harbor anyway."

"Why?" said Rosamund. She had a glass in her hand, and looked as though she needed it, what with jet lag and Ingmar in the offing.

"The view is better," Johnson said peacefully. "Also, it's less accessible. Dubrovnik's a walled city closed to traffic, unless you happen to want to get married. The only escape is through the gates or up the funicular: all easy to close if there's trouble. Come and see where the baby will sleep. Joanna, you'd better tell Lenny what to do if he wakens."

They had to wait for me in the end, because you can't just walk off a boat with a baby there. But I took care of the essentials quickly, and in the right order, leaving a feed in the fridge and the bathing and changing and feeding essentials still in their polythene wraps where they were handy and yet couldn't spill if *Dolly* sailed. They say that you can count a baby's luggage as roughly the same as two adults', and it's all too true.

Benedict's carrycot stood on the forward stateroom carpet, with each handle lashed to the bulkhead. He was still sleeping when I came back after washing quickly. I took off my apron and combed my hair and buttoned my coat and went out, leaving him. As I had guessed from the laughter, they were on their second refills and hadn't missed me. I followed everyone on to the jetty and Johnson took the wheel of the car. Looking back, I could see that Donovan was already standing by to cast off the shore line and that a thin cloud of smoke was rising aft from *Dolly's* exhaust.

Children don't waken on boats. I've seen a five-year-old sleep like the dead with an anchor chain roaring a foot away. Between the noise of the car and the harbor I couldn't even hear the sound of *Dolly's* engine, never mind the screams of Benedict, if any. It was Donovan who must have spotted my corrugated face at the back window and straightened to give me a thumbs-up. It didn't mean that Ben wasn't roaring; only that he wanted to cheer me. And he did. I was going to meet Mrs. Warr Beckenstaff on the *Glycera,* but I was a lot less worried about it than Rosamund.

The MS *Glycera,* chartered by the Warr Beckenstaff Corporation in the person of Rosamund's mother to mark the fiftieth anniversary of her cosmetics business, was a German ship: German-owned and German-crewed.

Not, perhaps, the most favored visitor in a Yugoslav harbor, within spitting distance of Hitler's underground prison and torture chamber on the other side of Dubrovnik. But congenial perhaps to those American guests who, unlike the Eisenkopps, had not forgotten their ethnic roots. And by any standard, a 6,000-ton mobile hotel whose food, appointments and general *luxe* could hardly be equalled, never mind bettered.

Pink and silver were Ingmar's trade colors and the *Glycera* wore them with all the chic which an expensive PR firm with an unlimited budget could demand from its favorite decorators. Wherever you looked, bunting, ribbons and awnings reminded you whose guest you were, and the scent of carnations and roses strove with the normal dock smell of tar, offal, diesel and bilge water.

The captain was waiting at the top of the companionway for Mrs. Warr Beckenstaff's daughter and kissed her hand, clicking his heels at Simon and Johnson. The nursemaid he ignored, which gave me time to look at the quilted satin and the massed foliage and the pink and silver garlands and the Louis Quinze grille behind which the Ingmar staff, in place of the purser, were hiding. I also enjoyed watching the stewards fancying Simon as he strolled past in his brown velvet gear, platinum hair carefully brushed and classical profile endorsed by the high flowered collar of his twenty-guinea voile shirt. Simon, whom Rosamund had wanted to marry so much that she had forced her mother's hand by allowing herself to become pregnant first. "What should I do if you stopped loving me?" he had repeated, laughing, to Rosamund in the flaming row I'd over-heard all those weeks ago. "Then I'd have to run to Grandma for help, wouldn't I?"

And Rosamund had shut up.

I was able to study the scene, since the head steward led the Booker-Readmans and Johnson right off to see their hostess, and I was left sitting upright in a deep-buttoned armchair in the Empfangs-Halle, watching their cases being wheeled off to their staterooms.

There was no other luggage about: the last of the guests must have come from the airport and were probably even now sleeping off their jet lag in their cabins. By my reckoning we had been fed eight times in the last twenty-four hours and no one would miss lunch, one would imagine. From the deck above, a murmur of music and laughter and the distant tinkle of plates told that the European guests, already well settled in, were making the most of the cuisine. Groups of people from the cabin area drifted upstairs from time to time to join them, or crossed the carpet to enquire about cashing checks or making telephone calls.

None of them looked at me, although like the stewards, I amused myself pricing their clothes and identifying them. The Eisenkopps hadn't been far out in their guesswork. Men and women, they were a credit to Ingmar, and I had a shot at guessing which of them had begged to come and which she had paid to do so. It wasn't an uninformed guess either. Private nurses and children's nannies know more about the personal lives of the idle rich than any gossip writer ever born. It's why half of them never hanker to marry, any more than the crowds at Brands Hatch want to change seats with the drivers.

Outside, I could hear a lot of muted activity: voices calling in German and machinery clanking and feet padding about, but inside it remained warm and scented and calm. Someone came and sprayed water all over the flowers, and someone else walked about letting fly with a ten-litre bottle of Ingmar's new scent, in a pink and silver aerosol. I shut my eyes and a man in a white jacket said, "Fraülein Emerson? Will you be so kind as to follow me, please?"

He took me up two flights of carpeted stairs to the Kleine Halle of the boat deck. To the biggest suite, of course, on the *Glycera;*

since Mrs. Warr Beckenstaff was the charterer. The only person for many months ever to employ my second name and reasonably, also, since she was paying for me. Since she had attempted to hire me right from the beginning, before anyone knew I was free, the week after Mike Widdess had died.

Then the steward took me down a long corridor, past the fire extinguishers and the drinking water containers, and stopped at a double door swagged in pink velvet. The voice which answered his knock was high, commanding and totally English.

"Send the girl in!" said Grandmother Warr Beckenstaff; and in my pudding-basin hat, my uniform coat, my brown gloves and low, polished shoes I drew a breath and walked firmly forward.

The clear, cold voice spoke again before I saw anyone at all in the room: behind the flowers, the cushions, the sofas: the ceiling and walls of pink and grey velvet.

"Tell me, girl," said the voice. "This extraordinary man Johnson Johnson: are you and he sleeping together?"

# Chapter 13

She must have been seventy-five anyway, which when you look around is no great age, I suppose, in a woman, and you would expect her to have everything tucked that would tuck; and she had. But she also had the poise and the drive and the dress sense of a woman who had married a small émigré pharmaceutist and turned him into a world cosmetics industry, with centres in London and New York and Paris.

The bewildered Warr Beckenstaff had a breakdown and died shortly after the tenth balance sheet; and thereafter nothing could stop her. And now she stood there in her pink silk jersey dress and examined me, the wealthy lady who had chosen the schools and colleges and finishing establishments which had made Rosamund what she was, and looked like making an equal mess of my Benedict.

Tall as her daughter, Ingmar Warr Beckenstaff was spider-thin, the brittle shafts of her wrists and shoulders emphasized by the weight of metal she wore, embedded with gemstones. Her eyes were Rosamund's: large and sunken and heavy-lidded; and if her chin was too definite, her cheek-bones were good and her mouth still had planes that could be tinted. The hair, a smooth bouffant silver grey, stopped just short of her ears and swept asymmetrically over in a wing which just cleared her left eye. Glimpsed briefly from the other side of a street, she would have had Donovan after her.

I must have smiled at the thought because she said, "You disappoint me. Why not answer? I thought you had character," and sat down.

"I'm sorry. I was trying to remember," I said. "Was that all you wanted to know?"

"How very prudish," she said. She had a gold and black onyx cigarette holder to match her necklet and was choosing a pink and silver scroll to screw into it. She looked up. "Sit down, girl. I am unlikely either to be shocked or to sack you for immorality. I am told that you have been a devoted and courageous nurse to my grandson, and I hope you feel that your services are being adequately recognized. I wish you to continue your excellent care of him. I also wish, in exchange, some information. My son-in-law sleeps around, and I don't like it."

I sat down, keeping my back straight, my ankles crossed and my hands with my gloves in my lap. "Not with me, Mrs. Warr Beckenstaff," I said politely.

"I think that's probably true," she said annoyingly. "Go on. With whom, then?"

I said, "I have a full-time job with Benedict. There really isn't much opportunity to study what else is going on in the household. In any case, it isn't my business."

"So it's the Eisenkopp woman. I was afraid so," said Mrs. Warr Beckenstaff. I wondered how I had given that away, and concluded she was the only piece of crumpet who lived so near that I was bound to have noticed. Or else she knew already, and it was merely a move in the game. The power game which, of course, she was playing with me.

I said, "I can't make any comment. I'm sorry. Would you trust my discretion on anything else if I did?"

I hadn't leaped forward to light her fag, and to do her justice she didn't appear to expect it. She put the lighter down and gazed at me through pink scented smoke. "It depends what else you know. For example, have you no questions about Benedict?"

"No," I said. "I haven't." Shot-gun weddings are not my affair. Or the reverse, as in this particular case.

"You haven't wondered," said Mrs. Warr Beckenstaff, her clear voice quite unaltered, "how, with a father of Simon's coloring, the child appears to be growing so dark? Or about other aspects of his appearance? Of course you have. And I expect you, not being uneducated or defective, to be able to give me a sensible opinion when I ask for it. Who does that grandson of mine remind you of?"

Because it was Ben, I hadn't said anything even to Johnson. But now, of course, there was really no help for it.

"Hugo Panadek," I said. "The Eisenkopps' Design Director."

Neither the pink swags nor the head of the Warr Beckenstaff Corporation fell to the ground. "Exactly," said Benedict's grandmother impatiently. "The Booker-Readman fellow, of course, must be completely infertile although my daughter, as is obvious, is besotted with him. I cannot imagine she could have resorted to a bald-headed Serbian otherwise."

*"I'll have to run to Grandma for help,"* Simon had said tauntingly to his angry wife. He wasn't afraid of this lady: why should he be? Rosamund had only to be nasty to Simon and he would spill the whole story: how he wasn't the father of Benedict, and how the heir to the Warr Beckenstaff fortune was the son of a bald-headed foreigner.

And Hugo . . . It was Hugo who had referred to both Benedict's parents, his lip curling, as *punks.* Hugo who had shown no surprise over the peculiar affair of the ikons and who had arranged Johnson's accident at Cape Cod, one might well reason, in order to expose Simon's liaison with Beverley. Hugo, one might suggest, in whose Wonderland Rudi Klapper, the shooting stall attendant who had given the Booker-Readmans their first kidnapping fright, had been employed; but who could hardly be interested in kidnapping his own son; especially as he, as well as Simon, had the power to blackmail the Warr Beckenstaff Corporation with the truth about its heir. I said however, to be sure, "If it's Mr. Panadek, will he make an approach, do you think, about Benedict?"

The large, lidded eyes continued to gaze at me through the smoke. "For money?" said the easy breath coming through the pearly capped teeth and silver-pink mouth. "If there were any person in this world who can induce me to pay what I don't intend to pay, I shouldn't be talking to you of all these matters now. Mr. Panadek is much too wise a gentleman to attempt blackmail. He has no interest, I am sure, in the child. While it would be a pity, there would be no permanent damage caused by Benedict's parentage being known. My will ensures that if Benedict dies, my daughter inherits no more than the barest minimum. If, on the other hand, Benedict has the ability, I shall be quite content to see him take over the business when he is of an age. I have made provision for that also. In the meantime, my main concern is to preserve the child from his parents. If need be, I shall do it by placing him totally in your hands. That is why you were chosen."

It seemed as good a chance as any. I said, "I was told that you asked for me even before I was free of my last job. Might I ask who recommended me?"

"You may, but I am afraid I cannot indulge you," Ingmar said. "There were a dozen of you, and my secretary made the enquiries which led to the final selection. We had the opinion, I believe, of another nanny and several employers. Indeed, in your case, the Princess at Cape Cod was one."

I'd never been employed by the Princess. But Hugo knew her. He had had lunch there. I said, "I think Benedict is bright. He's worth cultivating."

"In spite of the fact," said his grandmother, "that if he's kidnapped he could cost me a fortune?"

I said, "He's as safe as he can be. The yacht is very secure, and Mr. Johnson has taken every precaution."

"I believe he has," Ingmar said. She swung her feet slowly round, and removing her cigarette holder, took out and stubbed the cigarette. Then, one red nailed hand on her knee, she said, "Do you always sit like that? Yes. Your training, I suppose. Well, I must tell you I was taken with your Mr. Johnson when I first met him, and I have been impressed with him at each meeting since. Rosamund tells me the painting is quite astonishing. He is not, therefore, behind these attempts on Benedict and you are not, I now see, in collusion with him. I am glad to be reassured."

My mouth dropped open. I stared at her and then, despite myself, felt my face relax in a grin. "You thought . . . Of course, you might very well imagine such a thing."

"The projection of possibilities," Ingmar Warr Beckenstaff said, "is the structure upon which large businesses are founded and flourish. You had better return to your charge. I have arranged that from last month onwards, your salary will be increased by a third: I have also left instructions that all your existing cosmetics should be thrown away and replaced by those of the firm by whom you are employed. No excuse is acceptable: there is an anti-allergy range. What is it?"

She was talking to someone behind me. I turned my head and saw the blotched face of Ingmar's P.R. man. He said, "Madame . . ." and the telephone rang.

"Answer it," said Ingmar Warr Beckenstaff to me.

I answered it, squeezing between the pink sofas and around the silver baskets of roses and peonies. It was on a desk by the large boat-deck windows and as I picked it up and said, "Hullo? Mrs. Warr Beckenstaff's cabin," my gaze rested on the voile curtains and the deck and the harbor beyond them. And on the water.

Which was odd.

A voice said, "This is the Captain. May I speak with Mrs. Warr Beckenstaff, if you please?"

I put my hand over the telephone and said, "It's the captain. Mrs. Warr Beckenstaff, we're sailing."

"So I see," Ingmar said. "Give me the telephone." The door closed behind the public relations man and she spoke into the phone briefly, in German. She put the receiver down and I replaced the phone on the desk. "You don't understand German," she said. Beyond the pink swagged door, the ship's tannoy could just be heard, making a booming announcement. I thought of all the sleepers it would wake up, and of all the people, like the Eisenkopps, who were spending the afternoon at a hotel, and would return to the quay to find the *Glycera* absent.

I said, "No. I don't understand German. Why are we sailing?"

"To sever our connection with the land," said Ingmar Warr Beckenstaff, seating herself at her desk, and drawing pen and paper towards her. "You had better go, and send in my secretary. Fortunately, press and photographers are on board and, of course, all the European guests who joined us at Venice."

She was writing. "Mrs. Warr Beckenstaff," I said, "I have to get back to the baby. Why are we sailing?"

She half looked up. "Ah, the baby," she said. "He has been vaccinated, I should hope?"

Beneath my chaste lilac uniform, like a crab from its shell, the bottom fell out of my stomach. "Oh heavens," I said. "It isn't small-pox?"

"Ah, passion at last," she said, writing firmly. "Yes: an outbreak of smallpox was announced by Belgrade late this morning. Confined, they believe, to the Dubrovnik region, but we shall move out of the seaway for safety. No one comes aboard except in emergency, and unless he or she has been vaccinated. No one leaving the ship for the danger area will be permitted to come aboard a second time. The news reached the airport, I am told, just after our plane arrived and many if not all of the passengers are waiting there to take the next scheduled flight home. You didn't hear an announcement?"

"We left by car, before the others did. Mrs. Warr Beckenstaff . . ."

She put down her pen with a crack. "I am aware of your problem. It is minor. We shall make a temporary stop off Ploče to allow a launch to return you to the *Dolly*. I see no difficulty, provided the *Dolly* remains at sea and all those on board have been vaccinated. You will be safer than before, it seems to me. The militia have cordoned the area."

I couldn't get on deck then quickly enough. Johnson was hanging over the port side, his hair mixed up with his spectacles, watching the noisy approach of a launch full of luggage and people. Among them were the black and blonde heads and cashmere sports casuals of Comer and Beverley Eisenkopp.

Unlike the faces round about us, Johnson's was stamped with neither excitement nor horror. He listened with attention to all I told him of my visit to Ingmar and at the end said only, "She's right. I could do without the *Glycera* wandering about, but in a way, the cordon makes our job easier. It's almost bound to force the other side into a change of plan, and that always leaves room for errors. The other thing is the health hazard. Are you worried?"

Below, the launch had reached the foot of the companionway, and the captain and the chief officer had appeared there. No one had come aboard.

I said, "Ben is protected, and I'm all right. What about you and Lenny?"

"I'm a permanent walking chemical factory," Johnson said. "And I know Donovan is all right, and his invisible comrades. It's a mild outbreak. I gather the vaccinated can walk about anywhere so long as they have the right papers. And that's what the said other side are going to find awkward. I only hope, after this, the poor sods aren't moved to abandon the kidnap."

"Surely not," I said. Pained.

The shouting below had risen in volume. Craning over, we could see the wind lifting Comer's creamed hair, and hear the despairing twang of Beverley's accent. I said, "Comer's against vaccination as a matter of principle."

"Ain't that a bitch?" said Johnson sympathetically. "Then he's going to miss out on the Warr Beckenstaff gala. What do you think they've done with Bunty and the two Eisenkinder?"

"Sent them on to Herceg-Novi," I said. I tried very hard to keep the laughter out of my voice. "Bunty's vaccinated, you see. And when we were in Cape Cod, she got Dr. Gibbings to do the kids without telling Comer."

It was as well she did. The car, clearly, had been allowed to proceed to the seaside, and the Eisenkopps had had to return to plague-ridden Dubrovnik, to see the *Glycera* majestically sailing out of the harbor. No wonder they were clean out of alphas. I said, "I ought to get back to Benedict. I could take that launch. But I don't want the Eisenkopps on *Dolly*."

"I don't imagine you'll get them on *Dolly*," said Johnson placidly. "I'll come with you, if you like, to dissuade them. But if I know Comer, he'll take the first plane back to health, hygiene and sanity, and force Beverley and the kids to go along with him."

But he didn't. By the time Johnson and I boarded the launch it was empty of all but the rejected Eisenkopps and a number of tightlipped representatives of the Warr Beckenstaff Corporation. The Booker-Readmans, if appealed to, had clearly not come to the rescue. Neither had Ingmar herself although Dr. Gibbings, looking hurt, turned on his heel as we arrived and walked away from the head of the gangway. Comer said, his voice hoarse with declaiming, "I'm glad to see two folks with sense. You're gonna fly the kid out of the God-damned country."

The launch's engine started up and Johnson sat down, and so did I. Beverley said, "Are they going to fly the kid out of the country! Benedict's vaccinated; right?" to me.

I nodded. "I'm staying with him on *Dolly*. It's only a mild outbreak, Mr. Eisenkopp, and the health authorities haven't advised tourists to leave. I'm sure the children will be fine in Herceg-Novi."

"A bunch of gollies," Comer Eisenkopp said. "Some crap bunch of gollies on a coach tour to Meccaland, wouldn't you know it? And back they come with the plague. A hell of a mother my kids have got. She's left them down there with a girl that's pumped their guts fulla cow shit. A klutz. I'da bust her. I'da slung her out on her ass but their Mom here—oh, no. Herceg-Novi's not infected. Hell, Dubrovnik wasn't infected yesterday. Today like as not the bugs are right there in your belly, shoulder to shoulder and doin' a circle jerk. Ya know what she wants to do?"

The rope came inboard and we began to move away from the *Glycera.* Togetherness had melted from the Eisenkopp prospectus. Comer jerked a thumb at his wife. "She wants to get herself shot full of cow shit and go to the party."

I'd guessed that much. I also wondered how much she had paid in advance for her holiday course of plastic surgery. This time Johnson said, "I think it's been pretty well proved that vaccination saves lives, Mr. Eisenkopp. But if you don't fancy it, why not leave your wife with us? We'll see she gets her scrape, and I'll take her back to the *Glycera.* Then later on, she and the children can have a good holiday. Why, you might even feel like coming back in a few days and joining them."

He was a rat. I could feel Beverley stiffen at the prospect of bewitching her husband, all black eyes and skin-pink elastoplast. Comer said, "I've got a business to run. I can't do my head in like some guys in the play scene. Bev? You heard what he said."

"I want to get vaccinated," Beverley said. Her gorgeous face was blotchy with crying and temper, and strands of hair flew from her bandana. Her small, pretty hands were clenched so hard her rings were grinding together.

Comer said, "I reckon you mean to get your money's worth outta that costoom. And the beauty box. You know there's a white leather gift box in every cabin, fitted out with Ingmar's products in silver-topped crystal bottles, all lined with pink plush? The men get somethin' too. Sprayed with hormones, I guess. You'll look real good, honey, in spots."

We had arrived at the jetty. "You're no gentleman, Comer Eisenkopp," said his wife in a low-pitched, vehement voice. "Mr. Johnson, I thank you for your offer. Goodbye, Comer."

She jumped ashore. For a moment, Comer Eisenkopp looked

nonplussed. Then without a word, he strode on to the pier and made for a taxi, without waiting for his cases. The seamen began to lift them out and they stood in two matched sets beside us: his and hers, in leather-bound tapestry. A taxi containing Comer ambled across, absorbed one pile and vanished on the road to the airport. There were no farewells.

Johnson turned from the sea where *Dolly*, distantly swinging, disclosed the presence of Lenny with binoculars in the cockpit and Donovan lying stripped to the waist on the coachroof. They both waved, lazily. No cries floated over the water.

Her owner grinned down at his new companion. "Honey," said Johnson, who was no gentleman either, "you would look real good in anything. Come on and let's find a cow-doctor."

Johnson parked behind the north walls. From the highway above, Dubrovnik looks like a toy city packed in a matchbox, with a bite out of one end for the harbor. Of the two longer sides, one is built on the sea-rocks and the other crosses the peninsula neck under the shadow of wooded Mount Srdj. The city gates, once with their moats and their drawbridges, lie at either end of the matchbox; and the Placa, the broad main street which runs from the one gate to the other, is sunk like the floor of a boat, so that all the long streets on either side slope or step sharply down to it. The walls are seventy two feet high and eighteen feet thick in some places. Dubrovnik, old name Ragusa, was a rich city-state for four hundred years, trading like Venice with the Orient. It had a lot to protect.

It still had a lot to protect, and the enemy this time wasn't corsairs. Twenty-three thousand other people besides Beverley Eisenkopp wanted to be vaccinated, quickly, and it was clear long before Johnson slid into the Put Iza Grada car park that if Beverley was ever to grace the Ingmar anniversary celebration that evening, she was going to have to have the personal favor of St. Blaise, short of discovering a reliable but corrupt member of the Yugoslav nationalized health service.

Clear to me, that is. Beverley had already remembered what I had forgotten and Johnson wasn't supposed to know about. As Johnson got out of the car she said, "Now look at that view. Why don't you go up on the walls, J.J., and have yourself a nice walk while Nurse Joanna and I go and get this little business looked after? There's a real nice statue down there, you can't miss it; we could meet up with you there in half an hour?"

Johnson said. "Half an hour? Are you sure?" There were queues everywhere.

"I'm sure," said Beverley. The pinched look had gone out of her face and she tossed her Wig 'n Lift off her shoulders for Johnson's benefit. "Anyways, Nurse Joanna can come and tell you if I'm held up."

I telegraphed to Johnson, *I've got to get back to the baby,* and he replied with a flash of his glasses: *Don't miss the chance to find out where she is going.* In spite of all that, I said aloud, "Can Lenny manage?"

"Of course he can," said Johnson calmly. "First sign of senility, when you think you're indispensable. Run along, both of you."

And so we ran. Through the modern gateway, down the steps and the landings of the nearest plunging street and right along the Ulica Prijeka to a tall, crumbling seventeenth-century building with a wide, handsome door and brass plate. The Radoslav Clinic, naturally. Where Beverley was to have her plastic pick-up in three days from now, and the medics all knew her.

She said, ringing the bell, "I daresay Bunty has told you about this place. I guess there isn't much about my private life you don't know between you by this time. Maybe it seems weird to you, but you'd be surprised just how many big English names you'll see getting their image fixed up. And all those Japanese eyelids. You wanna come in?"

Nothing, really, would have kept me out.

Inside there was a black and white floor and a fountain, and a doorway leading into a patio with a pool and palm trees and wistaria, and a number of lemon trees in small tubs. There was also a queue, stretching three times round the hall and then out of sight up a staircase, of women in black skirts and headscarves, and men in thin dark suits and black berets, their collarless shirts displaying necklines of pristine white underwear. They were undoubtedly not there to have their chins lifted.

A nurse in white canvas boots and a blue overall came out of an office and there was a sharp exchange, in the middle of which Beverley wheeled round and pushing past the patient crocodile, began to make her way up the stairs. The nurse looked after her without attempting to follow, sighed and then, picking up a half-smoked cigarette, turned her large dark eyes on me. One of her sleeves had been taped up to uncover a new vaccination. "Don't tell me," I said. "You've cancelled the cosmetic surgery program?"

Her English was perfectly adequate. "Is it not reasonable?" she said. "The risk of infection. And all, all our doctors will be needed for many days for all these poor people. We will open again. Your friend will come back."

"The lady is my employer," I said, also with a sigh but smiling as well. "I am a nurse also. I look after the lady's two children." Well, I did, on occasion. And it brought me a seat in the office and a bowl of thick Turkish coffee. While my hostess said "Molim?" continuously through her cigarette into the telephone and Beverley jumped the queue, or failed to, for her vaccination.

Half an hour later I had seen over the clinic, inspected, with suppressed hysteria, the signed thank-you photographs in the doctors' private sitting room and located Beverley Eisenkopp, roughly two hundred and fifteenth in the double line of those waiting to be vaccinated, and weeping with rage. Equality, it seemed, meant equality; and if they lost the Eisenkopp overhaul business for the rest of their lives, they still weren't willing to oblige her.

I was on my way out to tell Johnson when this white-coated young doctor stopped me. Tall and brown, as most of the citizens were, with humorous brown eyes strongly under-lidded, and a slender nose with flattened high cheekbones. He said, without removing his cigarette, "The nurse tells me you are Mrs. Eisenkopp's nanny, so perhaps you are Bunty?"

Who would have thought it? I produced my most candid expression. "Well, she was nearly right. My employer is a friend of Mrs. Eisenkopp and I know Bunty very well. But my name's Joanna Emerson. Why? Do you know Bunty?"

I knew the answer just before he came out with it. "Ah, a great deal," he said. "But by name only, for I hear so much about her, and about you. It is you who have the aunt in Canada, is it not? For you see . . ."

"Don't tell me," I said. "You're Jesus Krysztof?"

Charlotte's boyfriend. As it happened, he wasn't. He was the other one.

"Lazar Dogíc," he said. His lids bunched with glee, and also against the clouds of grey smoke from his filter-fag. "Our names are difficult. Charlotte has much fun with mine. How is she; is she well? She is not with you?"

I explained. I further explained about Mrs. Eisenkopp. He knew all about her cancelled operation but not about her urgent desire to be vaccinated. In two minutes, equality had acquired a slight bend, and the American lady had been slipped from the queue by another nurse with laced boots with no toes and heels.

I followed. We were led to a neat room with clean parquet flooring where a trolley already stood by an armchair. While Lazar Dogíc administered the vaccine, I waited outside and tried to guess from the dialogue where he had punctured her.

Wherever it was, it made Dr. Dogíc's day: his fresh cigarette had dimples all round it when he eventually emerged. Beverley herself was rather blotched, and a line had sneaked out from the Wig 'n Lift and landed between her arched eyebrows. At the same time, you couldn't say she was mournful, either over the smallpox or Comer. It turned out that it was Dr. Dogíc's birthday, and Beverley had asked him to join us and Johnson in a drink. We all sallied forth to find the square, the statue and Johnson.

I remember at that point feeling momentarily free. I trusted Lenny with Ben. I believed Johnson when he said that the baby and I ran no danger when we were separate. I ought, no doubt, to be making a valuable study of my companions but my companions were getting along perfectly well together and had been here before and were going to be here again, and I wasn't.

Fate, or the Department, or Johnson had brought me to this mediaeval city-state without traffic, and I wanted to rubberneck. To drift with others along its main street, paved with brilliant white marble like parquet. To lift my eyes to the handsome stone buildings with their red pantile roofs and rows of green swallow-tailed shutters. To linger in front of each arch of the knee shops, door and window and counter in one, which for three hundred years had formed each side of the street into a range of mysterious caverns.

Too quickly we reached the square at the end, surrounded by

Renaissance and Gothic arched palaces and containing a free-standing pillar with the real nice statue of a longhaired knight with sword and shield in its niche.

Johnson wasn't behind the shield or sitting on the steps on the other side of the column, unless he had been flattened by the five hundred-odd people who were standing there instead, their backs to us. Beverley said, "What's going on? Are they running a sweepstake?" as she picked her way like the rest of us over a carpet of pigeons.

Charlotte's boy friend said, "No, they are watching the weddings. You see in front of you the Municipal Palace. There. Beside the belfry and the small fountain. And someone waves to you, perhaps your friend, from the Gradska Kafana? The City Café? On the terrace there?"

It was Johnson. But I wasn't looking at Johnson. Below the white balustrades of the City Café, and smothered bonnets, radiators, windows and boots with mixed flowers and greenery, were parked five desecrating automobiles. As we stared, a discreet croak behind us scattered first the pigeons and then the crowds to admit a sixth car which also halted in front of the Palace.

A girl in a long coarse white dress and short veil got out, followed by three men in good suits with carnations in their buttonholes and another girl in a long purple dress. They disappeared inside the building and the driver backed his car into line with the others.

"I told you," Johnson said when we joined him at his table. "It's the only thing they allow cars inside the city for. They'll be out in twenty minutes. Did you meet someone you knew?" Dr. Dogíc had lingered behind to speak to one of the drivers.

"A boy friend of Charlotte's," I said. "He's coming to join us. He gave Mrs. Eisenkopp her vaccination and it's his birthday, so we rather owe him something, if you don't mind."

"Perhaps I ought to go and bring him," Johnson said; and vanished, like the Cheshire Cat, while his voice was still displacing sound waves. I picked up the wine list. It was in the Roman alphabet, not the Cyrillic for a wonder, and I was reading under the Žestoka Pică or Strong Drinks and hovering between Gilbey's Gin and J. Walker at 15 Dinari when Johnson and Lazar came back and orders for Sljivovica went flying about like the pigeons.

Plum brandy at five in the afternoon needs to be treated with caution. I treated it with caution, which gave me a ringside view of Beverley lightly sloshed, going into her adored-little-girl act for Johnson and Lazar, both of whom had lost no time in chatting her up. Peals of silvery laughter greeted Johnson's every graven-faced observation, and he remained effortlessly prolific no matter how high he was becoming. On the other hand there was Lazar's charm, laid on with all the pure Balkan style which had placed him, obviously, on Charlotte's mailing list.

In between observing the Municipal Palace disgorge married couples like parking tickets, I watched the handsome brown doctor down four separate tumblers of Sljivovica with no visible change in his smile or his *macho*, and wondered how long it would take Mr. Eisenkopp's Beverley to recall that all the animation she was wasting on the habitués of the City Café would be better employed exclusively on Johnson and the other beautiful or powerful people on board the *Glycera*. Or Dr. Dogíc, who appeared to know the whole of female Dubrovnik, to cease smiling and waving and re-member the birthday party he had spent some energy fruitlessly inviting us severally to.

I wondered what sort of head Johnson had for plum brandy. Sober, I watched the setting sun flame on the ribbed pantile roofs high over our heads and light the wings of the swifts as they swept up from the dark of the ancient Platea Comunis and squeaked and wheeled against the rose-colored pines of Mount Srdj. Now the shutters were up and lights glimmered in all the arched windows and, a moment later, sprang along the main street as the people of Dubrovnik strolled out to take the evening air. A little wind started up and Beverley shivered and turned to pull on her green cashmere jacket, with help from each side. Then, smiling, she rose.

She had remembered. Beverley Eisenkopp had taken a great many pains to acquire that coveted invitation on board the *Glycera*, and she wasn't going to be diverted now.

We all left the café together. Three more people among the strollers, two of them ravishingly pretty girls, waved to Dr. Dogíc and he waved back, smiling. He was a popular boy. His polo-necked sweater, I noted, had been bought in Italy, and the thick gold ring on his little finger had a passable diamond in it. He said caressingly to Beverley, "You need help to find the way to your car? I come with you."

I watched him take her arm. I was still watching when he winked at me.

I didn't wink back, but I grinned. Conquering the impulse to look at Johnson almost killed me, both then and when we began to climb the steep street to the north wall and Lazar's hand, leaving Beverley, brushed the stout inverted pleat in my faithful green Maggie Bee trenchcoat.

I was entertained. Charlotte's boy friends always had bags of initiative, and no mid-European cavalier was going to offend the wealthier and more important of two possible dates by making up to both at once. None of that, however, was going to stop Dr. Dogíc from trying to have his cake and eat it. Also, one bitchily had to remember, the Radoslav Clinic knew to a day just how old Beverley was. I went on climbing steadily, and hoped, also bitchily, that Johnson had noticed.

It was getting dark. Overhead, the strip of sky between the tall leaning houses was inky blue, and the infrequent lanterns threw odd jagged shadows on the peeling walls and doorways and balconies. A gleaming brass plate announced ADVOKAT and another in English directed to *Disco-Bar with Disc Jokey*. There was a smell of cats, and Dijamant filter cigarettes, and cooking. Behind us in the square the last of the wedding cars, honking and afforested with waving arms, swept along the Placa, displacing the sauntering citizens.

It was all implacably foreign, and made one think of things I had heard about Yugoslavia during the war. How in one small town, every professional man, every doctor and teacher had been taken and executed in reprisal for German officers killed by the Resistance. How after the war, nine old women had been discovered living alone in one mountain village, where every other soul had either lost his life fighting or had been taken and shot. As we climbed higher I could see the neon sign of the Labirint, the night club built on the site, they said, of a wartime Gestapo torture chamber.

I said to Lazar, "Don't you see ghosts, when you go over there to dance?"

The street was wide enough—just—for three people. He tucked the hand that wasn't holding Beverley under my arm. "Why should we? Do you see ghosts in Dublin Castle? We are a collection of different races in Yugoslavia, with different languages, different religions, different customs."

"Then I suppose you were lucky," said Johnson from behind, "that a man like President Tito was able to hold you all together for so long. When he goes, what will happen?"

Still holding my arm, Lazar turned his head, smiling over his shoulder. "Ask the politicians. They control us. I am only a doctor. Here is the gateway, and there is the car park. You see, Izlaz means exit."

The sign, distressingly, said, ИЗЛАЗ. Lazar said "You have no Serbo-Croat?" And when we all shook our heads, "Ah, but you will manage very well. Most speak English. And now I must leave you. Goodbye, my dear Mrs. Eisenkopp. Goodbye, Mr. Johnson. Is it possible, Joanna, before you leave, that I might give you a message for Charlotte?"

The message, delivered in a smiling undertone as the others got into the car, was, as one might have guessed, a pressing invitation to Lazar Dogíc's birthday party. "The others will be on the *Glycera*, is it not? Then you are free."

"You don't know how tempting it is," I said. "But I'm looking after a baby on Mr. Johnson's yacht and we shan't even be tied up in the harbor. They're afraid of kidnapping, and we have to spend the night at anchor somewhere. I'm so sorry."

"So Mr. Johnson has said. But this is no problem. There are boats. There are two men on board, Mr. Johnson says, who attend to the baby this afternoon. Why can you not leave the baby with them for this evening?"

He patted me on the shoulder. "It is settled. I shall come for you."

"It isn't settled," I said. Behind us, Beverley had leant over and pressed Johnson's car horn. "Look, I have to go. Have a wonderful party. I'll tell Charlotte I met you."

He continued to grin. "I shall come," he said. He was still waving as we drove off.

Lenny Milligan brought the *Dolly* under motor to the quayside to pick us all up and take us across to where the *Glycera*, dressed overall with strings of colored lights, lay floodlit on the ocean like Selfridge's.

Ben, neatly stowed in his carrycot, was pinkly asleep and had been so, Donovan said, for four hours. After all, it was what I'd been counting on, but none the less I was pleased. I left him a few minutes longer while I got out orange juice and beef soup and the next bottle ready to warm, and found out how Johnson's galley cooker functioned. I spread polythene sheets and unpacked baby gear, while footsteps above, and voices, and the thud of dropped ropes gave way to the surge of the engine and the kind of motion that told we were now on our way to the *Glycera*.

Beverley's face needed fixing. She made straight for the heads, and didn't come near me again. Donovan put his head round the door and said, "My God, you should smell the plum brandy. Where've you lot all been?" and then withdrew when I grinned but didn't stop working. I had gone to lift Benedict when the engine stopped and we coasted, by the sounds, up to the *Glycera*.

They let Beverley on board this time: I heard her voice on the cruise boat's companionway, followed by the bumps of her baggage ascending. The door opened and Johnson said, "All right, Joanna?"

Because my whole attention was on Ben, I said "Yes, he's fine. You're off now, are you?" without thinking. It did strike me that he looked pretty sober for the amount of Žestoka Pića he had consumed. Benedict's eyes were still shut but his lips began to push in and out. I slipped my hands a little further under him, ready to lever.

Johnson said, "I don't know what the bloody hell your father was thinking of."

That found its way through the jet lag. My hands still under the baby, I gave Johnson my abrupt attention. "I'm sorry. I'm stupid. Don't worry. I do remember why we're here. Is there anything more I can do?"

From outside, we could hear calling voices. Johnson said, "No. We've been over it all. Don't trust the doctor."

"Lazar Dogíc? He was trying to lure me on shore," I said. "I thought you said that so long as Ben and I were separated . . . ?"

"I know. But don't trust him all the same. Good luck," Johnson said.

Even after he said it, he didn't move for a moment, although Lenny's voice had now joined the others calling his name. I said again, "Don't worry. It's my own father I'm doing it for."

It sounded discourteous but he understood probably because he gave one of his less glassy smiles before he walked off and boarded the *Glycera*. It was Ben himself, squirming against my two hands, who dragged my mind back to the baby.

My nose was pricking again, but that was jet lag as well as other emotions. Including, if you must know, plain terror.

# Chapter 14

Over supper Donovan and I revised our relationship. My second profession appeared to fascinate him.

"Like crossword puzzles?" he said helpfully. "I bet you sure beat the crap out of a crossword puzzle."

All he appeared to know about coding was that you needed a book by Charles Dickens and the ability to count up to twenty-six. I didn't ask him how he got into Intelligence work. I did ask him if he had ever played ice hockey in his life and he said yes, twice; but it was a great way to impress chicks. He was a great admirer of Johnson.

The *Glycera*, with Johnson on board, had sailed before we did. All the time I was feeding and settling Benedict, Donovan had given me a running commentary of the *Glycera*'s progress as she left her anchorage in the Daksa Channel and, dropping her pilot, turned south, reflected in the broken evening water, to begin her leisurely cruise into the calmer seas of the Boka Kotorska.

A cruise she would never have had to take, comfortably berthed at the quayside at Gruz, or at Venice. Listening to the rain pattering on the deck as Ben played with his bottle, and picked at my sleeve, and allowed the teat to pop yet again from the gummy pink arch of his smile, I allowed myself to hope, acidly, that all the Beautiful People were good sailors.

Beverley wasn't. Beverley, who had got her way and shed Comer and was now on board the same ship as her golden Ulysses, Sultry Simon. And who had shown the same sort of contempt for Rosamund as had Simon, Rosamund's husband. Nor was it hard to guess why. Beverley, too, must know that Simon was not the father of Rosamund's baby, lying here on my knee.

And the real father, Hugo? He also was on board; more at his ease than anyone there, for this was his country. Did his attitude of the sophisticated bystander extend to the baby, and was Ingmar right in believing he had no interest in claiming paternity; in staking an interest in the assets of the Warr Beckenstaff Corporation? Or was Ingmar herself not still a pretty good suspect? It was through her organization that this celebration was taking place tonight off Yugoslavia, instead of Venice.

And was Dr. Gibbings no more than a medical man paid by the Warr Beckenstaff to look after its employees, and specifically the Booker-Readmans? But for him, Sukey and Grover would never have been able to drive smoothly to their hotel in Herceg-Novi, taking their nurse Bunty with them. And the presence of a nanny might be quite essential to the plans for kidnapping a very young baby, particularly if Ben and I were to be separated. You couldn't discount even Bunty or Charlotte except that, of course, Charlotte was back in New York.

"This time," Johnson had said, "you won't see Rudi or Vladimir or any of the faces we know already. This time the other team aren't going to tip their hands. And by the same token, they mustn't spot, when they do appear, that you were expecting them. So no carrycot packed full of feeds and nappies, Joanna. None of Ben's equipment is going to be bugged: they'll be on the lookout for that. Your own things are something again. You'll be told about that."

I had been told about that. I had read all the notes he had given me about Yugoslavia. Even before Ben was fed this evening I had been shown by Lenny Milligan over every inch of the *Dolly*, including the sail locker, the engine and all the apparatus in the cockpit for running her. She was a beautiful ketch. The charts for the coast of Yugoslavia were already laid out in the saloon with an open volume of the Med. pilot, and he took me quickly through both. I believe, heaven help me, I even asked him what the Bora was, that was mentioned on every other page. *"To secure for a Bora, cables should be taken to the shore."*

Into the business-like Cockney voice of Johnson's skipper there had appeared a vein of real feeling. "That's the joker in the pack.

If you're a summer sailor you won't have struck it, because there ain't this difference between the low pressure in the Adriatic here and the high pressure zones away up there to the north-east behind the mountains. Everywhere in Yugoslavia, I don't have to tell you. The Bora's a wind, Miss. It blows in the winter and the spring, and it's caused by the cold air from the high ground spilling down into the sea through the mountain passes. There's no warning and when it comes, it comes like a bloody dam bursting, driving anything in its way to the south and the west. That's why there are wind socks on the cliff roads.

"If you're at sea, and you ever think a Bora's on the way, get into harbor and tie up. If there isn't a harbor, get under the land on a north shore and throw out cables . . . I'm going to get you and Mr. Donovan some supper now. Is there anything more you want to ask me?"

There was nothing more that mattered. We got under way soon after that, following in the *Glycera's* track just as far as the roadstead to the east of Dubrovnik where we were to drop anchor. I remember being mildly irritated, sitting down to table, to find Donovan deep in a Mickey Mouse comic, with a stack of others beside him. It wasn't till I saw some thumbed copies of the *Politika* beside them that the penny dropped. I said "Hey: you speak Serbo-Croat?"

I will say one thing for Denny Donovan: nothing except perhaps a bad case of leaf thrip ever disturbed him. He looked up from his comic. "Sure I do. So do you."

He shoved the pile over and I picked up Donald Duck and, it appeared, Tarzan. He was quite right. I could speak Serbo-Croat. So also could Grover. *"Ahhhh!"* I read slowly aloud. *"Buum-Buum! Jeek! Bu-hu!"* and *"Super Ideja!"*

"There's a hard one. *Krokidili!!!!*" I said to Donovan. "O.K. Explain away the newspapers."

"I don't have to. Lenny's just going to chuck them overboard," said Donovan annoyingly. "Two weeks' brain-flying tuition in Serbo-Croat, I would have you know, lies behind that innocent bunch of papers. Mr. Johnson's orders. All the time you've been ashore, Lenny and I have been working our asses off."

*"Super Ideja,"* I said, but I was impressed. "What about Johnson? Is he learning it too?"

"Didn't ask him," said Donovan. "It's a great language for swearing in. Hungarian's supposed to be even better but I'm sure as hell not going to any sweat to prove it. Sit down and have some Niksicko Pivo. The beer's not bad, at that."

His arm, I noticed, was giving him remarkably little trouble. I didn't follow it up. I did get the length of saying, "Denny. D'you remember what I had in my pockets in Winnipeg?" and see him look surprised, as Johnson had done. Then Johnson's skipper came in with coffee and said, "Not to interrupt, but I'm just going to throw the switch for the microphones. Just to remind you, miss. Everything you say from now on will be listened to by our own friends on shore. And there's always the risk that someone'll pick it up that's not meant to."

All according to plan. But now it was real, it wasn't so easy. I remember sitting voiceless for a moment, until Donovan weighed in with some nonsense.

We finished a meal I hadn't done justice to. Three quarters of an hour out of Luka Gruz, *Dolly* arrived at her new anchorage and Donovan went up to help Lenny while I cleared the dishes into the galley and washed them. Then I climbed up on to the side deck and looked about me.

It was dark and raining, in gusty showers fetched by a light and irregular wind; but all the lamps of Dubrovnik lay on our port side, while ahead the coast ran east and south in a string of clustering lights outlining the new resorts with their hotels and night clubs and restaurants.

Above rose the dark hills, with the beam of car headlights appearing and vanishing from the Adriatic highway slashed across them, and a starry nexus here and there to show where the villages lay. Looking at Dubrovnik below, afloat on her soft floodlit walls, graceful as the MS *Glycera* in the natural element of her waterway, you could see again the rich city-state full of palaces through which once flowed all the wealth of the East: the harbor in which thirty-five ships of the Spanish Armada had been built and fitted out to sail against England. A beautiful and alien city.

To the south was only blackness and wind. The *Glycera*, moving at twenty knots, was making for the Gulf of Kotor less than two hours away: sheltered waters where all the precious and pampered guests of Ingmar Warr Beckenstaff could dine and dance and listen to cabaret, could get drunk and fall in love and sleep with one another, could make deals and gamble and make and lose interesting social contacts, and face, and fortune. Could arrange, while doing so, for other people to hold a young baby to ransom, to cover the fact that my father was about to be blackmailed. And that I was going to be forced to decode for some murdering bastards a photographed document with the preposterous name of the Malted Milk Folio.

Denny Donovan said, "They've got some great date palms. I once grew a date palm in a plant pot. You know the cute thing about date palms?"

"The boys need the girls," I said. "It's a neat idea, and I bet it catches on. Where's the second anchor?"

"There, miss," said Lenny Milligan. "Everything in order for a quiet night. There's whisky in the cupboard, sir, and if you want me, I'll be in the cockpit or else the fo'c'sle." A smell of orange blossom poured into the boat and out again as we went below, followed by another spatter of rain, and all the rigging shook. Nodding, *Dolly* began a fresh meandering swing round her anchor.

Ben was asleep. I sat down again in Johnson's comfortable saloon and watched Donovan root for a pack of cards and the whisky bottles. "Or," he said turning round, "you might prefer the vintage champagne. What do you suppose they're doing on the *Glycera* now?"

"Oh," I said. "Pickin' and strummin' and clappin' and stompin'. And hunting out their stick-on seasick pills, if they're watching the barometer."

"I ain't afraid to say when I'm jealous," said Donovan equably. He handed me a large whisky and began dealing out cards. "I tell ya. I wouldn't mind waking up tomorrow morning with a hangover and a pair of Schlumberger cufflinks. You know who's doing the cabaret?"

"I don't suppose it's the Moofy Puppets," I said. "Who would you like to be sitting next to if you weren't playing gin rummy with me?"

"Any broad on that boat with an average unearned annual income of over three hundred thousand dollars who can't play gin rummy," said Donovan in an offended voice. "Hell, how much a point did I say we were playing for?"

"I've got it all noted down here," I said; "You owe me five dollars. My deal."

I'd milked him of seventeen dollars fifty when the bleep of Johnson's special radar could be heard changing in tone and the cockpit door opened to display Milligan's hand with a liquid rub-across message pad in it. The writing said, "Launch coming towards us from the harbor," I said, "What about another whisky?" to Donovan.

He had an excuse, then, to be on his feet and glancing out of the porthole. A moment later he didn't need an excuse, because the sound of several voices hailing the *Dolly* came quite clearly over the hum and twang and slosh of the wind and the water. Donovan said, "Anyone know twelve boys and girls in a big yellow launch out of Dubrovnik? They're all making this way and yelling fit to bust. Joanna?"

I went and stood beside him. The rain had stopped and the wind risen a little. It looked, out there, a good bit colder. The launch's own light and the glow from the *Dolly* lit the distant faces, and the white bow-water shot into the darkness. "Wait a minute. That's the doctor I met at the Radoslav Clinic. Lazar Dogíc," I said. "Good lord. He asked me to go to his birthday party. It looks as if he's come to collect me."

It was Lazar Dogíc: no longer in the white jacket in which he had given Beverley Eisenkopp her injection, or the polo neck in which he had taken plum brandy in the City Café with Johnson and the rest of us. Instead he looked extremely handsome, not to say romantic, in a loose white belted tunic with embroidered collar and cuffs and enormous wind-bellied sleeves, each of which was wrapped round a shrieking pinafored girl with the giggles. The water, cut up by the wind, was making the launch pitch and shudder and the rest of his friends, squeezed in behind, were also squealing. As I made for the deck, Donovan following, I could hear Lenny yelling at them to cut down the throttle.

His voice, caught by the wind, had no chance of reaching them, and in any case I much doubted if there was a man there sober enough to obey. The launch, its engine roaring, continued to come straight towards us, while Donovan semaphored with his long arms and Lenny Milligan, with the resignation of long years in Saturday anchorages, ran and threw over fenders, and I stood at the rails and used wildly, over and over, the universal cross and swing of the arms that means *No dice: skip it.*

They saw me all right. I could hear the groans over the water: sorrow blending into resistance merging into persuasion: all without the slightest slackening of speed. I thought they were going to ram us full astern; but at the last moment someone sobered, or someone lost their nerve. There was a sharp blow aft, followed by an alteration in the note of the launch's engine. Then the launch bounced past our port quarter, banged Lenny's fenders, headed out and then shot erratically back, to be met by the ends of two boathooks and Lenny Milligan's mahogany face.

Hungarian might be the best language for swearing in, but Johnson's skipper was making a brave try with English. Faced with two angry men and a demonstration of unmistakable abuse, the shouts of the birthday party diminished. The engine cut down to a purr and the launch rocked, idling just within the range of *Dolly*'s lights while Dr. Dogić, carefully disentangling himself from each of the girls, climbed up on a thwart and addressed us.

"Miss Joanna! We invite you and your friends to my Saint's Day. You are in Yugoslavia, and we do not think it polite to refuse. For any damage to Mr. Johnson's beautiful ship, of course we shall pay."

He then ruined the whole effect by breaking down into giggles: there was a chorus of remarks and a shout of laughter from behind him and the boat lurched, throwing him into a number of eager laps. Lenny said, "They're going to have that bloody launch over. Look at that."

What he was looking at were the two broad patches of peeled paint and bruised wood in the starboard bow of the speedboat where she had hit the *Dolly*. I just had time to wonder how serious the damage was and what harm the *Dolly* had suffered when the launch rocked still further under the shrieking, giggling crowd and dipping, must have shipped water.

Or it might have been a leak. It was enough, at any rate, to induce one of the birthday party to shriek, hanging over the side, that the launch was stoved in and sinking. And for the rest of the birthday party to crush over to see, and by tilting the boat, to propel two of their number with a splash and a shriek into the dark Adriatic.

You could have heard the screaming this time in Split. Man overboard. Nothing more urgent; no greater priority; no emergency, save only fire, more arresting in its demand for quick action.

*Don't trust the doctor.*

Perhaps not, but that boatload of drunken youngsters couldn't all be his accomplices.

*Don't trust the doctor.*

Lenny and Donovan were throwing lifebelts. The launch had righted. If they kept their heads, the swimmers would be picked up in five minutes. No one had asked to come aboard. So what was the point of the exercise?

No one was looking at me. Retreating softly, I sat on the coach roof. Beside me, upturned, was Johnson's old dinghy, offering cover and shade. Drawing up my legs I lay flat on the roof and then very quietly slid forward, with the bulk of the rowing boat between me and everyone else. To my left was the dark open sea and the shining side deck of the *Dolly*, lit by the uncurtained windows of the saloon. And as I looked, across the nearest yellow lit square slid first one dark shadow, then a second.

We had visitors. Don't trust the doctor indeed. We should have no fear of the launch. The launch was merely a diversion. While all our attention was to the port, the starboard side had acquired a neat rope ladder and a lashing, to which was attached, floating quietly below, a small and powerful speedboat with just enough room, one would judge, for four men, and a girl and a baby.

The second anchor was just where Lenny had placed it, but it seemed a pity to alarm anyone unnecessarily, and the rope ladder was nicely placed out of sight of the windows. I took off my shoes and slipped down it into the speedboat and with some regret, opened the sea cock. Then I came up and untied its painter. After that, keeping well clear of the windows, I put my shoes on and returned to my colleagues.

The two swimmers had been fished up and there was a short argument going on about whether or not they could come aboard to dry themselves. Noticeably, when Lenny refused, no effort was made to pursue the point. I remember remonstrating with him for the sake of appearances and because suddenly it seemed ridiculous that one couldn't bring two soaked and shivering people into the warmth and comfort of *Dolly*.

But that would ruin the plan. And on the success of the plan depended much more than the comfort of two over-hilarious party-goers. I got Lenny's message pad and wrote on it "Visitors below. Sunk their boat"; showed it to both men and then obliterated it.

In between we all went on calling and gesticulating. The launch came up near for the last time and slung aboard our lifebelts, bumping the stern again as she did so. Then, like a guilty child, she scuttled off to calls of "Oprostite!" and we could see the glint of the bottle repassing. Before they got halfway to the harbor they were all singing. A Eurovision song I had seen called "Look Woot You Dun," to be accurate.

Donovan said, "The rain's coming on again. Who's for a last drink? Come on, Lenny: you deserve one. You can inspect the damage later."

"Well sir, thank you sir. I wouldn't say no," Lenny said. "Although I must go round with a lamp right after. She's not taking water but she had a couple of nasty shunts. You'd think they'd never been in a bloody boat before, begging your pardon."

"They were tight," I said. I led the way down to the cockpit. It was empty. "And I can't help feeling it's all my fault. What on earth will Johnson say?"

I opened the saloon door and went down the steps. It was empty, too.

"I can't imagine," Lenny said. "But we've had worse before. She's not a pretty lady just for show, is the *Dolly*. She can take knocks if she has to." He shut the door on the wind and the rain, and came in doffing his cap, while Donovan opened the door of Johnson's bar and began taking out glasses. The gin rummy cards lay on the table where we'd left them, with my winnings.

The owners of the speedboat were almost as well-rehearsed as we were. Two of them must have been in the master stateroom and two in the forward passage between Donovan's room and the galley. Donovan had just removed the whisky when both doors to the saloon quietly opened.

Framed in each were two masked men, with cocked guns.

I screamed. In the forward stateroom Benedict suddenly wailed. One of the two men between his door and mine began speaking in distorted English, as if reciting by rote. "Put your hands up and stand still. We are taking the baby to ransom. The girl comes also to care for him. We wish no harm, only money." His mask, like that of the others, was only a black nylon stocking, inside which one could make nothing of his squeezed and distorted features.

"What is this? How the hell did you come on board?" said Donovan loudly, and without pausing, made a lunge for his jacket pocket.

They didn't shoot him. The leader just swung his gun and clipped the side of his head; and despite his nice thick hair, which must have cushioned the blow quite a bit, Donovan went staggering into the mast and subsided with a crash on the saloon floor where someone, kneeling, began to tie his hands and feet together with great professionalism. "Anyone else," said the leader, "want to try anything?"

"The child's too young," I said. "You won't get your money. I can't look after a baby as young as this away from all the things he's used to. You can't expect me to."

No one answered me. One of the two men from the stateroom had put a gun in Lenny's back, and the other was preparing to tie him up also. They were all big men, and dressed alike in dark sweaters and trousers, with heavy jackets and sneakers. They smelt foreign and reminded me of none of the men we had met so far in the kidnap game: I thought it a pretty safe guess that they were all natives. Except perhaps the leader, the only one who had spoken, whose English was good, although stilted.

I said again, "You can't take him. He's too young. He can't stand it."

The mask moved to some change of expression. "Why," said the leader, "we've been waiting for him to grow. Pack. Take what food and bottles you have. Trifun will help you. The child will not starve. Unless no one will pay for him."

I packed. Trifun helped me by standing masked at the door, playing with his revolver. I was still there when a spate of low, angry voices on deck told that someone was receiving, with disbelief, the tale of the vanished speedboat.

A moment later, the leader came into the cabin. "You. Where is the speed launch this yacht usually carries?"

My hands were shaking and I didn't bother to hide it. I said, "In the boatyard somewhere, I think. There was something wrong with it."

"Then there is an outboard motor?" said the mask.

I straightened again from my packing. "I don't know. Ask Mr. Milligan."

He walked away without answering, and when I struggled out shortly with my cases, I saw the reason. Both Johnson's skipper and Donovan had been manhandled up from the floor and each was now lying apparently sleeping on opposite benches. On the table between them was a syringe.

I dropped the cases and said, "What have you done to them?"

In the cabin behind me Benedict, awakened again, started crying. The mask tilted, listening. The voice behind it, irritated, said, "They will sleep for twelve hours, that is all."

Somewhere on deck a voice shouted, "Zorzi?" and added a number of words in Serbo-Croat which Donovan, if conscious, could no doubt have translated with ease.

The leader, it appeared, was Zorzi. He shouted something back, and then turned again to me. "Take the child into the big cabin. Mihovil will be with you, with his gun. We sail."

The mask told me nothing. "Where?" I said. And when he didn't answer, "But the baby—"

He cut me off. "The baby is nothing. You know it."

He turned away, leaving me standing. The baby is nothing. Vindication at last, after all these ambiguous weeks, of what the Department had said, and my father and Johnson. The baby is nothing. It is you, Joanna, they are after.

All that Johnson had planned was coming to pass. With no boat, they were trapped on the yacht. To go anywhere, they must use *Dolly*, conspicuous *Dolly* with all her cunning microphones. Except that these four men didn't look much like seamen. And if they were not, they must be at least as anxious as I was. For Lenny and Donovan, who might have sailed *Dolly*, had been stupidly put out of action.

Mihovil was the third masked kidnapper, and one of the obvious land-lubbers. While the other three tramped back and forth over our heads Mihovil sat with his gun in my back in the master bedroom. He showed no interest when I lifted Ben up for some orange juice and no relief when, the crying stopped, I finally tucked him up in his carrycot again. I didn't say anything either because I was listening.

But despite the temptation, no one tried to send for a launch through the R/T.

Radio telephone calls could be traced. Instead of a launch, Zorzi and his friends were going to have to sail fifty-four tons of gaff-rigged ketch to our destination and return before daylight. And it must be at least ten o'clock, maybe later.

Dinner on the *Glycera* would be over, but the night's program hardly begun. I wondered, if we were sailing south, how soon we would begin to bump into champagne bottles. I had another thought and turned to my taciturn friend with the gun. "I've just remembered. We were badly bumped by another boat. If your friend Zorzi is going to sail, he ought to check out the damage."

The only answer I got was a wave of the gun and a grunted word or two in Serbo-Croat. Mihovil didn't speak English. Then the boat suddenly drummed to the sound of the engine, followed almost at once by the grind of the anchor cable being wound up. I thought of all the receivers tuned in along the coast through which our voices were speaking, and I looked down at the sleeping face of Benedict, and I thought of my father. Then I saw the lights of the coast rocking past the porthole and knew that we were travelling south, in the wake of the *Glycera*, over a short, steep sea with a strengthening wind over our port quarter. We pitched suddenly and Mihovil swallowed. I raised my voice and shouted, "Zorzi!"

He came at once, the grotesque flattened face lodged in the doorway. I said, "Your friend here is going to be sick. And I need to lash the baby, too, if it's going to be rough. Do I really have to have a gun in my back? There are four of you. And surely I can't do much harm now we're sailing."

I finished up in the cockpit, with Ben lashed safely once more in our own forward stateroom. Also Petar, the fourth man, had been dispatched to look for damage with a hand torch. He returned with news of some surface splintering and little else. From the look of him, he had been in no trim for a vigorous examination, even had there been decent light, but Zorzi had a torch beam thrown into the bilges, and it was quite plain that we were tight and dry so far. The noise of the wind in the rigging jumped another tone or two, dropped and rose again, and with an imprecation, Zorzi changed hands on the tiller and as I watched him, peeled off his mask. Then, leaning forward, he switched on the chart light and pulled the chart towards him.

His face, despite the stubble of beard, looked the thick, dark texture of the peasant's but carried lines that hinted at city articulacy. An educated man, a professional perhaps, with the city man's superficial experience of pleasure craft. He could have run a launch successfully in to its landing-place, but instead he was sailing the Adriatic with *Dolly*, standing off from the shore to avoid the resorts with their bright, busy lighting.

The wind whined. I said, "I suppose I'm going to meet your chief anyway, wherever we're going. Are you allowed to tell me who he is?"

He didn't reply that time either. I told myself it was better than over-friendliness, the other thing I'd been afraid of. I found it hard to convince myself.

A spatter of rain hit the deck and then, like a pail of cold water, a sudden sharp wind that cut through my green English serge and sent *Dolly* heeling to starboard, so that I fell headlong against Zorzi.

From the impatient violence with which he thrust me out of his way, I might have been a shelfful of books. He was swearing, his fists cramped on the wheel and his eyes lifted up to the rigging. It had been a powerful squall, to catch our bare poles so sharply. And from the north-east, as the others had been. I said, "Zorzi. Do you know what to do in a Bora?"

As before, he made no reply. But I knew by his face that he didn't.

# Chapter 15

The thunder began at eleven.

There being nothing in the Margaret Beaseford College rules about wearing your uniform when caring for your employer's kidnapped child or children, I had changed into pants and sneakers and sweater, with a thick quilted jacket on top. Mihovil, who was occupying Donovan's bunk with a basin, was uninterested in my activities. Then back in the cockpit with Zorzi and Petar and Trifun I heard above the noise of the big Mercedes-Benz engine an explosion of sound which seemed to come out of the sky all about us. A moment later there was another loud crack, and then the peaks to our left were outlined twice in a blue sudden glimmer which might have been a major explosion, but was more likely, I thought, to be lightning. A rolling peal and then another proved me right. Thunder. Another of the first signs of the Bora.

By that time I knew exactly where we were, although not yet where we were heading for. I had learned my lesson well, from the books Johnson had supplied me with. I had watched the Rat Porporela diminish on the southern mole of Dubrovnik and the breakwater light open up from Mlini in the bay of Zupski to the south with Strebeno beside it. Then the village of Plat, and the lights marking the shoals and harbor at Cavtat. The current here was strongly to the north-west and the resulting jopple against the increasing gusts of north wind had been the coping stone of Mihovil's misery. Petar, I guessed from his face, was beginning to suffer the same sort of uneasiness. Zorzi at the wheel and Trifun his lieutenant appeared so far quite unaffected. They had all, by now, taken off their stocking masks and the three other faces, quite unremarkable, were as unknown and unrevealing as that of Zorzi.

We heard the thunder first just south of Cavtat, and as we pitched southward steadily in the dark I sat with my eyes on the land, watching for each flash of lightning. That way I saw the church at the airport, and then the aircraft light south of Rat Veliki Pač and a long time later, far ahead, the peninsula of Molunat, with its lights.

Beyond that, unseen as yet, was Ostri Rat, the western entrance point of the Gulf of Kotorska. If we left Dubrovnik at ten, we would reach it somewhere round one in the morning. If, that is to say, my kidnappers intended to sail so far south.

On the other hand the further south, the safer they would be. All the signs were that Johnson had been right. The original plan had involved nothing more than taking Ben and myself to some quiet stretch of shore near Dubrovnik, whence a car would have driven us swiftly up the winding mountain passes to some obscure hovel. With all the wild Montenegrin mountains to choose from, to hide us would be simple.

But the roads were barred because of the smallpox. Wherever they moved, they would be stopped and looked at and questioned, and commanded to deliver their papers. Their only hope now was to make their journey by sea, and to contrive a landing as near as possible to the fresh place they had chosen to hide us. And by the time they needed to move out, the emergency might well be over.

From time to time Zorzi or the others exchanged a few words but I didn't talk, nor did I give away, yet, that I knew where we were. They were edgy, and inimical. I didn't want to be drugged or silenced or blindfolded before I had a chance to speak aloud the name of the place we would stop at, for all those hidden microphones to pick up. Soon after that, Ben woke again, fretful with oversleeping, and minus a bottle. Zorzi gave me leave to go below and warm up a feed for the baby.

This time Trifun came with his gun and watched me and after a bit played with his foot against mine. I put up with it. I was going to be in his power for an indefinite time, and only a fool would arouse his resentment. With Zorzi above, he was unlikely to go further.

In fact it helped because Ben, unhappy with his new surroundings and my joggling lap, turned the feed into a marathon, with the yacht's motion increasing every minute. Eventually it was Trifun who got up hastily and bolting open the door, sat and guarded me from a bench in the cockpit.

With Ben bringing up wind on my shoulder, I watched the lights through the porthole. Ostri Rat, and we were veering east and north. We were going into the Boka Kotorska.

The Gulf of Kotorska, twenty nautical miles from end to end, consists of three enclosed basins connected by narrows, the whole being set among mountains. At the top of the range there is snow, and at the foot, palms, dates, vines, and every kind of sub-tropical foliage grow by the water.

The finest fjord scenery outside of Norway. The deepwater gulf which could hold in safety the whole of a large Mediterranean fleet. The perfect site for Peter the Great's naval academy. The indented wandering coast where still remain the crumbling relics of Rome and of Venice; the mosaic floors, the pillars, the palaces. And above all, the towering mountains, between which pours down the cold winter air from the eastern plateaux, driving faster and faster until, whirling down into the water, it strikes the small boats who unwisely or for their own good reasons have not fled to tie up in harbor.

And I dared not suggest that we ought to put into harbor, or turn aside, or take any action which would jeopardize my captors' safe landfall in darkness at their chosen rendezvous. Because for my father's purposes the kidnapping had to proceed without hindrance.

Only I wished that Lenny Milligan and Donovan had been conscious, to help and advise. What was more, I suspected that my captors rather wished it as well.

They had apparently reached the conclusion that I wasn't dangerous. Having lashed Ben's carrycot afresh to the sole in my stateroom, I aroused no protest when I crossed to the galley and washed up Ben's litter and stowed it. In the next cabin Mihovil was now snoring; and an empty bottle laid at his side explained why the bar doors were banging. There were books and cushions on the saloon floor as well and Donovan, sleeping still, had shifted nearer the edge of his bunk-seat.

I finished my business quickly in the galley and then moving about as best I could with the increasing motion, I began to stow gear, and to close and snib all the cupboards and drawers. I left Mihovil alone but found some rope in the fo'c'sle with which to moor the two drugged men to their benches. Then I checked the hatches and portholes and, last of all, found and pulled out all the life jackets and harness I could find, as well as a couple of ship's jackets from the hanging locker.

By then the whole cabin was heaving, and I was sore with being banged about, and weary, and frightened. Up in the cockpit, the two men with Zorzi appeared to be having some sort of argument: it ended with Zorzi's voice speaking sharply in Serbo-Croat: so sharply that the other voices were silenced. He kicked the door and it swung open, revealing his legs in long rubber boots as he sat with both fists on the wheel. A blast of cold air swept into the saloon and the freshness of it confused me.

It took a moment to pin down the reason. The air below decks on *Dolly* smelt different.

It was two in the morning, and I had just flown the Atlantic and lived through a long, tiring and difficult day, or surely I would have diagnosed it before Zorzi did, leaning down from the cockpit and sniffing. As it was, his raised voice told me nothing. I had to draw a long breath as he had, and then another. Then there was no doubt at all. A distinct and increasing aroma of diesel oil, permeating all the air and rising with fair certainty from the bilges.

I said, "We have a leak," in the same second that Zorzi, his gaze on the instrument panel, emitted a string of undoubted obscenities. There followed the clamoring speech of the other two, cut off by another sharp order. The lined face of Petar appeared and they pressed back as he knelt in the cockpit, in process of uncovering the engine.

Zorzi turned the wheel. Coming round to the wind, the yacht sagged and lurched. On the floor Petar coughed, and then rising, lunged for the lee rail. Then *Dolly* was round, pitching and rolling, and Zorzi cut the engine and picking up Johnson's big torch, directed it to where Trifun knelt in Petar's place, uncovering first the engine, and then the fuel tanks.

Then he began replacing hatches and floorboards and I said, "Well?" with my hand on the steps.

Zorzi favored me with a glance. "The deck tube has been fractured at the joint, and possibly the tank itself as well. There is a great deal in the bilges. The tank is almost empty."

I said, "I don't see how you can go through the Boka Kotorska under sail in this weather. Where are you making for?"

There was no point now in secrecy. Petar was vomiting still over the side and Trifun's face, cramped in the well of the cockpit in the reek of the oil, was sweating and pasty. Zorzi said, "You and the child are to spend the night on Gospa od škrpjela, an island off Perast. There."

He threw the chart down and pointed, and I swallowed too. The innermost basin of the Boka Kotorska is shaped like a butterfly on a pin, the pin being the narrows leading into it. And in the center of the basin is a shoal with the twin islands of Sveti Djorje and Gospa od škrpjela. Each had a church, I seemed to remember. And each, otherwise, was uninhabited.

I probably knew more than any of them about the narrows which led to that basin. They were named Tjesnac Verige, after the chain which, legend says, once stretched across them. Legend is probably true: at its narrowest point, the channel is only one and a half cables wide. And there is over a mile of it to navigate, facing directly north-east all the way.

I had said to Zorzi what anyone with sailing experience would have said. Under sail, it couldn't be done. And yet he had no real alternative. With the use of the engine, we might have got through the narrows and arrived at the island between three and four in the morning, with an hour to spare before it became light enough for the yacht to be noticed in the vicinity.

Long before the narrows, the supply of fuel would have run out; and we should be on a lee shore under sail with all the signs of a major storm brewing. To find shelter and wait out the storm was the sensible course. But there was not enough of the night left to do it in. I said, "You are risking your lives and the ransom."

He lifted the map, watching me. "You are not seasick, I see."

I said, "I used to sail with my father."

"In the Mediterranean?"

"We kept a small boat at Malta." It was true. And it explained how I recognized the Boka Kotorska. Or so I hoped.

Zorzi said, "As you see, my men are not mariners. You know how to sail?"

I said, "I know enough to tell you that you won't get through the narrows."

"I didn't ask your opinion," he said. "I will show you where we are to go, and you will tell them how to get the sails up. After you have made some food. Can you feed men, or only make messes for babies?"

"I can sail," I said, "or I can cook. I shall put some soup in a pan and you can order one of your puking friends to go below and watch it. He might try and sober up your other friend at the same time. We're going to need all the help we can get."

The hard, dark eyes stared at mine. "I do not recommend," said Zorzi, "that you speak to my men as if they are children. They might forget themselves . . . And what are you proposing to do?"

"See if there are any storm sails," I said. "Get up a sea anchor, if there is one. Cover the hatches with canvas. Put on a life jacket and harness, and see that you do the same."

"So now you care for our health?" he said.

"Only because I can't steer and look after sail on my own," I retorted. While I was speaking he had switched on the engine and turned *Dolly* back on her course again. The waves were big, but he knew enough to luff into them. I pursued it. "We ought to keep some fuel for emergencies. How much do we have?"

His teeth flashed briefly under the coarse, swollen nose. "The gauge shows empty. If you wish to save fuel, I recommend you raise sail without wasting more time. Trifun will heat soup. Petar will look for the storm sail." He grabbed for the chart as the deck tilted and then righted itself to another squall. We were all shouting.

I looked below, as I flung on my life jacket, at the bright, orderly, expensive interior of *Dolly* where a short time before Donovan and I had been sitting, whisky in hand, peacefully playing gin rummy. Where before that Johnson had been entertaining the Booker-Readmans. Where long before that Johnson had been living himself, with his own chosen company in other days, in other waters. Below the fear and the weariness I was aware of a dull kind of fury that I should be the one to foul up the *Dolly* with strangers, and bring to her boards nothing but violence and inferior seamanship.

Even Trifun was frightened. I got up on deck and shouted at him, and that made me feel better until under my feet I heard Benedict's awakened wail and remembered.

I don't know why I wanted to be a nurse. I don't want to be a nurse any more.

I've said that *Dolly* was beautiful, and that was immediately evident both in her profile and in her creature comforts. She was also beautiful in another sense, of which the closest parallel was the smooth-running orderliness of Johnson Johnson's painting arrangements.

In a white canvas bag clearly marked there was a storm jib and trysail, and next to it an excellent drogue. The trysail was already bent to its own pinewood gaff, with its sheets shackled on; and it was colored a soft Venetian red, and had been boiled with linseed and beeswax to keep it supple and light in the wet. The storm jib, its sheets ready bent on to it, was dressed in the same way with a wire span spliced to the head cringle to stop the sag between the head of the sail and the purchase block. I got them on deck and with Trifun with a lamp beside me, began issuing orders.

With Mihovil senseless below and Zorzi at the wheel holding the yacht hove-to, facing the wind and the sea, there were only three of us; and Petar didn't have English. In the dark and the wind and the violent pitching and rolling of the idling yacht I had to get the sail out of the bag without allowing it to catch the wind, and bend the peak and throat halyard blocks on to the strops on the trysail gaff, ready to hoist.

The luff of a sail of this kind is made to hold and run up the mast by being sewn at intervals with bracelets of ash parrel balls which have to be clipped round the mast one by one as you are hoisting. The sheets are double, and work through two blocks at the clew. From there, they run to a single block which is shackled to the mainsheet bolts.

Trifun didn't know what a mainsheet bolt was, or where to look for it. Petar, his arms embracing the boom, had to be shouted at by Zorzi before he would kneel on the slanting deck and fumble with luff toggles. If the mainsail had been up instead of stowed neatly round the boom, we could never have done it. The jib I bent on myself.

I had both sails sheeted in and was back in the cockpit, explaining to Trifun, when Zorzi started the engine again, turning the wheel at the same time to point *Dolly*'s bows across the heaving black expanse of the first of Kotorska's three basins.

Above the crash and slap of the waves, above the whining snarl of the wind there came only a coughing sound, quickly guttering to a halt. Zorzi tried again, and then a third time. No response. Water, perhaps in the exhaust. More likely the fuel was done. In either case, the engine was finished. Cut our losses.

I looked at the chart and the compass. "Bring the wheel round and keep the needle there. You see. If the wind stays steady, we can cross the basin and get through the first set of narrows without tacking. What about hazards? What depths do you have?"

"Read it!" he said, and pushed the Pilot at me, shouting angrily above the wind to the other two as he turned the wheel. I read it, lying beside me in the light of Trifun's torch while I sheeted in and waited for the moment to cast off the lee runner. Then our bows were pointing across the first of the three basins with the wind on our port beam, and we were moving, faster and faster. I settled down and began to explain, slowly and clearly, what the ropes were for and what had to be done with them. Then I made them all put on their life jackets and harness, and took the wheel, my own body-rope tied to a cleat, while Zorzi went below to change also.

Across the bay, nudged and blackened by all the intervening waves, lay the brilliant bouquet of lights that was Herceg-Novi. With a good pair of binoculars I could have picked out the hotel where Bunty lay fast asleep, with Grover and Sukey. A car headlight showed, on the winding road which edged all three waterways, and lights from a street or a jetty where the villages were. The fishing boats you might expect, lantern at prow, were quite absent. Those who made their livelihood from the sea knew when the sea was at its most dangerous.

When Zorzi came back I said, "It would be best if I have the helm. Do you agree?"

I thought perhaps that pride would stop him, but he consented: Long before I could steer for harbor, they could remove me. And my life as well as theirs was in danger. I took the tiller, instead of the wheel, so that I could sit up, my feet on the cockpit bench, and see all around me. I had it for five minutes only. Then, the lines in the darkness ran white, and I knew the first squall of the Bora was coming.

Like a dam bursting, Lenny had said; and it was just that. All the lights blackened and there was a roaring which drowned my voice screaming at Petar. I saw him pull in the runners. Then, sheeting in with one hand, I turned *Dolly* into the Bora.

She was half round when the wind struck, throwing her back like a card as her bows began to climb the first wave. Behind the blast of buffeting sound I could hear the groaning of overstrained timber. For a moment she balanced there, shuddering. Then her bows came down, the body of creaming black water moved backwards under her keel and I paid off, easing the sheets, shouting to Trifun, and strained my eyes, as the water swirled round the cockpit and ran down my neck and streamed from my sodden hair, to see where the next one was coming.

There was another, and another a moment or so after that. I took them each on the shoulder, and *Dolly* righted herself every time with a stream of water inboard on the weather side. I reckoned the last was a 40 to 50 knot gust. Then it died, though the seas it put up were still coming on, of an average steepness.

One experience like that in a trip and you would say you had been lucky; it had chipped the barnacles off; and the story would gain in the telling. But we were more than an hour from the island, with another basin and the next set of narrows to get through, and the Bora was only beginning.

I set Trifun and Petar to pumping out oil and seawater. I told Zorzi I needed to know how the baby was faring. Also the state of my two friends. He listened, then without comment vanished below.

From his point of view, Benedict had to survive. Nor did he want any damage to Lenny and Donovan which would invite police attention. I doubted if my lashings would stand up to another roll such as that. Of all of us, short of stoving in or capsizing, Ben was probably safest, but I wanted to be reassured about that. In a while Zorzi came back and grunted, which was all the reassurance I got. I took it that Mihovil was still senseless.

Between fright and seasickness, Petar was becoming less of an asset as well. After Trifun had been pumping alone for a while, Zorzi joined him and after some words between them, Trifun went below and I heard pans rattling in the galley. Someone had suggested soup, it seemed a long time ago. You needed something on a bad night or your efficiency dropped, with the cold and your spirits.

I shut the door into the saloon with my foot. Absolute darkness was imperative. The danger of the Bora squalls lay in their suddenness. Next time the wind would be stronger, the wave would be higher. And if I didn't see it in time we would broach, and fill and roll over. I had a hard weather helm and I held it with both my hands, my feet braced on the opposite locker, and kept my raw stinging eyes on the blustering dark to the north.

We did eleven knots, in uneven gusts, into the second basin, and Trifun put a hand on the helm while I drank my mug of hot soup. I think it surprised him how heavy it was. Perhaps he thought you don't have to be strong to handle seven pound babies. Most people think just that, who haven't lifted a pregnant mother, or an eleven- or thirteen-year-old spastic. It's partly a knack. It also develops fairly strong muscles.

When I'd finished the soup I took the helm back again. I had explained once more, as simply as I could, about the stresses on the sails and the rigging, and the various ways of easing the strain on the ship: of meeting the waves so that they did the least harm, using the sails to give her way so that she would answer the helm.

Elementary seamanship, including even a lesson in tacking. The booms, thank God, were on their crutches and lashed. A flying boom in a storm can kill more than landlubbers. That was why the trysail was up; small and strong and loose-footed to give just enough power without catching so much wind that the yacht could blow over. I thought, from the way the helm answered, that with another crew I might have risked a scrap of canvas on the mizzenmast, but that was out of the question. We should have to do as we were.

Now we had sea room, which was a mixed blessing, for the waves could develop. The wind also was stronger. I brought *Dolly* up to it, and she answered like a fine lady, sliding over the kicking, seething force of the sea with her port rail throwing spray from the water. Beside me, Zorzi jammed his feet on the lee bench of the cockpit and Trifun lay huddled on the same bench, his back to the saloon bulkhead. I could hear Petar retching below.

Across the bay lay the lights of the naval dockyard at Tivat. If a naval frigate appeared at this moment, sailing alongside, she could perhaps winch us aloft: six men, a girl and a baby; and put a seaman aboard to bring *Dolly* safely to harbor. But there was no frigate sailing helpfully in the basin, and even if I disregarded the men, and the guns, and got to the radio telephone and summoned them, we should be across the basin and into the narrows before help could get to us.

And I should be dead, or disabled, and when the boat sank, no one would save Ben from drowning.

Then Zorzi said, *"White sea!"* and the second squall hit us.

# Chapter 16

I had expected with the bilges cleared that I could count on turning into the wind that much more quickly. It was easy to allow the helm to drag my hands down, but although the bows swung to the left, it was an irregular movement which lost its drive as the wind smacked us.

It punched the masts, the sails, the rigging and took away all the air I was breathing. I could see Trifun, in the dark, with one hand clutching the saloon roof and the other stretched to the sheets. Then the first wave was there, a little too much on the beam, with the breaking spray avalanching into the cockpit.

*Dolly* rose, and hesitated, and then slid down the trough: paying off as I pulled the helm towards me, and then scooping round as I eased her ready to climb up the next. My sight kept blearing with the water dashing into my face and my lashes and I shook my head, trying to clear it.

The safety of all of us depended on my night vision. On judging the shape and nearness of every wave, so that I could present *Dolly* with a slope she could climb in spite of the wind force. This squall was fifty knots, and the waves were between fifteen and twenty feet, trough to cap. I had seen a yacht laid back at the wrong moment by a gust. That time, the wave fell on her mast, and rolled her clean over.

For us, the next wave was less frightening, though water came racing down through each of the side decks and poured in waterfalls through the scuppers as we bore away, and we had lost steerage again. The wave after that was less steep and I didn't luff, but we took more water and the next time I did bring her nearer the wind. Above the deafening noise I could hear the slamming and creaking of the standing rigging over my head, and wished I knew the boat, and how far I could push her. We heeled down into another trough and there was a shattering crash, this time below decks and beside me.

It was, I thought, the saloon table, but there was no time to investigate: under our feet green water was hurling itself backwards and forwards. I shouted "Pump!" to Zorzi and saw him lay hands on it. Trifun still had charge of the sheets on the lee side. Petar had not come up.

The squall lasted ten minutes, and at the end my hands were quite numb and my back and shoulder muscles pulled raw and burning. But when I wiped my eyes and took my bearings, I found we were nearly abreast of the light at Bijela. We had driven across the whole of the basin. Between us and the island which was our destination lay only the Verige, a mile and a quarter of narrows.

I did wonder, while we had sea room, whether to do anything about the mizzen. Or whether to try the opposite: to take Trifun with me forward and try to hand the jib, leaving us better balanced with only the trysail. What decided me against either action was the interval we had had so far between squalls. We were now at the mouth of the narrows. Even in the darkest part of the night I could see the white water within. Squeezed in that long, confined neck the steep seas would push and jumble, forming no pattern; and we should have to tack to make any progress. We would be facing the teeth of the wind.

There were horrors enough in that prospect. But if a squall hit us, I had no idea whether I could pull us through it.

Best to go now, without thinking.

I gave Trifun the tiller and clipping myself to the rail, made one quick cast over the boat with my torch. Then I opened the saloon door and shone the beam inside.

The floor of Johnson's comfortable sitting place was heaped with broken wood and rolling and smashed chinaware: a door had come off one of the cupboards and the table, as I thought, had uprooted itself and lay half across Donovan's legs. He and Lenny were still unconscious, lashed to their benches. Lenny had a long bleeding scratch by one ear, caused probably by flying glass. There was no sign of Petar or Mihovil, but no sign either of any water on the elegant carpet. We seemed to be dry.

I was closing the door when the wind moderated enough to let me hear, from the forward stateroom, a baby's thin, frightened crying.

I could do nothing about it. I closed the saloon door in Zorzi's face as, hearing it also, he stopped pumping and made to go forward. I said, "He is frightened, not hurt. I need you here."

He stayed. I think I disliked him more at that moment than at any time up to that point. He cared nothing for Benedict, and had shown it. He only wished to protect his investment.

The sailing directions for the Tjesnac Verige said that the bottom was mud, and there were no dangers outside a distance of about fifty yards from either side. Whatever I did would be a gamble. But if we were caught by a squall, a push to the right or the left could send us hurtling on shore and wreck us. We had to sail up the middle, and because the wind was dead ahead, we had to do it in short zig-zags, by tacking.

I took my class of two through the procedures again, hoarsely shouting, as the Nedjalja and Opatovo lights opened up, one on either side of the channel. Then I pronounced the magic words *Ready about*, and put the helm slowly down, and as the sails whipped, pulled in my sheets and slackened the runner. On the other side, Trifun did the opposite with Zorzi watching him. I pitched him out of his seat and took his place, my feet braced again where I'd been sitting as *Dolly* veered over and tilted. Trifun, who had not been expecting it either, stumbled down the new slope and just stopped himself from hitting the lee locker with a spectacular crash. They fitted themselves, tight-fisted, into their new positions and swore at one another as they got in each other's way. Zorzi had lit a cigarette while he was below and it hung from his lips, the tip glowing red in the windy dark. The wind blew the smoke past my face and it smelt, rank as it was, of land and of comfort.

It also smelt of whisky. He had had a quick private nip, had our leader, in those few minutes below; but had made no effort to allow us to share it. More face-saving, perhaps. And the kind of leader who can't admit that he's scared is not the man I would choose to rely on.

A little while later I said *Ready about* again, and this time they were smarter in getting to their new positions, but the boat herself lingered for a fraction of a second in the eye of the wind. Then she came over and we settled on the new tack, but I could feel the sweat running down inside my soaked jersey.

Sailing close-hauled in a lumpy sea, there is always the danger that your boat will hang in stays, pointing into the wind without moving into one tack or the other, and so quite at the mercy of the weather. And with her ill-balanced sail, *Dolly* had been given a much harder task than she merited.

The helm kicked, and I straightened my shoulders and pulled against it while I watched and thought. The motion was fearful: I could see the pallor in the two men's faces by the swimming blue light of the compass: my own was probably even whiter. I had reached no conclusion when we reached the end of the short leg I allowed myself and, waiting for the fractional easing of wind that might help, I shouted again to go about.

I should perhaps have seen the heavy seas that were coming but I didn't, largely because they formed no regular pattern but approached simply as a mass of heaving black water. They threw *Dolly* off her course just as she was swinging and this time what I was afraid of had happened. Instead of veering she stayed pointing ahead, her keel crashing and slamming as the waves struck her.

There is a trick and I used it. If she couldn't come round by her bows, she would have to turn the other way. I put both hands round the helm and instead of easing it down brought it up. I slackened the trysail as she turned and went on turning, until her stern faced the wind and her trysail and jib flapped and shuddered and whipped. Then she was round and they filled, and we were on the new tack by courtesy of a jibe which she had suffered only because she was the lady she was. I drew a breath of relief and then a sharp explosion from above made me hold it. With my mind on the backstays and mast, it was a moment before I saw what it was. The jib halyard block had given way, freeing the top of the scarlet triangle to crouch and snap over the foredeck.

If I had been there, trying to hand the sail, I should have been swept overboard. As it was, it beat for a few moments longer and then, as the snap shackles gave way, freed itself from the sheets altogether. For a while it flew like a handkerchief, but with a strain like that, even the strongest cringle must rip. The last I saw of the storm jib was when it flew undulating into the white-surfing black upon black which was the shore. We were under trysail alone, and better for it. Then Trifun shouted *"Gospoda!"* and I looked, but it was too late.

The wind and sea came together, and the first wave was twenty-five feet high and almost on us when I saw it. We went through the edge like a corkscrew, the sail throwing water backwards and forwards and a solid weight of green sea crashing down on the saloon roof and side deck and pouring full-throated into the cockpit.

Zorzi and Trifun were both swept off their seats to the floor of the cockpit. I fared better, braced with the tiller. I could see nothing and hear nothing but the water pouring over my head and shoulders but I could feel the boat slide into the trough and her bows buck and tremble and falter in their swing round to the next wave and the wind.

The tiller was running with water but I gripped it and pulled the whole weight of the ship up towards me as the next wave appeared and grew bigger. The bows began to respond. I was shouting to Trifun to ease off the sheets when the wind, outracing the wave, pushed the *Dolly* as with the flat of a hand and held her, shuddering, as the thing towering over us grew and advanced.

It struck us on the starboard quarter so that the port rail went under and the two men huddled on the floor of the cockpit received the first over-spill, coughing and choking, from the lee side. Because I was more exposed on the weather side, the water took me this time with a force that nothing at all could resist. I was spooned from my seat and flung upwards and outwards over the near-vertical cockpit. The force, had I landed on the deck or the rail or the cabin roof, would have smashed my ribs and very likely my spine, but the violence was of a greater order even than that. It threw me clear of the boat altogether, and into the sea.

It seemed reasonable to suppose that was the end. Zorzi and Trifun had no reason to help me. Profit no longer mattered, only surviving. Then my head came above water and I found that I was still clipped on to my harness, and that my harness was still attached to the backstay, and that the toe rail of the boat was just under my nose. Against which, the piece of wood I was clutching with both hands was the broken tiller.

Trifun had already struggled up to the pump and Zorzi was bailing when I heaved myself on board and took the wheel, helping the yacht to come round into the wind as slowly she lifted her mast to the sky again. They glanced at me and then away again, that was all.

I waited for the mast to crack with the strain, but it didn't, although the gusts pushed and swung it and the seas threw the keel this way and that. Nor did another wave of like dimension fall upon us, although from moment to moment I was awaiting it. With no way on the boat, there was nothing I could have done to counter it. And the only reason I could see for its absence was the surfing line of the shore, and its configurations. Somewhere here there must be cross currents and eddies which had deformed the regular pattern. Two waves had been thrown up, which had all but capsized us. But there were no more.

Slowly, we realized it. As the water went down and the ship lightened, she began to answer again to the wheel and I had to take the next risk: to go about before the shore rocks could hole us. And to lay on sheets, stays and sail, a strain there was not all that much hope of their taking.

I had to shout this time before the men would listen to me, or even look for themselves to see how near the shore we now were. They wanted to lie in the yacht and be taken to safety. So did I. But there is no such thing in life as lying down and relying on someone else's goodwill, or strength, to get you out of a hole. I nagged them until they returned to their posts, the water still slapping about our ankles and pouring off through the scuppers as *Dolly* nudged through the jostling sea. Then I filled the sail and went about while she was running, and she swung round this time and landed foursquare on the opposite board, the trysail filling again. The rigging had held, and the mast, and the precious stormsail with its double sheets. Trifun said something in Serbo-Croat and after a moment, Zorzi threw it at me, in English. "The wind is dying."

The squall had ceased. The sea remained, something to reckon with even after both men had taken turns again at pumping and baling. We had to go about again very soon after that, and again, and again. But each time it became easier, and more automatic; the men knew what they had to do, the helm was lighter. It was just as well. I had no strength left now to call on, whatever the emergency.

We sailed out of the mouth of the Verige at four o'clock on Thursday morning.

The seas, joppling over the race, became easier as we turned to the north, over the broad lagoon which swept to left and to right of us. Ahead, the pin between the wings of the butterfly, lay two black patches, denser than the rest. The island of Sveti Djordje and the island of Gospa od škrpjela, on which Benedict and I were to be landed.

One had to hunt for them, because the eye was caught by something far beyond them, also lying on the water in the northeastern basin, about where stood the town of Risan. A floating palace of light, long and low and brilliant, with colored lamps swagged and flickering still in a geometric canopy over her. The *Glycera* in shelter, her portholes and windows ablaze, her beautiful people still celebrating the fiftieth year of the Warr Beckenstaff cosmetic empire.

I said to Zorzi, "You can sail her now," and left the wheel so that, after standing a moment, he had to move quickly to right it. I wondered as I turned for the saloon steps if he would pull me back, but he didn't. If he and Trifun couldn't manage her now, they were worse fools even than I thought them.

Below, the carpet was soaked and the door of the washroom had broken, showing Petar wedged within, his eyes shut, his breathing stertorous. The table had shifted off Donovan's legs and he lay as he had done all along, breathing quietly. Lenny also seemed quite unharmed. They were, one supposed, the lucky ones.

I didn't stay to examine any of them, only looked as I made my way over the rubble as quickly as the heaving of the boat would allow.

Mihovil lay on the floor beside Donovan's bunk among the glistening crumbs of the whisky bottle. He had been sick: not a pretty sight. But he was alive. Then I opened the door of the forward stateroom, behind which there was no sound at all.

Because I had snibbed and stowed away everything, nothing had fallen. And because Benedict's carrycot had been lashed by each of its handles, it stood still on the floor where I had placed it. And inside, lying half on the side and half on the bottom but enclosed still in his quilted coat with its neat, furry sleeping bag was Benedict asleep, his fine skin blubbered with crying. Across his cheek, thickening where it had bled a little, was a long scratch and a red bruise where he had been thrown against something, perhaps the side of the locker. But that was all. His breathing, almost inaudible, was just as it should be.

I wondered when he had been hurt, and hoped it was lately, during the squall at the narrows. It was the first time since I had come to care for him that he had been injured or frightened without someone to comfort him. It would have been a comfort for me to waken and lift him, but that would have been selfish. He was best where he was.

I watched him for quite some time, and then moving slowly got together again the things we should need, he and I, for our stay on the island, however long it was going to be. I did what I could, too, to make Lenny and Donovan a little more comfortable. The other two men I left alone. After a bit, I heard my name called and went out to find the island quite close. There was nothing on it really but a church. I could just make out a huddle of roofs, and a cupola, and a belfry. A man standing on the quayside was waving a lantern and shouting. After a moment he put it down and caught the rope Trifun threw him: I helped them winch *Dolly* in, and hung tenders over, and sheeted in. Then Zorzi and Trifun stepped ashore, and signed me to wait in the cockpit.

I must have closed my eyes, for the next thing I knew my cases were at my feet and Trifun was emerging from below, Benedict's carrycot in his hands. The man from the quayside, my torch in his fist, was walking round *Dolly*'s deck, inspecting her: as I looked, he bent and tested a shackle. Someone who knew boats at last. Someone, of course, who was going to sail *Dolly* away from the Gulf of Kotorska, and back to an anchorage less revealing. With, it seemed, Petar and Mihovil still on board.

Ben was waking in the cold air. I took the carrycot over from Trifun, and left him to carry the cases ashore. The newcomer left *Dolly* also and followed. Instead of walking round to the church they both advanced to where Zorzi stood, on the far side of the quay. I walked behind, smiling at Benedict. Then I reached them and looked up.

At the foot of the quay steps lay a motor launch. "We go," said Zorzi.

Through the wan, turgid lens of exhaustion, I stared at him. "We were to stay on the island?" In less than an hour it would be light. Wherever he landed, he would face the police and the road barriers. To leave the island surely was madness.

And disaster from my point of view. This was the island whose name had been spoken last night for the benefit of all those unseen watchers. Now, away from the microphones of the *Dolly*, our hiding place was to be altered.

They pushed me when I hesitated, and I picked up the carrycot and climbed down to the launch.

The ride to the shore was a short one. My knees gave way, stepping on to the shingle, and I put down the carrycot and sat on a rock while the launch was pushed off, and then the newcomer switched on his engine to pilot her back to the *Dolly*. Trifun picked up the cases and I stood up and climbed the beach between them both to a clearing in the scrub overhanging the roadway.

Standing parked with its lights out was an ambulance. The only vehicle, of course, which could drive anywhere at all without being questioned.

I was put in the back. I couldn't see who the driver was, but heard the sound of a harsh voice barking in Serbo-Croat at Zorzi. From Zorzi's tone he was being conciliatory. I was glad someone was chewing him out, but beyond caring too much over what. Ben had started to snuffle. I talked to him, and as he came more awake, lifted him out and had a good look, while I rocked him and talked.

He was all right. But a crying match wasn't too far in the future. I couldn't heat him a bottle but I did have some orange juice made up for this kind of occasion. I rescued it from my bag, and let him see it, and then inserted the teat between his gums. What it is to have all your troubles settled by food. I could remember being hungry. At that precise moment my stomach felt it never wanted to eat again.

The ambulance doors opened and Zorzi and Trifun climbed in

carrying something. Zorzi said, "Americans like to use bugs. Tell me where they are."

To think, to answer, to keep alert was almost impossible. Behind the stubble of his beard Zorzi looked as bad as I felt, and angry. This was not his idea. I said, "None. We don't need bugs with a bodyguard."

That didn't even raise a sneer. He simply signed to Trifun, and Trifun stepped forward with a bug-alert.

Benedict resented being separated from his bottle, and anyone passing on that road would have heard it. No one passed. They found nothing on Benedict, nothing in the bags or my clothes, down to my shoes. I let them hold my arms and I didn't struggle. The door to the ambulance was locked, and there was a third man in the driver's seat. I had nowhere to run to. And I wasn't supposed to run anywhere anyway.

Johnson had told me that a bug-alert would blow it, and it did. They found my small, expensive dental operation and held my jaws open in their dirty hands while they picked at my teeth.

The bug was in a capped tooth, but it had been planted firmly enough not to come out while I was chewing, and by the time they dragged it out my head was ringing with pain. Nor was my jaw much improved when Zorzi hit it. "Well?" he said. "Bug on you: no bug on the baby?"

I didn't know what they knew. I had to pretend I didn't know they knew anything. I said, "My father is nervous."

"What?" said Zorzi.

I tried again. "When I go abroad, my father wants me to be safe."

They looked at me. Then from the frosted panel in front came a rapping. The driver spoke, and Zorzi, leaving me, opened the door and climbed out of the ambulance. He took the bug with him.

He came back five minutes later, and smiling. "Your tooth," he said. "It goes on a journey."

Damn.

The ambulance started up.

The coast road to Kotor is spectacular. As the sky paled I saw it fitfully above Benedict's head as he sucked, his eyes fixed on mine, and brought up the air he had swallowed, scented with orange, and then lay, smiling and semaphoring with his arms, while going through his repertoire of noises after each of my sentences. I got an impression of red roofed villages, and date palms, and vines and magenta judas trees and orange blossom, and porches and balconies covered with windblown creeper and geraniums. The lower hills were green and yellow with scrub and gorse, with chrome-grey scars of rock in between, and cypresses set upright here and there like runes among the bushes. Higher up, as the light strengthened, the mountains looked as artificial as peaks out of papier mâché: wild and serrated and surging, with snow on the top.

When one is being kidnapped one should pay the greatest attention to the route one is taking. When one is in charge of a baby, one should never . . . never . . . never allow oneself to fall asleep.

Benedict slept, and I slept with my arms folded round him. I woke once, and we were still driving along the waterside opposite a walled town of antique, pale yellow buildings, skeined all over the opposite hillside. It occurred to me that it could be Kotor.

The next time I woke, we were driving on the same side as the town, and looking down on it.

My eyes stayed open that time, because of the road, which on my side dropped sheer down the mountain. As I looked, the ambulance turned to the right, nearly throwing me out of my seat. It was near enough like being on shipboard again to remind me of the ache in my back and my arms and my shoulders and to make even Benedict's weight seem oppressive. I laid him still sleeping back in his cot, and planted a foot on either side of it, and held on, as I saw Zorzi and Trifun were doing.

We climbed the mountain in twenty-five zigzags, with the ambulance engine whining with effort, and the gulf below becoming smaller and more distant at every bend. On the edge of one curve I saw a wind sock. It was true then. I hadn't believed it.

After a bit I stopped looking even at that, because my head got too heavy to hold up. I think the others were sleeping that time before I was. Even when the lurching eventually stopped and the wheels turned on to a long, level surface and ran for some time without deviating, I found it an effort to open my eyes, and to turn and peer out of the window.

I didn't believe what I saw, but if my brain had been working I would have known it was quite real, even if it was one possibility that Johnson had ruled out of court right from the beginning.

The ambulance stood on a wide gravel drive lined with bushes.

Ahead was a sweep of blue water, culminating in what appeared to be a drawbridge. And at the other end of the drawbridge, catching the pink light of dawn on its stairs, its archways, its batlements and pepperpot towers, was the Mad Ludwig castle from Missy's Golden American Wonderland.

The fortress of Kalk with its moat, which was a whimming place.

In which the owner, Hugo Panadek, was wont to whim, according to Grover.

lenses, told nothing at all except that he was concentrating on the road. Which was sufficient answer, I supposed, in itself. He took the next bend rather fast.

I was glad Hugo was with us, and I was also sorry. There was a lot I wanted to ask. There was a lot, too, I wanted to rejoice about. With Hugo there, I couldn't talk about my father. And I wanted to talk. I didn't want to think about Benedict.

The next corner rolled me right over against Johnson's arm. I got off as soon as I could, and heard from the graphic curses behind that Hugo had also been thrown off balance. He said, "Friend: we hold the slalom competitions in the winter. Do you mind? My molecules are easily disconnected."

Johnson said, "Are all these bends the same width?"

"No," said Hugo. At Johnson's tone his own had changed altogether. "Some are wider than others. Why? Your steering? Or your brakes?"

"Brakes," Johnson said. That was all, for, his wrists turning the wheel, he was guiding us hurtling round the next bend. The second, or third of the famous, the notorious twenty-five serpentine road-bends of Lovćen.

And I knew why the brakes weren't working. *I guess he'll just have to have a small accident,* Grandpa Eisenkopp had said. And after I had gone from the room, someone had been sent out to arrange just that.

The wind banged on the walls of the car and the tires culled a long, tenor roar from the road and the headlights, dazzling on the tarmac, swung again and lit up segments of hillside, plucked out of the dark: a green bush, its black shadow spiked on a rockface; a boulder brilliant-cut like a diamond; a loop of grey-textured, sinuous back. In some parts of the hills there were jackals . . . .

The car began to fetch round into the other arm of the loop, like *Dolly* coming round for her jibe. But on a precipitous road, with a cliff plunging straight into blackness below us.

Then Hugo said, "*Now.* You have enough width now." And Johnson turned the wheel full lock, scientifically, in a racing skid that slid the car back on its wheels downwards and in reverse into the mountain, gaining space but losing momentum while the powerful engine roared and clawed to pull the dead weight of the slewed car into the other half of the flattened U bend that would set it climbing again, the way we had come. A U bend which couldn't help but bring us to the edge of the road, where the wind thrust and fretted and whipped in the glare of the headlights.

I didn't think then that Johnson knew himself whether or not he would make it. I could see the damp grain of his skin bright as crêpe-de-chine under the mess of his hair and a vein suddenly underlined with the effort. Then Hugo leaned from the back, and putting his strong, long-fingered hands over Johnson's, added his strength to pull the wheel round.

There was a moment when I felt the rear wheel falter and sink into the soft, crumbling edge of the precipice. There was a moment when the car was not fully round and the wind, suddenly gusting, caught the high structure and rocked it, first forwards and then back as if it had been a child's wooden horse, or perhaps a cradle. Then, his hands still on the wheel, Hugo flung his body weight sideways and I leaned over, my shoulder pressed against Johnson's and my weight on his side, to keep the fulcrum inwards, on the mountain side of the road.

Then the tires gripped, and the engine note lost some of its shrillness and the car began to pull away from the side and to climb, uphill back to the castle and safety.

That was when Hugo, leaning still over the wheel, removed one hand and thrust it inside Johnson's coat.

I saw Johnson's hand come off the wheel, snatching. One of Hugo's fists knocked it aside. The other freed itself from Johnson's coat, dragging with it the long manila envelope containing the Malted Milk Folio.

Both Johnson's hands came off the wheel as he lunged for the papers. The car rocked and swayed and then, with a scraping of earth, began to slide backwards. Hugo's door crashed open and jolted there, dragging its edge on the ground. And Hugo himself, already half out, leant over and gave us, by way of his last parting benison, a full turn of the wheel to jerk us round and straight over the cliff-edge.

# Chapter 20

There was nowhere for me to jump. I was on the precipice side. But there might be a chance for Johnson. I don't remember even troubling to shout out. I just put both hands against him and shoved.

"Don't push," said Johnson reprovingly. "Keep your head. Drive with consideration. And when in doubt, apply the brakes."

The car was stationary.

"What?" I said. Any other of a dozen interrogative pronouns would have done as well.

"Hang on," said my friend Johnson amiably. "We *are* a bit close to the weather balloons." And reving up, he engaged his lowest gear and began gently to take the car up and into the center of the road.

The headlights, beaming round, lit a dark figure and pale features staring at us. Hugo. Wondering as I was, if it was all an illusion; and the car was in reality jumping and somersaulting down the face of the cliff. Something glittered in one of his hands.

"If I were you," Johnson said, "I should lie down. Donovan is supposed to be waiting for him, but he's probably got a revolver." And as he spoke, there was a flash of flame in the dark and a bang, followed by a jolt from under the car.

"Damn. I thought he'd do that," Johnson said. "Ah, well. This is where we take to the bushes." He bumped on one flat tire to the side of the road and pulled on his brakes, which were working perfectly. Then he twisted round, delving at the same time into a pocket. A revolver emerged, and he tested it quickly and looked up. "Nimble Fingers Inc. I reckon he has five more bullets. Want to risk it?"

"If you mean," I said, getting out, "do I want to avoid being a hostage yet again, then the answer is yes. . . . You know, he's got away. You haven't a hope in hell of catching him."

"Nonsense," Johnson said. "I told you. Donovan's tracking him. Also, he's dead keen to get rid of me. Until you bellowed the tidings back there, he didn't have any idea that I knew about the Folio also."

*Bellowed.* I treated it with the contempt it deserved.

On second thoughts I shall be more honest and say I hardly noticed it. A recollection had struck me, and for some reason I was consumed with mirth. I said, "Oh heck, I forgot. I'm hellish sorry about *Dolly*."

He had gone. I stepped out sideways, searching. "And so you bloody well should be," said his voice conversationally, just ahead of me. "She would have done thirteen knots under bare poles in that weather. And there you were, skipping about, hoisting sails like a one-handed paperhanger. It put me right off my sleep."

There was a crack and a whine. I said, "Shut up!" and then was silent as another bullet went by. I changed my position and found I was beside Johnson again. In spite of everything I said, "*What do you mean . . .*" and broke off as another bullet hit the rock in front of us.

A second gun spoke, ahead to the right, and was answered by the first one again. "Donovan. One to go," Johnson said.

I said, "What do you mean, it put you off your sleep?" and heard him give a comfortable laugh.

He said, "We'll really have to stop and get on with the job. But yes, when the *Glycera* dropped her pilot, she dropped me as well. Awfully sorry and all that. Really. But I was alongside, on the shore road, all the time you were sailing *Dolly*."

With that he disappeared. The slag. The klutz. Fending off rocks and a quantity of thrashing bushes I followed as best I could, and soon I had no breath to talk with anyway, which was probably the idea. At least, I noticed, he always kept within reach. As I had discerned, he wasn't going to risk having to rescue me for a second time this evening.

Not, come to think of it, that he had rescued me the first time.

Hugo himself had done that, by leaving the nursery clues which only a children's nanny would be best primed to follow. Because, one had to think, he wanted me free and Gramps' little lot exposed. Because, somehow, Hugo Panadek knew about the Croatian Liberation Army all along, and was quite willing that they should do all the dirty work and receive all the kicks while he walked off in the end with the Malted Milk Folio. Was it possible that he had even made sure that Gramps knew about the basement of the castle of Kalk? Was it possible that even without the smallpox and the nuns' visit—or was that a fabrication too?—the first two hiding-places Gramps had chosen would always have been put out of action, somehow, by Hugo?

And yet . . . And yet Hugo hadn't intended to come in the car with Johnson just now. I could hardly be mistaken about that. He had been quite content to let us go, knowing that Johnson carried the Folio in his jacket. Then at the last minute he had changed his mind. Why?

There was a burst of firing ahead and something else, as we rounded a corner. The gleam, through that long drive of trees of a lit window, shining alone and isolated over water. We were back within reach of the castle. I said, "Oh Christ, if you let him get back in there you'll never catch him."

"I rather think," Johnson said, standing up, "that we have let him get back in there. Donovan?"

A combined smell of mud and aftershave lotion signalled the appearance of my bodyguard, who said, "Hi, baby!" and kissed me, with one arm round my shoulders.

"Donovan?" said Johnson repressively.

"I'm afraid you're right, sir," said Donovan cheerfully. "There's another underground entrance over there. It's open if you want to follow him in."

"I rather think not," Johnson said. "Is everyone inside?"

"All deployed, sir. He can't get into the castle itself, or out through the other moat exit. As soon as he went in there, he was trapped in the basement. It's just a case of starving him out. Or whatever."

"I rather fancy whatever," Johnson said thoughtfully.

I said flatly, "You knew this would happen? You just wanted the official police out of the way?"

"Check," said Donovan. "You knew we had Mr. Johnson's men all round the gulf? You see, there was this driver."

"I think we'll save the saga," Johnson said. "Denny, you might go and make sure this side of the tunnel is quite secure. I'll meet you at the moat entrance."

Donovan left. I said, "What driver?" We were walking up the road to the castle.

Johnson said, "The fellow who drove the wedding taxi, remember? Your nice Dr. Dogíc from the Radoslav Clinic went over and spoke to him. To tell him, actually, not to stand by any more, for the baby wasn't with you. I told you that wedding cars were the only traffic allowed there. It would have been a snip for a snatch."

"So?" I said. Someone loomed up and spoke to Johnson in English and when he answered, faded again.

Johnson said, "So I had him followed, that's all, and he led us here. It let us warn the police even before the kidnap note gave Donovan his excuse, and let me get my own men around. That, of course, was all part of the basic ground plot organized by the elder Mr. Eisenkopp. We were on to him by that time, thanks to you and Beverley."

*"Beverley?"* I said.

He had stopped to look about. He came back. "Well, yes. While Grover was locking you both in the bathroom, Donovan took the chance to slip through and fiddle his way through Gramp's door. The wheelchair was there, but Gramps wasn't. Also we found the receiving end of the bug in Donovan's plastic plant. Careless that; but of course Gramps had no idea who Donovan was. He merely wanted to get information about Benedict's movements. But that in turn, helped by you again, led us to Hugo."

"I've been a great help all along," I said. I was feeling aggrieved.

"You have." He settled down to walk beside me, hands in pockets. "To begin with, Donovan came across a bug in Gramps' room. Which raised, as you might imagine, all kinds of questions. Then, when we began to check out the theory by feeding Gramps' plant scraps of nonsense, we were alarmed and gratified to find not only Gramps, but Hugo acting on the false information. Then we checked Hugo's phone calls. One of them was to Lübeck, the home port of the *Glycera*. Somehow, of course, he had to shift the venue of the

Warr Beckenstaff gala from Venice to Dubrovnik and he did. And then, there was your jumping bean."

"The Widdess toddler's," I said. "I did wonder, if neither you nor Denny mentioned it, how Hugo knew it was the sort of thing I carried about in my pockets. I suppose it entertained Vladimir, and he included it in the tale when he reported the Eskimo story to Gramps. . . . You might have told me."

"I might. But you wouldn't have let Hugo kiss you any more," Johnson said. "Anyway, the whole thing was pretty delicate. The militia have been very good, and haven't asked any awkward questions. But this part of the operation, naturally, I wanted to keep in our own hands."

"Why does Hugo want the Folio?" I said.

Johnson smiled in the dark. "Because, I rather fancy, he is on someone else's list of Government agents. Or perhaps he is a gifted freelance. Wild as a fox. But, you know, bloody amusing."

I agreed, but I wasn't going to say so. I said, "Why didn't he want to come in the car then? He knew you had the Folio."

We had reached the entrance to the moat tunnel. "I must say," said Johnson, "I felt rather for him at that point. He knew I had the Folio. He knew I knew he knew I had the Folio. And he was free to establish his perfect innocence by aiding, abetting and encouraging me to drive off with the said Folio without let or hindrance from Hugo. Any suspicions we might have had would have been utterly disarmed."

"But he *was* letting it go," I said. "He couldn't have hoped to get it back from you after that. He didn't know Gramps had fooled with the brakes. . . ."

I caught myself up. "No one fooled with the brakes," said Johnson patiently. "I had to get him to show his hand somehow, hadn't I? And his reason for letting the Folio go was perfectly simple. He thought he had a copy. The machine you transmitted the coded lists on has a memory. He thought he had only to return to the room and make himself a print-out. But then. . . ."

"You said you had wiped the machines," I said, remembering. "I thought in a stupid way you meant you had turned them off safely. So he realized there wasn't a print-out, and he'd have to pinch the original from you. And he flipping well did."

"Well, we've trapped him," said Johnson mildly. He seemed surprised by my vehemence. He might have said more, but someone else came up and spoke to him, and a little further on a man appeared with a rifle and showed us obsequiously through a door. I looked round and felt immediately queasy. It was the office and workshop where I had stood, with Benedict at my feet, facing that easy chair with the spiral of smoke ascending from it.

There was no one in the chair now. The room was a shambles, where men had thrown litter and overturned cases in their haste to get out, and other men had rummaged through, searching. The only people there now seemed to be Johnson's own. One of them said, "We've located him, sir. He's in the large storeroom. Without ammunition, so far as we can gather. Do you want to challenge him yourself?"

"I think," Johnson said, "that after taking all the trouble, Joanna and I should have some of the fun. . . . What the hell is that?"

A burst of gunfire, echoing hollowly round one of the underground rooms, died away to the sound of running feet and men's voices. We were brought up at the door by a man with blood on his face, breathlessly reporting. "He seems to have got a fresh weapon, sir. We can't see what it is, because he's shot all the lights out."

Johnson said, "Have you sent anyone else in?" and when the man shook his head he said, "Well, don't. I know the customer and you don't. Joanna, stay behind. You, get some arc lights and cable. Set them all in the passage, but don't switch on until I tell you. I may need back-up fire, but on no account follow me into the warehouse. This man is an exceptional shot. He can stay there and pick us all off till kingdom come if we let him."

I said, "He's got to come out some time, or starve."

He said, "I know. But Panadek is a Yugoslav citizen, and we are in Yugoslavia. I want this finished tonight. It will be. He doesn't want to lose his life any more than I do."

I don't know why I found that so reassuring. Or I do, but the reasons are personal. I went with the others to the doorway of the big warehouse, and saw, through the open door, how the darkness transformed it into a place of shadowy racks and benches and shelves and tables. Then there was a flash of red and a crash and the combat man behind me pulled me violently back from the threshold where the light from the passage had betrayed me.

A moment later the lights in both the adjoining passages went out and I heard the men beside me shuffle, blocking the door in the darkness. Then Johnson said, "All right. Let me through," and they parted.

We waited. Presently, within the depths of the warehouse, Johnson's voice spoke quietly. "I have a gun and twenty men. You're going to get taken anyway."

Silence. Then, "No doubt," said Hugo Panadek's impudent voice. "But we may as well have some entertainment, may we not, in the meantime? It has been one hell of a joke, my Britannic friend. It is worth one hell of a pay-off."

The bark of Johnson's gun drowned the last words, but did not stop them. I heard the zing of a ricochet, and then a hissing sound, like a porcupine on an airbed. Without further warning, a dozen jets of pink light leaped up from the floor of the warehouse and wavered there, lighting up all the toys on the shelving; lighting up the dark shattered lights in the roof; lighting up the figure of Johnson, flattened against a row of shelving.

I didn't see Hugo, but I saw the spark from his gun, and heard the bang, and saw Johnson's head jerk before the rosy lights died as if pinched by a snuffer. In the silence there was a small clatter, followed by the tinkle of broken glass.

I waited, my hands clamped round the doorpost, for the sound of Johnson falling. Instead, after a moment, he spoke, mildly. "You bastard," he said. "But I will say you can shoot." And then I realized, of course, that Hugo had merely shot off his bifocal glasses.

I had a gun. I also had perfect vision. I moved before anyone could stop me, through the door and into the warehouse. Then I halted, for I couldn't see anything.

I could hear something, though. A trundling noise, making its way in a straight line along a distant path between racks, from the sound of it. A noise which dwindled and then oddly became louder, as if, having rounded the racks, it was now traversing the next row. The sound, still at some remove, drew level with me, passed me, and dwindled to the right again. A moment later, I heard it coming back, a little louder and nearer. This time, as it drew level, it hesitated, picked up, hesitated again, and then resuming, made its way to the left.

No one moved. The object, whatever it was, began to come back.

This time it was nearer again: perhaps two rows of racks from where I was standing. And this time as it drew level it slowed down and nearly stopped.

The silence was so ghostly that I jumped with fright when a booming voice spoke suddenly from the ceiling. It came this time from a loudspeaker and was relayed there, unmistakably, by Hugo. He said, "How very odd. Are there two of you? I could have sworn Johnson was up by the railway track. . . . I want to introduce you to Fred. Fred is one of my favorite inventions. You remember the pool bug at Cape Cod, Johnson? Fred works the same way, with a sensor bar on his nose. If there is anyone human in this room, Fred will find him. Won't you, my pet?"

Whether spurred by his master's voice or not, Fred had resumed his trundle and was now passing down to the right. I wondered where the microphone was that Hugo was speaking into. It not only disguised his position, it effectively covered any footsteps. On the other hand, it allowed Johnson to move as well. I wondered if he was by the railway track, and thought I might as well move that way myself, before I found Fred curled up at my feet, with Hugo no doubt behind him, if not riding howdah.

Then it occurred to me that once I was free of the racks, the sensitive Fred would merely trundle straight for me. The game was to wait until he was halfway along, and then dash out at the opposite end of my row, and as far as I could get over the warehouse. Hoping not to collide with Hugo on the way, or even Johnson, without his glasses and with his revolver.

I never did do it, because just as Fred got to the end of the row and started coming down the one next to mine there was a jangle and a buzz, and I saw that someone anyway was on the railway platform, for the trains had started to run. And very pretty too they looked in the dark, with their carriage windows flashing by, and the lights on in the stations and the signals. A troop train came into view followed by a rocket carrier. The train disappeared but the carrier halted, fizzed a little, and then without more ado, let fly a rocket.

It was, I suppose, a small firework. It burst in the air, throwing sparks and black shadows everywhere. Johnson, who had set it off, was prudently out of sight. But there, clear in my line of vision, was Hugo Panadek at the end of my row of stacking shelves, with a dark shadow at his feet which must be Fred. And I, of course, was equally plain to Hugo Panadek.

He fired without compunction straight at me, and from where I was lying on the floor, I fired back. That neither of us hit the other was due to the fact that he tripped on Fred's cable, and that in any case, I fired at Fred. I hit him, too. I had hoped he would go up in a sheet of flame so that at least I could see where Johnson was, but he just crepitated mournfully and gave off a lot of disagreeable fumes.

A voice from the ceiling said, "Get out, Joanna. Panadek, I think that's enough. In a moment I shall ask them to switch the lights on. Before you can shoot them all out, they will have you. Throw your gun down."

So Johnson had found the microphone, which was foolhardy, for of course, Hugo knew where it was. Instead of throwing down his revolver he ran. I could hear the footsteps receding and knew he was crossing the room. I hoped Johnson had had the sense to move quickly. It came to me that now I had virtually stopped him from shooting. He would never know, when he saw or heard anything, whether it might be Hugo or me.

I wondered fretfully just how bad his sight was. It was, I said bitterly to myself, a bloody silly trade for a man with bifocal glasses.

Johnson's mind, I suppose, was running along the same lines. At any rate his voice came again, this time without the microphone, and from somewhere on my right. He simply said, "Lights," and all along the wall on our left, the white faces of high-power lamps sprang into dazzling being.

No one shot them out. No one ran. No one moved. What the lights did show up, with merciless clarity, was a closing black square on the wall by the railway. This, of course, must be the door by which Hugo had made his entry. And by which he was hoping to leave—and might leave, if the sentry at the other end was less than watchful.

Johnson reached the door just as it was closing and prised it open. It would have shut behind him if I hadn't caught it and followed. If he hadn't the sense to know when to give up, then I supposed I was stuck with my role as his guide dog.

I followed him into warm darkness. Behind me the heavy door closed with a series of murmuring clicks. Then, in a white searing blaze, the lights came on to show me where I was.

Not, as I thought, in a passage. But in a box: a small empty room whose walls and ceiling and floor were made of sheets of bright, glittering metal.

In front of me was Johnson. And no more than ten feet away, his gun on the floor, stood Hugo Panadek.

He was smiling. "If you were counting," he said, "you will know that it's empty. May I hint that it was a fraction unfair, calling in quite so many minions? I much prefer one to one ... or one to two: it makes little difference. You *can* see me, I hope?"

Beneath his knitted black brows, Johnson appeared to be concentrating. "I think so," he said. "You're either a distant bald man or a fingerstall. There's an armed combat expert behind the door at your back, and another at the field end of the entrance. It would be nice if you just kicked the gun out of your way and came towards me, slowly, with your hands raised, as in the movies."

"But it wouldn't be so nice for me," said Hugo Panadek. "Or so much fun. I know you don't want to take your eyes off me - You *can* see me, can't you?—but you might ask Joanna to look up at the ceiling. It's the very last toy, Johnson; and the switch which operates that has also locked both the doors. I can't get out, but neither can you. And when they do get in to fetch us, I doubt very much if either of you will be interested."

Before he had finished talking, I was gaping upwards. A trap in the ceiling had opened. I was prepared, I suppose, for something spectacular. The mouth of a machine gun. A nozzle of gas. A spray of quick-lime or acid.

I had forgotten Hugo Panadek's unique temperament.

Instead, there appeared in the ceiling an immense silver ball. For a moment it hovered there, in the frame of its trapdoor. Then slowly, paid out on a strong iron chain, it descended. Heavily, so that it reminded me of the weights used for house demolition. I was speculating about the unseen overhead girder that carried it, when it came to a halt, perhaps six inches, no more, from the floor; and hanging dead in the centre.

With a low rumble the trapdoor above closed itself over, leaving only an eyelet hole for the ball-chain. We looked at it, and at Hugo, who was watching us. Then across the ball, I saw Johnson make a small movement.

He had put his finger to his lips, in the universal signal for silence. His naked eyes were on mine. Their expression I couldn't interpret. I shook my head in puzzled query, and looked at Hugo.

The room was very small. He had retreated to the wall at his back and was leaning there, with his arms lightly folded. He looked quite at ease, and also expectant. The ball hung, without moving, between the three of us. Distantly, in the silence I could hear the sound of muffled banging. It stopped, and a voice shouted, "Mr. Johnson! Sir! Can you hear us?"

Johnson didn't reply. I looked at Hugo. He was still smiling. When I looked at Johnson again he shook his head and again made the signal for silence. Then he opened his hands and began to speak in dumb language.

It was a long time since I used it—at school, I think. I remembered the vowels, which are easy, but not too many of the consonants. He gave me the same letters several times before I got what he was trying to say. *Don't speak.* And then he pointed to the ball.

I knew then what he meant, and I wondered if he was right. If he was, it was Fred all over again. Except that Hugo was in the room with us, and therefore the ball had to operate on a basis to which Hugo could make himself immune. By, for example, staying silent.

I nodded to let Johnson know that I understood and he smiled, and leaning back, folded his arms as Hugo had done. Distantly, we could hear voices still, first on one side of the door and then beyond the other door, in the corridor that led to the field. I realized as Johnson's men talked that they didn't even know there was a space between the two doors in which three people might possibly shut themselves. They had watched Hugo run through the door from the warehouse and they had seen it close behind Johnson and myself. Now it refused to open, and when they walked down the tunnel from the field end, the passage would seem to be empty. I could hear the guard at the other end distantly protesting that no one had passed him.

Then I heard Donovan's muffled voice say, "All righty: let's blow the *bogomil* down. The workshop's bursting with nitro. Go on, you. Get off your butt and go get it."

Opposite me, Hugo's smile showed wide and white under his moustache. A smile of total enjoyment, for all he was no better off now than we were.

For Johnson's men were going to tape explosives to the door at our backs. And they had to be stopped. For between the blast and the ball, it would kill us.

I beat Johnson to it by a fraction. Just as he drew breath, I opened my mouth and screamed *"Stop!"*

The ball hung, sombre and silent, between us. As the first sibilant reached it, it stirred. Stirred, trembled, teetered, and then, polished and enormous, swung towards me.

There was an image on it of myself, pinheaded and bloated. It advanced, wider than I could dodge: too vast to hope to slip under.

From behind the ball Johnson's voice, clear but not loud, said, *"Repeat."*

Before the word was halfspoken, the shining thing had stopped its advance. It halted, shook, and then slowly began to recede. The pin-headed figure dwindled. Air and space came in its place. I watched the ball, mesmerized, pick up speed. It was on its way, hurtling towards Johnson when it came to me what he had said. I shouted *"Stop!"*

The ball answered. It was uncanny. It was like calling a dog. In front of Johnson's face it steadied, shuddering, and then began the return swing towards me. Voices outside exclaimed remotely. Someone said, "What is it?" and someone else said, "There's someone in there."

The ball loomed: I came face to face again with my image. Johnson said, quickly and loudly, *Johnson, Joanna . . ."*

I waited as long as I dared. *"And Panadek,"* I added. The ball swung towards me.

Johnson said, *"Don"t explode!!"* and the ball turned again.

Donovan's voice shouted, "Got it." Insulated by the walls, sounds outside seemed to leave the ball quite impervious. The voice, stifled, continued, "What's wrong? Can you tell us?"

In five syllables? It was all we could risk, and even that made the swing longer than was comfortable. I watched the ball and shouted,

*"Demolition . . ."* As the ball left him, Johnson smiled. Then just before it reached me, he said " *. . . ball.*"

It was like bloody Scrabble. I waited, selecting and discarding, and came up with *"Sensitive."* The ball swung my way.

*"To sound,"* said Johnson; and as the ball was coming, made a fast drawing movement with his hand over the wall behind him.

I thought I knew what he meant, but I didn't want to blow it. I said, *"Try to . . ."*

And as the ball swung to me, Johnson finished it, *". . . Cut wall."*

The ball receded. I stood there, limp with relief and exhaustion and actually watched Johnson's eyebrows go up before I recovered my senses.

Message received, over and out. Except that it wasn't over and out. We had to go on talking.

There was no time to think of words. I just screeched, and the ball stopped and came back to me. At the right moment, Johnson said politely, *"Thank you,"* and grinned again. The ball turned towards him.

*"What now?"* I said. The ball turned.

*"Verse?"* he said. The ball left me. Something hit the wall behind us. I found I was smiling too. Verse, of course, with its regular beats, and its effortless feed-belt of words. I wondered what verses he knew. I said, *"Incy . . ."*

*"Christ. Wincey . . ."* he said. I was right. Everyone knew that one.

*"Spider,"* I said portentously.

*"Climbing . . ."*

*"Up the . . ."*

*"Spout."*

The ball swung like clockwork. The spider continued its saga. With time to think, I could hear the hammering going on between words, and then the high-pitched sound of a drill. In his workshop Hugo had every tool anyone could conceivably need. I even had a moment, between words, to glance at Hugo.

Leaning against the wall without moving, he really looked no different from all the other times I had been in his amusing, versatile company. In the gorilla suit in the Eisenkopps' flat; shooting rustlers at Missy's Golden American Wonderland; swimming out to save Johnson at Cape Cod in the little exploit which exposed Beverley so successfully. Inviting Simon to the party which reinstated me as a member of the Yugoslav expedition. Repairing the Brownbelly tape because it didn't matter to him whether Vladimir was identified or not, because Vladimir was Gramps' man, as all the men at the Wonderland had been.... For Hugo all along had been the lone man, the jackal, the scavenger.

He looked the same, except that the smile under the moustache had resignation in it, and perhaps even a shadow of admiration. He could not, of course, speak. He didn't have to.

We had got on to the Gondoliers, as I remember, by the time the oxyacetylene cutter finally began to draw a line through the wall. Johnson, it turned out, had a moderately melodious tenor, and I had been one of the Kings of Barataria myself in my schooldays. It was a scramble to get some of the lines in, I distinctly remember, but we managed:

*"Replying we—"*
*"Say, as—"*
*"One indi-"*
*"Vidual. As I—"*
*"Find I'm a—"*
*"King, to my—"*
*"Kingdom I—"*
*"Bid you all. I'm a—"*
*"-Ware you ob—"*
*"Ject, to pa-"*
*"Vilions and—"*
*"Palaces, but you'll—"*
*"Find I re-"*
*"Spect, Your Re-"*
*"-Publican fallacies . . ."*

We didn't have to go any further. At just that point, a section of the wall fell out. It drew the ball to the sound. And, well trained as I was, I shouted, briskly, to summon it back.

I think Donovan must have thought Hugo, seen clear through the gap, was in process of torturing us. As I suppose he was. At any rate, he lunged through the opening and fired.

It caught Panadek in the shoulder and he yelled. And the ball turned and made for him.

It would have been poetic justice to let it go, but I had had enough poetry for one night. So had Johnson, it appeared. We shouted *"Stop!"* at the same moment and then, feeling stupid, alternately until someone found the switch and the ball rose slowly into the ceiling and both doors opened.

Hugo still leaned against the wall, his hand gripping his shoulder and blood running down between his long fingers. "All right," he said. "You ought to have been the toy designers and I ought to have been the nanny." Then he felt in his jacket and drawing out the brown manila envelope, tossed it towards us. "If it contains a page from the *Politika,* I don't want to know it."

"It contains a page from the *Politika,*" Johnson said.

They had replaced the burst tire on the Mercedes-Benz. Johnson drove down the mountain very carefully. We didn't say very much because we were both flogged. Indeed Johnson's hands, when he took them off the wheel, were trembling. And I was wrestling, as it happened, with my conscience.

Then, instead of going round to the harbor where *Dolly* was, Johnson drew up at the Hotel Mimosa in Herceg-Novi.

There was a blue and white police van standing outside, under the orange trees. I said rudely, "Oh bloody hell," and sat there with my eyes full of tears.

Johnson glanced at me and then away again. He said, "There were some things that neither Hugo nor Eisenkopp could have done. Engineering the Warr Beckenstaff for you. The MMA badges that identified the party at the Wonderland. The torn note in your pocket. The introduction of Lazar to Charlotte. The way Panadek found out about the whole of Gramps' scheme, right from the beginning. . . . But I didn't know you knew."

"I didn't," I said. "Not until I saw that futile apron nappy round Benedict's legs in the basement. He's been wearing a kite nappy for weeks now."

Bunty came out between two policemen as we went through the doors. She too looked just the same, with frizzed hair standing out round her earrings. She had her high-heeled boots on and if she was pale, the makeup hid it. She just looked annoyed. In fact, she pretended not to see me as they went past. I wondered where Gramps had picked her up and how they came to have joined forces.

She was a hard case; out for herself and for money: the fate of the Croats would mean nothing to Bunty. Was it through the nanny network, for example, that she found out that Mike Widdess worked for MI5, which let her sell the information later to Gramps? I didn't know yet if she worked alone, or with partners. Or if her team or Gramps had faked that car crash in which Mike Widdess died. Perhaps we should be surprised, looking over her record, to find how often she had been employed in a household where the child had been threatened with kidnapping.

One had to suppose that she had played along both Gramps and Panadek in other ways too. Panadek for merely the hell of it. I expect he gave her gifts. He certainly rummaged her rooms and her mail, and when he found out what she was up to, he had merely to plant his microphones and stand by for the prize money. Or rather, the Folio.

Panadek, whom she thought of simply as a sucker to go to bed with, had been too clever for Bunty all along.

Johnson was speaking to someone in Serbo-Croat. He turned back to me and said, "Their room's on the first floor." I didn't think he had remembered. Then I saw I was looking again at the reflection of myself in his face. I said, "Where did the glasses come from?"

"I keep a spare set in the car," Johnson said. "Didn't you notice?"

I hadn't. Indeed, if you asked, I could have sworn he did at least half of that journey down those serpentine bends without any glasses at all. Then I forgot about it, because we came to a door and Johnson stopped and said, "You go in."

It was Sukey's crying that burst on the ears as soon as I turned the handle. Grover wasn't crying although his face was all swollen with past excesses, and there were green tracks down to his chin, and he had wet himself all through his Daniel Hechter trendy tapestry two-piece. He was trying to feed Sukey with an arm round her lolling head and a cup of water pressed overflowing into her toothless mouth. Wherever Bunty had been, she hadn't been near them for hours and hours.

Then I went in and Grover looked round. His face, so like Comer Eisenkopp's, was white and defiant and frightened. Then he recognized me, and said, "You was not hurting Sukey."

"I know you weren't," I said. "Sukey's going to have a nice dinner now, and so is Grover."

I was in the middle of saying it when Beverley burst through the doorway beside me. They must have sent for her. Her red dress was stained and her careful blond hair was a mess. What she had, she was going to have to make the best of. No more money for the Radoslav Clinic. Not as Comer's wife, anyhow.

Then she ran to the bed and kneeling, flung her arms round both Grover and Sukey, crying so that both the kids began screaming at once. But it was the right kind of yelling; open and hearty and angry, with no panic in it. I backed to the door, and came out, and faced Johnson.

"I know. Bloody kids," he said, and gave me his handkerchief. Then we drove to the *Dolly*.

I flew home next day, to my father.

I only ever fell in love with one man, and he was married. Then his wife died, and the next time we met he had bifocal glasses, and a yacht and was a walking chemical factory.

Meanwhile I had other girls' children.